MY
SON'S
GIRLFRIEND

BOOKS BY KERRY WILKINSON

ROMANCE NOVELS

Ten Birthdays

Truly, Madly, Amy

THE JESSICA DANIEL SERIES

The Killer Inside (also published as *Locked In*)

Vigilante

The Woman in Black

Think of the Children

Playing With Fire

The Missing Dead (also published as *Thicker than Water*)

Behind Closed Doors

Crossing the Line

Scarred for Life

For Richer, For Poorer

Nothing But Trouble

Eye for an Eye

Silent Suspect

The Unlucky Ones

A Cry in the Night

THE ANDREW HUNTER SERIES

Something Wicked

Something Hidden

Something Buried

MY
SON'S
GIRLFRIEND

KERRY WILKINSON

bookouture

Published by Bookouture in 2025

An imprint of Storyfire Ltd.
Carmelite House
50 Victoria Embankment
London EC4Y 0DZ

www.bookouture.com

The authorised representative in the EEA is Hachette Ireland
8 Castlecourt Centre
Dublin 15 D15 XTP3
Ireland
(email: info@hbgi.ie)

ISBN: 978-1-83618-517-8
eBook ISBN: 978-1-83618-516-1

ONE

MONDAY

Daniel was calling.

Jennifer's son was twenty-one, of the generation brought up on texts, WhatsApps, and probably some other messaging thing his mother had never heard of. He didn't really *do* phone calls, let alone when it was almost eleven at night.

Late-night calls could only mean something was wrong. Something bad.

Jennifer slid the green button sideways to answer, then held the phone to her ear.

'Dan?'

Silence at first. Someone was breathing hard, as if they'd been running. Maybe they still were.

'Daniel?' Jennifer tried. His full name. Things were serious.

The breathing continued, then something more. A man's voice. Her *son's* voice.

'Mum?'

It was one word, though so much more. There was anguish, a million cries for help that only a mother could make out. Something terrible really *had* happened.

'What's wrong?' Jennifer asked, though she was barely able

to hear anything over her own racing heart. She pushed forward until she was sitting on the edge of the sofa. It was gloomy in her living room, no big light, only the lamp at the back.

The silence was an agonising second and then: 'It wasn't me.'

For a moment, Jennifer wondered whether she'd heard her son correctly. Her 'What wasn't you?' sounded as confused as she felt.

She waited, though there was only silence. It took her a few seconds to realise the screen was blank, that the call had cut out. Jennifer stared at the phone, trying to ignore the way her stomach seemed to be squeezing itself.

'What wasn't you?' she repeated, knowing she would get no answer.

Daniel had gone.

TWO

Jennifer tried calling her son back, though he didn't pick up. She tried a second, then third, time – but there was no answer.

Daniel had never been one for pranks. When he was six or seven, his father, Jennifer's husband, had hidden behind a door and jumped out with a loud 'boo!' That was Andrew's type of humour: he found nothing funnier than someone falling over. Except Daniel hadn't reacted with anything approaching humour, instead bursting into tears and shutting himself in his room for the rest of the day. He was a sensitive sort, more like his mum than his dad. This wouldn't be a misjudged joke. The single 'Mum' had been enough to tell Jennifer something was terribly, awfully, wrong.

Jennifer stared at her phone, then opened messages. She started with a simple: 'Is everything OK? I think we got cut off'. It felt so understated, even as Jennifer's throat had suddenly dried. She listened to the plip, watched the message send, and then continued staring, willing her son to reply.

Daniel was living hours away at university, having not long entered his second year. That first year of him living away from home had taken some getting used to. Daniel was never far from

Jennifer's thoughts after he'd moved out, with endless daydreams about where he was, and whether he was safe. Someone at her work had gone through the same with her daughter the year before. She'd told Jennifer that it got better over time. That those little worries never quite went, but the gaps between them got longer.

And Jennifer was worried now.

It was suddenly hard to judge time. Jennifer was sure it had been only seconds that she'd been looking at her phone, willing something to happen. Yet, when she looked up to the clock, it was almost half-past eleven. Somehow more than thirty minutes had passed. In a panicked trance, she had sent two more messages, first asking: 'Are you all right?', then adding: 'Please can you call me back?'. Both had gone without reply, apparently unread.

The blueish light of Jennifer's work laptop burned through the gloomy living room. It was at her side, on the sofa, with the home page of her son's university website on the screen. She wasn't sure when she'd opened it, but she'd been looking to see if there was some sort of urgent news posted. She'd also opened tabs on the BBC News site, plus one for the local newspaper where he lived. There was nothing relevant, though Jennifer doubted anyone was working this late.

Daniel's 'It wasn't me' was sounding more ominous as the minutes passed.

Jennifer wasn't sure what to do. It was almost midnight and it would take her more than two hours to reach her son. She had no idea how to contact him and spent a minute or two trying to think of any of his old school friends who might be up this late. If she could somehow contact one of them, they might be able to message him.

Except, why would he have called *her* if he didn't want to talk?

Jennifer picked up the laptop and searched for a phone

number for Daniel's local police force. Calling 999 felt like an overreaction, but there might be some sort of non-emergency number. Somebody might be able to visit his house and at least see if he was home. She didn't have numbers for any of his housemates.

Before that, Jennifer figured she would head upstairs and ask Andrew if he had any ideas. He'd be asleep, likely snoring, as he always was. It had been about half-six when he'd suggested sharing a bottle of wine, though, as always, Jennifer had sipped from a small glass, while he'd polished off the rest. They both knew the deal when it came to sharing alcohol. There wasn't a lot of equal distribution going on, even if that wasn't really a problem, compared to the other issues they had. Jennifer had been considering suggesting separate bedrooms for a while, though that would mean putting Daniel's stuff in the attic. It would be hard to see that second bedroom as anything other than his – but a night without Andrew's snoring really did seem appealing.

Not that Jennifer would be sleeping any time soon. She needed Daniel to reply.

Jennifer was on the second step when somebody knocked on the front door. She froze as a creak from the step echoed through the empty hallway. They had a doorbell, yet someone had chosen to knock. They would have surely seen the lights inside and guessed someone was still up.

For a moment, Jennifer thought it must be Daniel. He wasn't at university and had called when nearly home. Except... if it was him, why wouldn't he have simply opened the door? He had a key.

Jennifer trod back down to the hall and turned towards the door, where a large shadow stood on the other side of the rippled glass.

After clicking the chain into place, Jennifer eased the door open, allowing a gust of chilled air to bristle her cheeks. She gasped at the cold, then blinked as she took in a pair of police officers in uniform. There was a man at the back, with a woman closest to the door.

The female officer smiled humourlessly as she peeped at Jennifer through the gap. 'We didn't know if there'd be someone up,' she said, before quickly adding: 'Are you Jennifer Farley?'

Jennifer's eyes felt dry from the air, and she couldn't stop blinking. Nothing good could ever come from a late-night police visit. She managed a croaky 'Yes', as the officer shuffled nervously from foot to foot.

'Do you know where your son is?'

Jennifer stared for a moment, feeling as if she had missed something. She mumbled a 'hang on', then closed the door momentarily, unlatching the chain, before opening it fully. It only took a couple of seconds but that was all that was needed for Jennifer to know instinctively she should keep quiet about the last forty minutes or so.

'He's at university in Ashington,' she said. 'I assume he's there. I've not seen him since September.'

It was around seven weeks since Andrew had driven up their son to begin his second year. Since then, the darkening nights had mirrored Jennifer's mood.

The officers remained on the doorstep, though the man was now at his partner's side. They glanced to one another, as if trying to decide who should do the talking. Their breaths misted the air.

'Do you have any way of contacting him?' the male officer asked.

Jennifer eyed him for a moment, trying to think of how to answer the question. She obviously had a phone, because everyone did. That wasn't really what they were asking.

'Is something wrong?' Jennifer asked, fighting the quiver in her voice. There had to be.

The male officer cleared his throat. 'There's been an incident with Daniel's girlfriend,' he said.

Jennifer hadn't told them her son's name, and it felt ominous that they knew.

'What sort of incident?' Jennifer asked.

The officers glanced to one another again – and it was impossible to miss the shift in atmosphere. The night felt dangerous.

'We're making this call on behalf of our colleagues from another force,' the man said, sounding rehearsed. 'Your son's girlfriend is dead.'

THREE

Jennifer waited for a follow-up. Some sort of clarification that Daniel's girlfriend wasn't *actually* dead. This was police-speak for something else.

She waited but there was only a stilted, solemn, silence.

'Ella?' Jennifer said. 'Ella's dead?'

But she was so young. Just a kid.

Jennifer's words didn't feel real, even as she spoke and the officers nodded in unison. 'That's what we've been told,' the man said. 'Our colleagues are trying to find your son, which is why we're here. Do you have any idea where he might be?'

It wasn't me.

Suddenly Jennifer knew why Daniel had called. He knew the police would come knocking – and he wanted his mum to know that, regardless of what they might say, it wasn't him who had killed Ella.

'I've not seen him since September,' Jennifer repeated, which was true.

'When did you last speak to him?'

Jennifer let out a long *let me think* breath, as if to say that she couldn't remember – even though it had only been about forty-five minutes. For now at least, it felt like something to keep to herself. Daniel wanted her to know that whatever had happened to Ella wasn't down to him, which had to mean something.

Luckily, the female officer was starting to shiver from the cold. She rubbed her hands together and jumped in, which stopped Jennifer from having to answer. 'My sister went off to uni in September. Mum's always complaining that she never calls.'

Jennifer eyed the officer, aware she was now firmly of the generation who looked at police officers as being young nowadays. She'd long since passed the point of thinking all new music was rubbish. At forty-four, she was officially old.

'Daniel texts sometimes,' Jennifer said. 'But I've not had anything from him for a few days.'

That was also true. He'd messaged her a photo on Friday or Saturday of a puppy he'd seen in the park: a brown and white spaniel, all bandy legs and oversized paws. A way of keeping in touch without having to actually talk about his life. It was a big jump from puppy pictures to whatever had seemingly gone on that evening.

'Do you know what happened?' Jennifer added.

'Nothing past the fact that Daniel's girlfriend is dead, and that our colleagues are trying to find him.'

That sounded rehearsed, too. Could Ella possibly be dead? There must have been a mistake somewhere. Perhaps it was someone who looked like her? Or someone with a similar name?

'Do they think he had something to do with it?'

The blink-and-miss-it glimpse between the officers was enough.

'It's very early,' the man replied. 'Our colleagues are looking into it.'

As the officer's eyes shot upwards, Jennifer thought they were going to ask to come in. They would want to look around, just to make sure Daniel wasn't there. As if prompted by the unasked question, she said: 'My husband's in bed. Do you want me to get him up?'

That got a shake of the head, though they were at an impasse.

The female officer handed across a business card and told Jennifer to call the number if Daniel either came home, or contacted her. With that, they re-crossed the road and headed towards a marked police car that was parked under a street light. If any of the neighbours were up, they'd have some serious gossip for the morning.

Jennifer closed the door and headed back to the living room. She would get Andrew up to tell him what had happened but, before that, she needed some time to herself.

Ella was dead.

Jennifer had met her at Christmas the year before, when Daniel had brought her down to meet his family. As far as Jennifer knew, they'd been together for about a year. It wasn't quite clear where they'd met, other than that she lived in Ashington. Ella was definitely in a band, although Jennifer didn't know whether Daniel was involved. She seemed nice enough, albeit a little quiet. That was probably expected given a first meeting with her boyfriend's parents. Daniel and Ella had spent much of their time either in his bedroom, or out with friends. It was the first time that Jennifer had realised properly that her son had a life of his own. That he didn't *need* her any longer.

And now Ella was dead.

Police were at Jennifer's front door asking questions about Daniel. Were they also visiting Ella's parents? Telling them their daughter was never coming home again?

That fear from Daniel's late-night call, the glacial, sinking sensation, that the worst had happened... it had come true – but for Ella's parents.

Jennifer sat on the sofa, staring at the living room wall and Daniel's old school photographs, which had been faded by the sun. Andrew had been vaguely talking about redecorating the living room, which would likely mean taking down all those old pictures. One more admission that time was passing.

Her husband always had something on the go. Before that, he'd been talking about a full security system for the house, even though there was barely any crime where they lived. In the end, he'd installed a dummy camera above their front door because it was cheaper.

Jennifer's thoughts were racing to anywhere that meant she didn't have to face what was in front of her.

The police hadn't said that Daniel was a suspect in whatever had happened to Ella, though it was heavily implied.

It wasn't me.

Daniel knew the police would think it was him. He knew they would be searching for him. What could have happened?

Jennifer checked her phone, though there had been no further calls or messages.

She didn't know what to do – but she had to talk to her husband.

The stairs creaked as Jennifer headed up. The house had felt so quiet since her son had left. Before, there would always be a steady undercurrent from Daniel's music, or him talking to his friends while they were gaming. Without his soundtrack, the house itself felt louder.

As she reached the top of the stairs, Jennifer was met by the grunted echo of Andrew's snoring. There was a time in which rolling him over would do the trick but now it made little difference whether he was on his side or back.

Jennifer sighed as she opened the bedroom door and stood in the frame, watching her husband's chest rise and fall under the covers.

They'd not been getting on for a while, which she knew was

classic empty nest syndrome. He probably knew it as well. It was such a cliché – but that didn't mean it wasn't real.

She crept into the room and perched on the edge of the bed, before resting a hand on her husband's shoulder. His skin was warm, though he didn't shift.

'Andrew…?'

Jennifer shook her husband gently and repeated his name as he blinked himself awake. The light from the hall skirted across the bed, lightening the gloom as he stared up at her.

'Are you OK?' he managed.

Jennifer told him everything that had happened in the last hour or so. About Daniel's call and then the police. Andrew had shuffled himself into a sitting position and he fought away a yawn as Jennifer finished.

They had been together since she got pregnant twenty-two years before. They'd got married because it felt like what a couple should do when they were going to have a baby. She'd taken his last name because that's what people did. Times changed and she wasn't sure that expectation would be there for either of those scenarios any longer.

'I need to go up there,' Jennifer told him, even as she wondered when she'd made that decision. The realisation had been sudden and yet inevitable. It was *her* that Daniel had called. He might be twenty-one years old – but Jennifer's son wanted his mum.

She couldn't quite explain why she needed to go, or what she was going to do once she got there. There was a vague notion of finding Daniel, hopefully before the police. Maybe he'd already be in custody by the time she got there, so she could be there for him? It seemed like such an unbelievable outcome. Her baby boy, her only child, suspected of the worst possible thing. A poor young woman apparently dead.

Either way, there wasn't a lot she could do from home.

Andrew rubbed his eyes, though Jennifer could barely see him through the murk.

'I can come with you,' he replied, even though Jennifer wasn't convinced he meant it. It wasn't that he didn't care for their son, more that Andrew didn't really deal with things this serious. Jennifer had always been the one to march into school if there was a problem. It had been her who'd got into an argument with the neighbour who'd objected to Daniel skateboarding years back. The neighbour insisted 'reckless' skateboarders might scratch his car, even though the *might* was doing a lot of heavy lifting – and he was parked half on the pavement anyway.

Andrew was the fun dad. The one who took Daniel to football, when their son was interested in such a thing. He'd insisted on taking Daniel for a pint on the night he turned eighteen, even though Daniel had quietly told his mum that he didn't really like alcohol.

'Someone should stay here in case Daniel comes home,' Jennifer told her husband.

Andrew kicked himself out of the covers and twisted so that he was sitting at her side. She felt him breathing and the warmth of his body.

'What do I do if he comes home?' Andrew asked. 'Do I call the police?'

Jennifer started to say 'of course' but stopped herself. Was it that simple? A terrible thing had happened and the police apparently thought Daniel had something to do with it. If it *wasn't* him, should his parents really turn him in? What was the alternative?

'I don't know,' Jennifer said – and it felt like the first bit of true honesty they'd had in their marriage for a long time.

No forty-something wanted to separate out the assets, sell off the house, and start again. No forty-something wanted to be a divorcee in the age of dating apps. It was much easier to talk around their issues, else pretend they weren't there. They didn't really do honesty any longer.

But they were now.

'Do I call you?' he asked – and Jennifer almost laughed. She was Daniel's mum – not Andrew's.

'I'm sure you can figure it out,' she said, though it came out harsher than she meant.

Or maybe it was exactly as she meant.

They sat in silence for a moment, swallowed by the night, thoughts as dark as the shadows at what might have happened.

'Are you really going back *by yourself*?' Andrew asked – and it sounded like genuine concern.

'I've got to.'

'It's just... after everything that happened to you there. You didn't want to go up for the open day, or to drop off Daniel for uni...?'

Andrew was right, of course. Jennifer already knew that.

'This is bigger than that,' she replied. 'I've got to find him and I know the town better than you.'

There was a pregnant pause and then Andrew couldn't help himself. 'You *knew* the town. It's been a long time since you were there yourself. There are all sorts of new buildings and so on.'

Jennifer had known what he was going to say. He was right, although he could have kept it to himself.

'I have to go,' she said.

'Now?'

Jennifer was already on her feet, ready to turn on the lights and pack a bag. She was *really* going to return to the place she'd promised herself she wouldn't.

'I have to,' she repeated.

TWENTY-FOUR YEARS AGO

Jennifer was having a jacket potato for the twelfth day running. It was 90p in the university canteen, along with either a pot of tuna mayo, beans, or cheese. A bargain – that was certainly better than cooking in the grimy shared kitchen. Not only that but Hayley had read in a magazine somewhere that potatoes were supposed to be good at curing hangovers.

As it was, neither Jennifer, Natasha or Hayley were hungover that lunchtime, although it had been an early 11 a.m. start with lectures. How anybody was supposed to be paying attention at that ungodly hour was the biggest mystery of their course. Hayley and Jennifer had spent an hour listening to their lecturer waffle on, while Natasha took notes. Among their trio of friends, she had seemingly taken it upon herself to take notes for them all – which was fine by Jennifer. After class, they had headed to the canteen in an attempt to wake up.

Trays clattered across tables, as cutlery clanked off plates. The canteen was always a symphony at lunchtimes. The oily smell of chips hung on the air, as it always did. It might be the twenty-first century – just – but cuisine was yet to move much past chips and pizza.

Jennifer was halfway through her potato when the shouting started. She turned to see a lad stomping down the steps. He was broad and lumbering, with the sort of hunched walk that made it look like he was permanently wearing a heavy backpack. He bellowed 'Jo', while stumbling towards the windows, a handful of tables away from where Jennifer was sitting.

A girl with purple hair was sitting by herself, reading a paperback as a pizza slice sat largely uneaten on the table in front of her. As the man approached, she put down her book, pages splayed, spine cracked.

'I told you what you had to do,' she said, firmly.

The canteen had gone quiet, the underlying din silenced as students stopped to watch whatever drama was about to unfold.

'I can't,' he said, though there was a quiver to his voice. He was carrying a crumpled Tesco carrier bag and his bottom lip wobbled, as if he was about to cry.

The girl sighed long and loud. 'I'm not going over this again, Craig,' she said.

Craig was towering over her and he bobbed on his toes, seemingly unsure what to do.

Jennifer flicked a quick glance to her friends, who were both watching the scene unfold.

For a moment it felt as if Craig was going to twist and blunder away. He half-turned, before spinning back and reaching into the supermarket bag. It felt like slow motion as he pulled out a kitchen knife and wafted it around clumsily. It was the type of long, pointy, triangular blade that Jennifer used to slice vegetables in their shared kitchen when she wasn't buying a potato every day.

Nobody spoke.

Jo gawped up, mouth open, while Craig stared down at her. Neither seemed quite sure what to do. The knife was swaying in Craig's loose grip, as if he had surprised himself.

But then, from nowhere, Jennifer was on her feet. Neither of her friends had moved but, within a moment, Jennifer had stepped around the tables and was standing in front of Craig. She wasn't entirely sure how she'd got there, or what she was planning to do. It had been instinctive and impulsive. She was in between Craig and Jo, staring up to the taller man.

That was the thing with having an alcoholic mother. She might not wave knives around, but there was often shouting and vague threats. Lots of tears, too. Jennifer had got used to soothing people on the edge. She knew when threats were meant – and when they weren't.

Which is why she could see that Craig's heart wasn't in this. As they looked to one another, he knew it, too.

'It's OK,' Jennifer said, her tone calm and flat. She was well practised from trying to talk down her mother after she'd come home from the shop raging at the lack of food in the cupboards. Either that, or complaining that she couldn't find her cigarettes. Jennifer would ask which route she'd taken home, something like that. Her mother would blink, confused, and distracted. It wouldn't always work, but it often did – and that was enough. 'We can talk this out,' Jennifer told Craig. 'There's no need for the knife.'

His wide eyes stared into Jennifer's, before he angled his head to goggle at the blade. It was as if he didn't remember taking it from the bag. That it wasn't him who'd brought it.

His wrist flickered and, for a moment, Jennifer thought she'd misjudged him. The blade was so close that she'd have no time to move if he lunged.

So close...

Except he didn't lunge. He was still holding the empty Tesco bag in his other hand and lifted it, before dropping the knife inside.

'It's, um...'

Craig never finished the sentence. He stepped backwards, still eyeing Jennifer, before spinning and hurrying towards the steps. A moment later and he was around the corner, out of sight.

FOUR

TUESDAY

Purple was licking the horizon as Jennifer navigated the empty backstreets of Ashington. The red-brick terraces of the outskirts were the same as they had been when Jennifer had been a student almost a quarter-century before. Someone once told her the houses had been built a hundred years before, back when every man in the town worked at the mill. The boys, too. They were identical relics of an industry and a time that no longer existed.

The town was different but the same, like seeing an old boyfriend a couple of decades after splitting up.

Andrew had driven Daniel up for the open day and starts of term. Jennifer couldn't quite believe that her son had chosen this university of them all – but it was the only one which offered him the music course he wanted.

Despite the lack of aptitude shown from either of his parents, Daniel had always been a natural at music. One of those who could pick up an instrument and make it sing. As he got older, he'd decided he didn't want to be in a band. Being front and centre didn't appeal, which was very him. Very Jennifer, probably. He wanted to compose and create, to be the person at the back who could say he'd made something, rather than the one at the front belting it out.

Which was why, when it came to this *specific* music course, he said he didn't have a choice. There was truth to that – except there was *always* a choice.

Daniel knew what this town meant to her. He knew why she had dropped out so many years before. Jennifer didn't blame her son for coming, but she also didn't *not* blame him. She figured it would be three years, then he'd come home – or move somewhere else. There was no scenario in which she considered returning herself.

Jennifer had driven for more than four hours and it was a little after six in the morning now. It would have taken longer had there been any traffic in the early hours. She yawned her way across town, heading in the once familiar direction of the university. The main buildings were all signposted but many of the students lived in the small houses that dotted the maze of side streets.

Like most students nowadays, Daniel couldn't get by with only his loan and a bit of money from his parents. When it came to finance, things had changed so quickly since Jennifer had been a student – and undoubtedly for the worst. Everything was so expensive for young people, especially rent.

Some of his friends worked in shops, pubs, or the university library. Others offered IT help, or personal training. Daniel had started tutoring music at some point earlier in the year. He'd set up his own website, with associated social media accounts. When he'd got his first client, he'd called his mum, sounding as enthusiastic as Jennifer could remember. It was so rare that they spoke but, in that moment, he'd been an excited child once more. The boy who'd eagerly told her about the goal he scored, back when he was into football. Or when he'd seen a cheap acoustic guitar in a charity shop, and realised he could buy it himself with the money made from washing cars.

That moment was short-lived. Whenever Jennifer asked how things were going with his tutoring, Daniel would say they were 'fine', or something similarly neutral. That tended to be his way, and perhaps most young adults were the same with their parents. It was all the minimal amount of information until something was needed, or someone was heartbroken.

Or, or course, until something went tragically wrong.

Jennifer mulled over that as she parked on one of the side streets parallel to where Daniel lived. Years since she'd left but those little side streets with student houses were the same as ever. She had received no messages while driving, but tried calling Daniel. She didn't expect him to answer, but it was still disappointing that he didn't. She'd had so many hours for dark thoughts to creep in. Those officers on the doorstep might not have said as much – but, at the absolute least, her son was suspected of being involved in something terrible.

Find My Friends showed Daniel as being in his shared house, barely a couple of hundred metres away, except it also said he was 'not found', which perhaps meant his phone had been turned off somewhere near the house.

In the last year or so, Jennifer had often looked at Find My Friends for comfort in knowing where Daniel was. It always felt like spying and she wondered if he'd mind. They'd set it up when he'd first got a mobile phone. It had been a condition of buying him one for his birthday. She'd told him it was a safety thing and, when he'd been in his early teens, it probably was. Now he was in his twenties, he could buy his own phone and didn't need his mother to look out for him. Jennifer didn't know whether her son had forgotten to turn it off, or if he simply didn't mind her knowing where he was. A large part of her didn't want to risk asking, in case he had forgotten and decided to turn it off.

Jennifer fought away a yawn. She'd barely considered her husband on the drive – but Daniel was his son, too.

Andrew picked up on the first ring. His voice was pained and tired – and she doubted he'd slept much.

'I made it,' she told him, talking about the drive.

'What are you going to do now?' he asked, practical as ever.

Jennifer had had a lot of time to consider this, though she didn't have a great answer. She'd thought being in the town would be enough to trigger an idea better than finding her son. A part of her wondered whether the police had arrested him while she had been on the road.

'I'm going to head to his house and see if any of his flatmates are up,' Jennifer replied.

Andrew grunted with something that might have been approval. It was hard to tell, especially as they were both so tired. 'I think there might be someone watching the house,' he added.

'What do you mean?'

He *hrmmed* to himself. 'Not sure. There's someone in a black car over the road, just sitting there.'

Jennifer thought for a moment. 'Maybe it's someone waiting to pick up a neighbour for work?'

It didn't sound convincing, even to her. There was every chance the police had sent someone out to watch the house in case Daniel appeared. More fool them. If they were really lucky, they might catch a glimpse of her husband opening the curtains while in his underwear.

'Maybe...' Andrew replied, also not sounding persuaded.

He said they should keep in contact and then offered an awkward 'bye', before hanging up.

The air was crisp; the sky a gloomy grey as Jennifer got out of the car. Lights were beginning to flicker on inside some of the houses as people woke up.

Jennifer hadn't lived in this area of town herself, though she had definitely walked these streets on the way home from nights out. Drunken students would sway along the centre of the road in the early hours, back in the days when it was a pound a pint.

Daniel had lived in halls for his first year but moved into a shared house with his friends for the second.

Jennifer had barely turned onto the street where her son lived when she spotted the police tape. It was looped around a lamp post and then tied to a gatepost, blocking off access to a house. A pair of police cars were parked on the street outside. Someone in a white paper suit was shuffling out of the house, while a pair of uniformed officers hung around on the pavement. Jennifer had been about to check her phone to confirm her son's house number, though this felt like something of a giveaway.

It definitely wasn't a good sign.

She saw faces in windows as she headed along the road, knowing it would be quite the shock for people waking up to see such a police presence.

That knotting, twisting sensation was back in Jennifer's stomach as she buried her hands in her jacket pockets and hurried towards the tape. She wondered if the officers would be able to tell her what had happened, or whether Daniel had been found.

She had almost reached them when Jennifer passed a neighbour's overgrown bush, then realised there was somebody sitting on the wall at the other side. The young man was in loose joggers, with an oversized hoody: vaping with one hand, scrolling his phone with the other.

Jennifer stopped and turned to take him in. They had never met, though she'd seen photos of him with Daniel.

As the young man realised he was being watched, he lowered his vape pen to look up and take her in. His eyes widened slowly with recognition.

'It's Mark, isn't it?' Jennifer said.

'Uh.... yes,' he replied, sounding unsure – though Jennifer

didn't blame him for not wanting to talk to her. He was one of the students who'd moved in with Daniel at the start of their second year. There were four of them sharing a house.

'What happened?' Jennifer asked.

Mark slipped a glance towards the police officers, who were only a few metres away. Neither of them had seemingly noticed her – but, suddenly, Mark was staring at the ground.

'I don't think I can, um...'

'I know the police are looking for Daniel.'

That got no reaction as Mark continued to look to the floor, deliberately avoiding any sort of eye contact.

'You can tell me,' Jennifer added.

Mark clucked his tongue, seemingly thinking it over. He lifted his vape and inhaled, before guffing out something sweet. The air was suddenly heavy with chocolate or toffee.

And then, the darkness was back.

'Daniel killed Ella,' he said.

FIVE

There was something about the words coming from Daniel's housemate that made it sound more real. The police were used to talking about crimes and other terrible things. They were always looking for someone, always knocking on doors.

But those three words – Daniel killed Ella – felt so real in this young man's voice.

Ella really was dead – and people thought Daniel had done it. Not long before, it felt as if it could be a mistake, or a mix-up with people or names. Now, it was fact.

Jennifer needed a moment. She took a breath and glanced towards the house and the fluttering tape.

'Did you see it?' she asked. The sentence felt heavy in her chest, as if someone had shoved her hard.

Her question got a shake of the head.

'What happened?'

Another shake. 'I got home and Dan's door was open,' Mark said. 'She was on the bed...'

He took a long breath, before finding solace in his vape once more. He was blinking and shattered. People always said they knew how others felt in a moment of crisis – and Jennifer had to stop herself from saying the same. But she really *did* know how he felt.

Except that wasn't the only thing going through Jennifer's mind. Mark hadn't *seen* Daniel kill Ella. He'd not *heard* it happening. But it was no wonder the police were looking for Daniel if Ella had been killed in his room.

'How did she...?'

Mark gulped at the question. Jennifer watched him inhale heavily and wondered whether she'd get an answer.

'There was a lamp cord around her neck,' he said solemnly.

From nowhere the chill of the morning rippled through Jennifer. 'A lamp cord...?' she repeated, though it wasn't really a question.

It couldn't be that. Not again. It was impossible.

Mark was nodding. 'That's what I saw.'

Jennifer felt the urge to comfort him. Perhaps in anticipation of such a gesture, Mark was suddenly on his feet. He brushed down his front, pocketing the vape pen and phone.

'I've got to get off,' he said, dragging up a bag that had been sitting on the ground behind the wall. 'I have to shower at the uni gym, because we're not allowed in the house.'

He flicked a glance towards the police officers, who were paying him no attention.

'Do you know where he is?' Mark asked, finally looking at Jennifer properly. There were red rings around his eyes, the gentlest dots of tears in the corners.

'No,' Jennifer replied, and then: 'Do you?'

'If I did, I'd have told them first,' Mark said, nodding towards the police. There was a hint of aggression, though Jennifer didn't necessarily blame him.

'I'm sorry for what you had to see,' she said. 'Is there anything I can do?'

That got another shake of the head. 'I've got lectures, then I do afternoons at the Red Lion.' A pause and then he motioned towards the house. 'They said we should be allowed back later...'

There was something in the way Mark said it that made it seem as if that wasn't necessarily a good thing. Who wanted to sleep in a room next to where someone had recently died?

Jennifer thanked him again, though Mark's back was already turned as he hurried off in the direction of the university. She watched him for a moment, before turning back to the house.

Someone in a white paper suit was carrying out a series of items in what looked like transparent sandwich bags. Jennifer couldn't quite make out what any of it was, before he loaded the items into the back of an unmarked white van that was parked across the road.

The pair of officers had noticed her now and were muttering between themselves. Jennifer again considered asking them what was going on, though she doubted they could tell her any more than Mark had. For now, she wasn't particularly keen to identify herself as Daniel's mother, just in case they decided to question her more formally. She had driven through the night, after all.

Instead, Jennifer turned and headed back towards the car, where the cool air had invaded the inside. Her fingers ached from the chill as she fumbled with her phone.

Now she'd been told Ella was killed by a lamp cord around her neck, she knew Daniel couldn't have done what Mark was claiming he had. Daniel knew why his mum had never graduated, he knew what had happened to make her drop out.

Jennifer started the car, with no particular plan of where to go. The radio blipped on, with the fading bars of Ed Sheeran, before it cut to a presenter teeing up the news. Warm air gushed from the car heaters as Jennifer held her quivering fingers in front of the blowers.

The newsreader launched into her script with no messing

around: 'Our top story this morning. Police are investigating a murder in Ashington...'

Her tone was low and serious and the longer she spoke, the more it sank in for Jennifer that this was as serious as anything could be. It wasn't simply a death, the police were calling it a *murder*. And then, as that was becoming reality, Jennifer's body went cold at the newsreader's next words.

'... Police are searching for local student, Daniel Farley. He is considered dangerous and should not be approached.'

SIX

Jennifer continued listening to the radio, though little else went in. Her little boy, whom she'd once watched dig a big hole on a beach when he was six or seven, was now considered dangerous. The same boy who she had once been able to hold in a single hand. The same son who had cried the first, and only, time he'd watched *E.T.*, because he couldn't take the 'I'll be right here' line near the end. Now police were saying he shouldn't be approached.

It didn't feel real.

Jennifer found herself browsing local news websites, where similar details had been hastily put up, in among the avalanche of adverts. What a contrast to try to read a serious news story, while a video for something called *Mr Pete's Meat Emporium* kept appearing over the top.

Daniel was named in all the pieces. As far as Jennifer could tell, there were no pictures yet published, but it wouldn't be long. She suspected there would already be some on various Facebook forums. People would be reading his name, then looking him up. Any silly videos or photographs he'd ever posted would soon be pored over for signs he was a secret psychopath.

Those dark thoughts from the long drive now felt as if they were nowhere near dark enough. This was so much worse than Jennifer had feared.

And what of Ella's parents? That poor girl had been found alone, dead, strangled. Daniel wouldn't have done that. Should she try to contact them and say?

The engine was idling as she called Andrew instead. He hadn't seen the reports, though said the police had already returned to the house. They'd largely repeated everything from the night before, asking if he knew where Daniel was – and then emphasising strongly that he must contact them if their son got in touch.

After Jennifer hung up, she realised the call had somehow left her feeling even worse.

She tried to remember whether Daniel had said anything else on the previous night's call. He'd definitely said 'It wasn't me' – but was there more?

She wondered whether he'd discovered Ella's body before Mark? If that had made him run? He must be so frightened, knowing he was going to be accused of something he hadn't done. Knowing Ella was dead.

That poor girl.

As Jennifer tried to remember the call, she found herself scrolling through the messages she'd swapped with Daniel over the previous months. There were the semi-regular dog photos, plus the various check-ins, where he assured her he was fine. Definitely nothing to indicate he was in trouble, nor that he and Ella were having problems.

With nothing obvious, Jennifer loaded her email and searched Daniel's name. He'd forward her the odd thing here and there, though it was usually admin he didn't want to do. She'd encouraged him to make sure he kept some degree of receipts from his tutoring, just in case the inland revenue came calling. It was supposed to be a joke with an edge, but he'd taken it seriously and passed on every invoice since.

At least it kept her in his life.

Jennifer scrolled through a long series of PDF attachments until she stumbled across an email from a year before. Not long after he'd started at university, Daniel had asked if she'd pay for a locker. It was close to the university, which meant he could leave all his books there, without having to lug them to and from his halls. There was an annual fee, which she'd agreed to pay. Because the credit card needed to match the name on file, everything had come to her email – and then she'd forwarded the details.

Jennifer checked the locker's address against the Maps app. It was ten-minute drive, or twenty-five minute walk. She had never seen the locker before renting it and figured it was worth checking, considering she had little idea of what else to do. At worst, there'd be nothing inside, at best, there might be some sort of clue as to Daniel's location.

The town suddenly felt busy as she drove through the narrow roads. Drivers were bumper-to-bumper, heading to work or school with their children. Jennifer batted away the yawns, trying to stay focused, until she realised she was in the area where she used to live.

Like Daniel, she'd been in halls her first year, before moving into a shared house. As she pulled to a stop at a set of traffic lights, Jennifer strained against her seat belt to get a view of her old first-year block of flats. The building had been run-down twenty-five years back – and they were long past that. Blue chunky fencing ringed what used to be the green at the front, while the block itself was boarded up. Large 'Keep Out' signs were clipped along the fence line, and there was something about an upcoming demolition that Jennifer didn't have time to read because the traffic light had turned green.

She continued along the road, following her phone directions towards the locker, as her thoughts drifted.

It wasn't long until Jennifer pulled into a grotty car park around the back of a grottier-looking lecture hall. An overflowing clothes donation bin was in the corner, along with an upturned shopping trolley. It felt like the sort of place in which little good ever happened – and Jennifer didn't hang around as she hurried along an alley, following the phone's instructions.

It was still too early for lectures and the area was largely empty as Jennifer emerged next to a glass-fronted building that she was certain used to be a bank. Jennifer vaguely remembered one of her friends sitting in the atrium when they were walking home from town. There had probably been too much alcohol drunk, though Jennifer's memory was hazy – which perhaps confirmed as much.

It was definitely not a bank any longer. Instead, the sign across the top read 'Safe And Secure Storage', which felt as if someone could have probably taken a little longer with the branding.

Jennifer tried the door, which was locked. There was a keypad to the side and it was only as she re-read the email that she realised she'd been sent two PINs. The first got her through the door, which led into a room laid out a lot like a swimming pool changing room. Lockers were stacked floor to ceiling around the walls, with three more rows in the centre. It was impossible to miss the cameras in the corners, watching Jennifer as she walked into the space. Nobody else was inside.

After checking the number from the email, Jennifer followed the bank of lockers until she found Daniel's. It was at ground level, almost in the corner, nearly directly under one of the cameras. Number fourteen. She crouched and felt her back creak and crack. She'd been sitting in the car for far too long, not to mention she'd barely slept in the last twenty-four hours. That left her sitting on the ground as she tapped the PIN into the locker. The panel beeped, then flashed green as the lock disengaged.

Jennifer braced herself, assuming the worst. It was that sort of day... which made it almost a disappointment to find the stack of books sitting at the front. It seemed like a relic that so much teaching was apparently still done from heavy textbooks.

Jennifer rested her head against the nearest bank of lockers and sighed. She closed her eyes for a moment, half wishing she could fall asleep here. At least it was warm. It was hard to think through the fog of the past day. Did Daniel want her to find him? To help him? Did he simply want her to know that, when the police came calling, he wasn't guilty of what they'd say he was? If that was true, wouldn't it have been better to work with them? It looked so bad that he'd seemingly run. Most people would assume he was guilty because he was hiding.

It wasn't me.

That's what he wanted her to know – and, somehow, Jennifer needed to show everyone else.

She opened her eyes and blinked back into the room.

Jennifer was about to close the door when she realised the locker was far deeper than the books. She moved them forward, a few at a time, restacking them on the ground, and giving her access to the back of the space. It was dark and she reached to the wall, her hand closing around what turned out to be a cloth supermarket bag-for-life. The sort nobody ever remembered to take out of their car boot.

The bag was far larger than Jennifer first thought, and plopped to the ground with a solid *thunk*. It was so full that the top couldn't close, leaving the contents easy to see.

Jennifer didn't need to go digging to see what was inside.

It was cash.

Lots of it.

SEVEN

For a moment, Jennifer wondered if she'd somehow got the wrong locker. She rechecked the email – but the number was correct and the PIN had worked. Then there were the music textbooks at the front. It had to be Daniel's.

Except... there was so much money.

Far more cash than Jennifer had ever seen – and this was the age of the cashless society. When Daniel was paid for tutoring, it was through bank transfer. Jennifer knew that, because she sorted the invoices and receipts for him. Almost everything nowadays was electronic. And yet...

Jennifer opened the bag properly, instantly realising it wasn't only cash. A mobile phone was wedged into the side, along with a loose key, unattached to any fob or ring. The sort of Yale key that opened a front door, without any indication of what it was for.

As she continued digging around the notes, Jennifer pulled out a rectangle of plastic that turned out to be a driving licence. Except, when she turned it over, the face and name didn't belong to Daniel. It was from someone she'd never heard of, called Benjamin Davies. Benjamin had a plain, expressionless face; brown dead eyes staring forward. His date-of-birth showed that he was a few years older than Daniel, though still in his twenties.

She wondered whether the cash belonged to this Ben – or if Daniel had sublet him the locker. Except Daniel's books were still inside. Was he sharing it?

Jennifer couldn't see any other items in the bag, but there was so much more money. All the notes were bundled into piles with paper wraps – and it didn't take long for Jennifer to flick through the first and count five-hundred pounds in tens and twenties. She didn't count the rest, not properly, but there was at least another hundred bundles, probably more.

Fifty grand – and that was an absolute minimum. It could be closer to a hundred. The notes were crumpled and used, not the sort to have recently come from a bank. It had all been in circulation.

Jennifer closed the handles of the bag as best she could.

She knew she should call the police. It wasn't only what had happened to poor Ella, but there was so much money. It wasn't a cliché to say people would kill for such an amount, and Jennifer wondered if somebody had.

The other items were still on the ground and Jennifer picked up the old phone. She could feel her heart thundering again. It was an old Samsung, with a scratched screen and scuffed back. It definitely wasn't Daniel's. He had an iPhone and took a lot more care with his things. He hated the idea of scuffs and scratches on his guitar – and his phone was no different.

That meant a phone and driving licence that wasn't his, a key that probably wasn't, and all the money. Plus, of course, so many questions.

Jennifer was still holding the phone when it started to ring. She jumped and almost dropped it, before realising it was a different phone that was making the noise. She fumbled with her bag, digging into the side pocket before pulling out her own device. It was an o7 mobile number she didn't recognise, though Jennifer's first thought was that it could be Daniel calling from another phone.

She swiped to answer, offering a hurried 'Hello?'

A woman's voice replied: 'Is that Mrs Farley?'

'Who's asking?'

'My name's Helen and I work for the *Ashington Gazette*. I was wondering if—'

Jennifer hung up. The last thing she needed was reporters chasing her, even if they did have reason. She considered turning off her phone, though didn't want to miss anything if Daniel called or messaged. She assumed the police would be trying to trace his proper phone, although that might be because she'd seen too many crime dramas. She wasn't sure if they could actually do that. Either way, her phone needed to be on – so she blocked the reporter's number and then returned the device to her bag.

Not that she had ever really taken her eyes from the money. It had a pull that was impossible to ignore. Jennifer had never been one of those people who always had some sort of money-making scheme on the go. What was it they called it? Hustle culture?

And yet...

Jennifer couldn't stop looking at it in the bag. The neat piles had been stacked into a cube that felt like just the sort of tidiness of which Daniel would be capable.

A minute or so passed until Jennifer remembered the cameras. There was one ahead of her facing the door that might be recording her if it had a wide enough lens. She was fairly sure the one above her wouldn't be able to capture directly down, which meant the money might not have been spotted. She had no way of knowing if anyone was monitoring it anyway. The cameras might only be used if something went wrong. In any case, the locker was in her name. Technically, this was *her* locker, with no connection to Daniel, and the police wouldn't know to look for it.

She knew she should call them, yet the 'It wasn't me' haunted her. Daniel didn't trust the police to believe him, which is presumably why he'd run. Did that mean Jennifer should feel the same?

Jennifer returned the bag of money to the rear of the locker, then stacked the books in front. It was more or less as it had been when she got there. She closed the door, though changed her mind before locking it into place. Moments later and the books were back on the floor. Jennifer reached into the bag and retrieved the phone, driving licence and key, before pushing the rest back inside. This time she did lock it.

She was still sitting on the floor as she struggled with the phone, trying to turn it on. It was heavier and clunkier than anything she'd used from the past few years, so likely eight or ten years old.

It took a while for the phone to boot, though there was no passcode needed before the main app screen appeared. Jennifer had never used an Android, so it took a few moments to figure out how things worked. After a bit of fiddling, from what she could tell, there were no stored texts or messages, no missed or made calls, and nobody saved in contacts. It felt like whoever owned it made a point of deleting everything they did. Which definitely couldn't be a good thing if it was related to Daniel.

Jennifer put the key, phone and licence in her bag. The notes could stay where they were. She wasn't naïve. That amount of cash was rare, and likely only kept by drug dealers, or – perhaps – prolific sex workers. Jennifer couldn't imagine Daniel being involved in either of those things, and yet the money's presence in his locker was undeniable.

She pulled herself up, checked the locker was actually shut, and then headed back into the cold. Jennifer retraced the route to the grimy car park, where she sat in her vehicle. It wasn't warm – but it was *marginally* toastier than outside.

Jennifer had so many questions for her son. She'd driven through the night without much of a plan, somehow trusting that she'd have some idea of what to do once she arrived. Now, she felt more lost than before.

She searched the internet for 'Benjamin Davies', then 'Ben Davies', hoping the driving licence might give some clue about the locker contents – except the name was too common. There were loads of Ben Davieses.

Jennifer needed help – and she knew exactly who to call.

Someone from the area who'd been at the back of Jennifer's thoughts throughout the drive. How could she not be?

Jennifer tapped the screen to see Natasha's details. It had been more than twenty years since they'd last seen one another, though they were always in a vague degree of contact. They never called or messaged regularly, yet through Facebook and the like were always aware of what the other was up to. Not good enough friends to attend each other's wedding, but on decent enough terms to know when and where it was happening. Natasha knew Jennifer had a son who was at university, while Jennifer knew Natasha had three kids of her own. She knew Natasha worked in the office of a car dealership and that her husband had something to do with haulage.

Friends but not friends.

They shared a history of course – and Natasha knew this town better than Jennifer ever would. She'd stayed, while Jennifer had run.

Jennifer's thumb hovered over the phone number, trying to convince herself it was a good idea. It had been a long time since they'd been eating lunch in the university canteen, when Craig had walked into their lives with that knife in a bag.

A long, *long* time.

Except Natasha answered on the second ring and it

sounded as if she'd been waiting on this call for two decades. As if she always knew it would come.

'Jen...?'

'Did you see the news?' Jennifer asked, not bothering with a hello.

There was a pause, a breath. 'About the girl at the uni?'

'She was strangled by a lamp cord,' Jennifer said.

Another beat. 'How do you know?'

'It's Daniel's girlfriend who's dead. He's the one the police are looking for. They think he did it.'

Jennifer could hear her old friend absorbing the news and then, finally: 'Do you want to talk?'

TWENTY-FOUR YEARS AGO

Jennifer, Natasha and Hayley were sitting on the steps outside the students' union building. The crumbling stairs banked down like an amphitheatre, even though the only thing at the bottom was a smoking shelter next to the double entrance doors.

It had been a little over a week since Craig had lumbered into the canteen, before eventually turning around again. Jennifer hadn't seen either him or Jo since – and it almost felt as if those few minutes had been a dream. She knew it had happened, that she had been in the middle of it, and yet there was a wispy, translucent feel to the memory. As if she could never quite remember it properly.

Jo hadn't said much after the incident. Jennifer assumed she was in some sort of shock, because she'd mumbled a 'thanks' and then hurried away.

Jennifer's friends had treated her with awed reverence in the immediate aftermath, asking how she'd been brave enough to stand up to him. Jennifer wasn't sure what to tell them. She didn't think she was special, it was just one of those things. In the moment, she had somehow known what to do. There had been vague talk between the three of them about contacting the police, except none of them knew either Jo or Craig, so what were they going to say?

After that, they had continued with their regular lives of lectures, tutorials, and a couple of nights out.

They hadn't returned to the canteen, though. None of them had said it out loud but it felt wrong to be there after what they'd seen. Baked potatoes had also lost their appeal for Jennifer – which is why they had moved onto shared lunches on the steps outside the union.

The days had been getting warmer and it wouldn't be long until what felt like the entire population of students would be spending their lunchtimes dotted around the steps, eating sandwiches and chatting.

Their conversations flitted around their course, the people on it, those in charge – and then far more important topics, such as where they should go that evening. The nearest pub was doing a pound a pint, but it was grotty and always crammed. There was some sort of doctors and nurses night going on at the club in town, but that would be full of pervs and creeps. The union itself was hosting a comedy night but that was hit-and-miss.

And then, as the trio continued chatting, Jennifer saw them. It was Jo's purple hair that caught her eye as the double doors opened and a couple pushed their way into the sun. They passed under the smoking shelter and then started climbing the steps, heading roughly in the direction of the library. Jo was at the back, clasping onto Craig's hand as he hobbled up the steps. The walk was unmistakable.

Natasha had been saying something about maybe joining drama club but had stopped mid-sentence as the three of them gawped at Jo and Craig holding hands. It was as if they were a normal couple, as if he hadn't pulled a knife on his girlfriend a little over a week before.

For a moment, the trio had gone unnoticed but then, as Jo

reached the top, she stopped, released Craig's hand, and turned to stare. She was focused on Jennifer, who felt herself shrinking under the stare – not that there was any respite from Craig. He was glaring too, the pair of them gazing from one side of the steps to the other.

Jennifer felt as if she could read their thoughts, or Craig's at the very least. *How dare you get involved in our relationship. How dare you.*

And then, as if it had never happened, Craig reached and re-took Jo's hand. With a swish of purple hair, she turned and the pair of them headed towards the library. A moment later and they were out of sight.

It felt as if Jennifer, Natasha and Hayley all breathed in at the same time. It was then that Jennifer had the feeling that something awful was going to happen. Maybe something inevitable. She wouldn't be able to stop it, even if she wanted to, even if she tried. An idea that something had happened in the canteen that went beyond her understanding – and that her life would never quite be the same again.

EIGHT

Jennifer walked along the cool harbour's edge. She passed between a pair of railings and emerged into a small car park, where a butty van was parked underneath a swaying tree. A line of people snaked from the front of the van onto the path that looped out towards the road and the trading estate beyond. The large whiteboard advertising the £2 breakfast bap special was likely a reason why, not to mention that drifting smell of egg, sausage and bacon.

Natasha was sitting on a bench close to the van, knees crossed, facing the water. She was in a big coat, a belt knotted across the front. A napkin sat on the bench at her side, with a half-eaten breakfast bap oozing yolk onto the paper. She'd gone blonde since the last time Jennifer had seen her, though Jennifer had gone darker. Those little greys had been conspiring against her in increasing numbers over the past few years.

When she spotted Jennifer, Natasha stood and smiled. 'You made it,' she said – as if this were a long-planned reunion.

For a minute or two, it was. They talked about how great the other looked, how it had been such a long time, that they should've met so much earlier. All that. It felt good for Jennifer to play the game, if only for a few moments. In another life, they'd have been better friends. They'd have seen each other several times a year, maybe even been maids of honour for one another.

Jennifer sat on the other side of the bench, as Natasha took a bite of her sandwich, while carefully holding the napkin underneath. A small goop of yolk drizzled across her fingers as she licked it clean.

'Messy business,' Natasha said. She took another bite and then put down the bap on the bench between them. 'It's only two quid if you want one. Best bargain in town.'

Jennifer's stomach grumbled at the idea of food. As well as a lack of sleep, she hadn't eaten in about fourteen hours. If it wasn't for the queue, she'd have likely indulged.

'Are you still at the car dealership?' Jennifer asked. There were much more important things to talk about – but she could hardly launch into that right away.

'I've been laid off twice this year already,' Natasha replied. 'They bring me back for a couple of months at a time, then let me go again. I should probably go somewhere else...'

The pair of them sat for a moment, gazing across the rippling water of the docks to the bank of metal containers on the far shore. Shipping had always been part of the economy for Ashington. The big boats would come in, unload the various imported cargo containers, swap them for others, then head out again.

As if reading her mind, Natasha spoke: 'The only real work in town is the uni or the docks. They keep talk about expanding but that would mean knocking down some old flats – and there isn't enough housing anyway.'

Maybe she *could* launch into things right away. She hadn't called an old, old friend to chat about blocks of flats.

'They're saying Daniel's killed his girlfriend,' Jennifer

managed. 'He can't have but I need to find him. I don't know where to look...'

Jennifer tailed off, unsure how to finish.

Across the water, a large crane was lifting a metal container from a dock ship and they listened as the mechanism groaned and creaked on the breeze.

'Daniel lives in a house a bit like our old one,' Jennifer added. 'One of the terraces.'

Natasha was silent at first, probably picturing the area. There was no way she could've forgotten what happened. 'Why did you let him come here?'

It felt like an honest question but Jennifer couldn't stop herself sighing. 'He's an adult. It was his choice.'

'Did he know what happened with us?'

'I told him long before he ever applied. Only a few universities offer the music course he wanted – and the others rejected him. His grades weren't brilliant. Exams have never been his thing. It was here or nowhere.'

Jennifer felt more defensive telling this to someone else than when trying to rationalise it to herself. She knew it was true and yet a part of her could never quite get over her son's decision.

'Huh...' Natasha said. It was perhaps more of an exhalation than a word and Jennifer wasn't quite sure what to make of it. 'I didn't think you'd ever come back,' she added.

'I didn't think you'd stay.'

That got a snigger of a laugh, though there was no humour there.

'Neither did I. I suppose I couldn't pull myself away.'

Natasha waited a moment as a soft boom grinded across the water. The crane had placed one of the containers on top of another, the metal grating as they touched.

'I did go and watch on the day they pulled down our old row of houses,' Natasha added. 'They flattened it, as if it had never been there. It's all student flats now. Much nicer than what we had.'

'Good,' Jennifer replied, and she meant it.

She had read an article about it a few years back, probably forwarded by Natasha. The house in which she'd spent some of her second year had been left standing far too long.

'I saw our old halls are getting pulled down, too,' Jennifer said. The place where they'd lived in the first year. It wouldn't be long before any trace of her university life was gone.

'I think that's due in the next month,' Natasha replied. 'I drive past it most days. There's been fences up for ages. I read they're starting with Cabot, then moving onto Drake and Livingstone.'

More quiet as Jennifer tried to remember what their other blocks were named. Cabot, Drake, Livingstone, Magellan and... something else. Her block, Cabot, was one of five, each of which were named after famous explorers. When he was busy fighting the Spanish, Francis Drake probably didn't expect himself to be synonymous with horny students getting off with one another in a shadowed corner of a building named after him.

Not that it mattered. There were more important things to talk about.

'He's been here a bit over a year,' Jennifer added. 'The police came to the house last night, asking if I'd seen him.'

'Have you?'

'Not since last month when his dad drove him up for his second year. They said his girlfriend was dead. After that, I just, sort of... had to be here. I wasn't really sure what I was going to do when I arrived. The police are still looking for him.'

Natasha was staring towards the water and nodded a fraction. She had clearly seen the news and perhaps done a bit more reading since their brief phone call.

'You said there was a lamp cord...?'

'I spoke to Daniel's housemate. He found the body.'

'Oh...' The pause was devastating: no instant rebuttal, only acceptance. 'Did Daniel know *exactly* what happened with us?'

'He knew.'

'What do you think?' Natasha asked – and it was such a loaded question. What she was *really* asking was whether Jennifer thought her son was a murderer.

'He wouldn't do this,' Jennifer said. 'I just want to find him.'

'Why did he run?'

It was a fair question, the one everyone would be asking. Most people who were innocent of killing someone would hang around for the police. Jennifer didn't have an answer. It was feeling like a mistake to meet.

Natasha picked up the remnants of her sandwich and finished it in two bites. She dabbed her chin, then dropped the paper into the bin at the side of the bench.

'Are you asking me to help you find him?' Natasha asked.

That's exactly what Jennifer had been thinking, except, in the moment, she knew she couldn't. Natasha didn't owe her anything, and certainly not this.

'Not really,' Jennifer lied. 'It's just I don't know the town any more. It's the same but different. *Really* different. I guess I was wondering if you could think of anywhere I might look?'

It felt like a silly request now she'd said it. It was unlikely Natasha was going to know the town better than the police officers who served it – and that was if she *wanted* to help.

'Does he drive?' Natasha asked.

'No.'

'He couldn't have got far, then.'

Jennifer had already figured that out – even if there was an officer sitting outside her home at the other end of the country. If Daniel had called from somewhere near his house the night before, he was almost certainly still in the area.

'I don't know if there's anything I can say,' Natasha said.

'I'm guessing the police will be looking for his phone records to see if he was in contact with friends, that sort of thing.'

That was another thing of which Jennifer was sure. At some point they would discover he had rung her, and want to ask what he'd said. She hadn't exactly lied to the officers the night before, but she hadn't told them he'd called. It was a potential problem for later.

For a moment, it felt as if Natasha was about to get up. She uncrossed, then re-crossed her legs. The smell of sausage was still strong in the air and, when Jennifer turned, the queue for the van was a quarter of the size it had been.

'Do you want a coffee?' Jennifer asked. She knew it had been a waste of a meeting but perhaps it was good to see Natasha's face again after all these years.

That got the slimmest of smiles: 'If you're buying.'

Jennifer rounded the bench and joined the back of the line, shuffling forward at regular intervals until it was her turn. She knew she should eat, though couldn't force herself to be hungry. She also didn't think her stomach could handle so much grease in one go. Instead, she ordered a pair of coffees, guessed that Jennifer wanted milk, no sugar, then carried the polystyrene cups back to the bench.

Natasha had been typing something into her phone but stopped as Jennifer neared, dispatching the device into her bag.

'I think it's instant,' Jennifer said, passing across the cup.

'I'm not a coffee snob,' Natasha replied, as she sipped from the top.

'Me either.'

Jennifer copied her old friend, though, in truth, she was a bit snobbish against whatever this was. Coffee was probably a technical truth, even though it was bitter and had a sort of bin juice tang about it.

She drank anyway. It would wake her up.

'Did you hear about Jo?' Natasha asked, in between sips.

Jennifer had cupped her hands around the polystyrene, absorbing the warmth of the drink. Her breath was a gentle mist against the cold. 'What about her?'

'I think she found God. I didn't recognise her at first, probably because she doesn't have purple hair now. She wears glasses and looks so different to when we knew her. I only realised it was her when I was up close. She was in town, next to one of those little stands where they hand out leaflets and try to convert you.'

Jennifer thought on that a moment. They hadn't known one another well – but Jo hadn't seemed the religious type back when she'd been in Jennifer's life.

'Did she give you a leaflet?'

'Not really. I was walking past and felt like I was being watched. That little thing when the back of your neck tingles. I looked over and she was there. She did this blink, like when you know someone but you're not completely sure who it is. I stopped dead on the street, then went over to say hello.'

'When was that?'

'Maybe a year ago?'

'What did she say?'

That got a gentle laugh: 'Just went into her spiel. Acted like we'd never met. I've seen her a few times since. They're in the same place every week, near the optician on the high street. Sometimes it's her, sometimes it's someone else.'

Jennifer could picture the area. The Woolworths would be gone, probably the HMV and Debenhams, too – but she doubted the high street was *that* different. There would still be the large spherical bollards near the top that someone drove into every few months. Still the Christmas lights that went up in October and didn't come down until the spring.

'I suppose, after everything with Craig...' Jennifer said, talking about Jo and her apparent conversion. When there was no reply, she added: 'I guess you'd just want to forget?'

The crane across the water was heaving another container from the cargo ship. The groan echoed across the docks and Jennifer shivered as she slipped through time. She'd forgotten that the creak of those containers would echo through the town if the wind was blowing in a certain direction. There were mornings when she'd be lying in bed, woken by the moans of metal on metal.

Natasha pushed herself up and brushed invisible crumbs from her front. 'I don't know how to help you,' she said. 'I don't know where young people hang out, or where someone might hide.'

This was what Jennifer had feared. She'd driven through the night without much of a plan. She'd found a lot of money that couldn't be explained – and then got in touch with one of the few people she knew, in the hope someone would have a better idea than her. The tiredness was overtaking her, clouding her thoughts and ideas.

'Maybe he texted you something in the past?' Natasha added, almost flippantly as she stood up. 'Sent you a picture? Something like that?' She half-turned towards the cars. 'I'm sorry but I have to get to work. It was nice seeing you again.'

Jennifer agreed but it felt like an end, not a beginning.

Natasha had taken a few steps towards the car park when she stopped.

'If you need help, I'll be around,' she added, although she was looking towards the cars as she spoke. It didn't sound like a real offer, not that Jennifer blamed her. A person couldn't realistically offer too much when someone was wanted for murder.

'Thanks,' Jennifer said – and, as she headed back towards the docks and her own vehicle, she realised it had been more or less the last thing they'd said to one another twenty-odd years before. Except, that time, it had been outside a courtroom.

NINE

Jennifer was stuck again. That hoped inspiration about what to do had never come. Meeting Natasha hadn't helped – and had simply left Jennifer feeling worse about the way she'd let things drift with someone who was supposed to be her friend.

She tried calling Daniel, knowing he wouldn't answer. This time, it didn't even ring. His phone must be off, or perhaps even thrown away. Jennifer really had watched too many crime dramas.

She sat in the driver's seat, as the windows steamed, trying to think of what to do next, before figuring it couldn't do any harm to take Natasha's idea.

She clicked into the messages shared with Daniel over years. There were the dog pictures, of course, but nothing that felt negative or worrying. She found herself scrolling back to the early part of the year, when he'd messaged to say he had his first private tutoring client. He was going to be teaching music to a boy named Charles and had sent Jennifer a photo of a large house with the word 'Posh!'. He'd added that the parents owned an antiques business in town. He'd not named them in the messages but there had been a phone call at some point, when he'd said the dad was named 'Gary'. Jennifer had forgotten the mum's name but, on the call, she'd said something about nobody being called Gary any longer.

It was easy enough to search 'Ashington', 'Gary' and 'Antiques' and find the business. According to the Companies House website, Etherington's Auctions was based at a large house a short distance outside town. Jennifer checked on Google Maps, where a street view image appeared of the same house Daniel had sent her.

As a new place to start, Jennifer figured she didn't have a better idea.

The presence of an Ashington posh bit really was something of a surprise to Jennifer. When she'd lived in town, she'd spent more or less all her time in and around the university, which was anything but upmarket. She would frequently leave her house or flat to find seagulls picking at a dumped takeaway on a wall or the pavement outside.

She doubted there were many kebabs eaten in this part of town, let alone slopped on the ground. The imposing detached houses, with big gates, gave off the vibe of people who drank green smoothies and pretended they were tasty. There'd be a lot of Peloton bikes in an area like this.

The driveway gates were open as Jennifer walked up towards the house. There was a tidy patch of lawn at the front, with flowerbeds pressed against tightly trimmed hedges. A double garage was attached to the house, with a black Audi parked outside.

It was a little after ten and Jennifer had been awake for an entire day and more. The coffee from the sandwich van had done little more than offend her tastebuds. It was only as she reached the front door that she realised she wasn't sure where she'd be sleeping that evening. She would have to look up hotels at some point.

Jennifer rang the bell and heard the chime from inside. She leaned her forehead on the frame, resting for a few seconds, while questioning what she was doing. A small voice told her to leave things to the police, except she couldn't forget Daniel's 'It wasn't me'. There had to be a reason he didn't want to leave himself in the hands of the police.

A young woman was dead but she still trusted her son. She had to.

She just wished she knew how to help.

Nothing had happened, so Jennifer tried the bell again. She fought away a yawn just as the large wooden door swung inwards, revealing a man in jeans and a fleece. He was probably late-fifties, that silver fox-type who went to Coldplay stadium gigs and drank Guinness when the rugby was on. He'd definitely read Sun Tzu's *The Art of War*.

He eyed Jennifer with a slightly raised eyebrow, likely expecting someone else. 'Hello...?'

If she wasn't so tired, Jennifer could have come up with something better than her own, somewhat bemused, 'Hello.' They looked to one another for a moment, before she realised she should probably say a bit more. 'I'm Jennifer. I'm, um, Daniel Farley's mum.'

The man's eyes flared, even as his salt-and-pepper eyebrows dipped to almost meet in the middle. For a moment, Jennifer thought he was going to order her off his property, perhaps even call the police. His features hardened – but only for a flicker. 'Oh, you poor thing,' he said. 'Do you want to come in?'

It wasn't quite what Jennifer had expected. It was hard to know if he felt sorry for her because her son was missing and wanted by the police, or because he knew Daniel – and assumed, like Jennifer, that he was innocent.

The man held the door wider, as the warmth radiated. The

idea of being inside somewhere other than a car suddenly appealed more than anything. Jennifer thank-you'd her way inside as he introduced himself as Gary. He hung her coat on a rack near the door, then said she could keep on her shoes, despite the rack underneath. The hall was wide, with a high ceiling, filled with little in the way of anything. That was the thing with rich people versus poor. When someone had very little, they kept everything, just in case. Those with money could live in big, open spaces – because, if they ever needed something, they'd simply buy it.

Gary led Jennifer through to a show-home kitchen. There were gleaming pans hanging from hooks over the top of an island. The cooker was double the width of anything Jennifer had ever owned, with a series of stainless-steel appliances lining the counter.

'Take a seat,' Gary encouraged, pulling out a stool from underneath the island. Jennifer did as much, as Gary started to fill a kettle from one of those taps with a hose. 'Do you want a tea?' he asked. 'Or we've got coffee pods?'

He nodded towards a machine next to a giant fridge that had a stack of aluminium capsules at the side.

Jennifer was still hoping something would wake her up, so opted for the coffee as Gary fussed.

'My wife's out at the moment,' he said. 'We couldn't believe it when we heard about Ella on the news this morning.'

So he wasn't blaming her for whatever Daniel was accused of.

'Do you know her?' Jennifer asked.

'Of course. She and Daniel are here together most weeks, working with Charles.'

Jennifer hadn't known Ella did the tutoring sessions along-side Daniel – not that Gary seemed to pick up on this.

'We've not told Charles yet. He's at school, so we'll talk to him later. Charles has really come out of himself since Daniel started working with him. He's so much more talkative than he used to be. Daniel's always been so generous with his time. We always offer overtime when he stays, but he always says no. Daniel and Ella would sit in the music room with Charles, composing their little songs on the piano and guitar. Charles is going to be devastated.'

Jennifer needed a moment to absorb that. There was a gentle tone of condescension from the 'little songs' but it felt as if Gary's heart was in the right place.

'What sort of songs?' Jennifer asked.

'They sounded like jingles, or nursery rhymes. That sort of thing.'

'How old is Charles?'

'Six.'

The coffee machine started to whine as the brewing began, leaving a punctured gap as Jennifer wondered how a six-year-old could understand what had happened. What would they even tell him? One of his tutors was dead, and the other accused of doing it? Charles wouldn't even necessarily see them as teachers at his age. And both of them were so young. They'd be friends of a sort, working on music together. It would be fun, rather than a teacher-student relationship.

As the coffee machine finished its cycle, Gary removed the cup from underneath and placed it in front of Jennifer.

'Harriet has a son from her first relationship,' he said.

'Is that your wife?'

'Right. He's in his twenties – so there's a big gap between him and Charles. They don't really have a lot in common, so Daniel and Ella have been invaluable. We brought Daniel in because Charles was interested in songs and music. We didn't realise he'd end up being happier and chattier from it all.'

Jennifer gulped. It was partly because she was so tired –

but, after everything, she needed to hear something positive about her son. There would be so many awful things said and written about him in the coming hours and days. This is what she would cling to until the truth came out. She didn't know what had happened with Ella, or why he'd run – but *this* was her son.

'The police think Daniel killed her,' Jennifer found herself saying. Gary had slid a box tissues across the counter, which was his way of acknowledging the tears. Jennifer dabbed her eyes and then gulped the coffee.

Gary gave her some time as he fiddled with the machine by clearing out the drip tray. There was a radio on in the background, though Jennifer couldn't make out the song. As Jennifer composed herself, Gary didn't press. He fussed around the kitchen, brushing non-existent crumbs into the sink.

He settled on a stool of his own once Jennifer was ready. 'Were there any, um, *problems* with Daniel and Ella?' she asked.

Jennifer couldn't think of a better way to phrase things. That police statement telling people not to approach Daniel would be everywhere by now. She wondered whether Gary believed it. He'd been so kind when talking about Daniel, which wasn't usually how someone would talk about an alleged killer.

'Not that I know of,' Gary replied, although he was chewing his lip.

'You can say,' Jennifer encouraged.

He thought for a fraction more, then nodded shortly. 'When they were here at the weekend, it felt as if they might have had an argument. They weren't really talking to each other when they got here and there was a bruise around Ella's eye.' He waited a moment. 'Harriet and I didn't want to assume or accuse.'

That mention of the bruise felt like an accusation, even if he'd not specifically said.

'I should tell you something,' he added, suddenly sounding

more serious than before. 'When I said Harriet was out, it's because she's with the police. They were here first thing, asking if we knew where Daniel might be, or if we knew anything about what might have happened with them. We told them about Ella's eye – and they asked Harriet to go in and give a formal statement.' He took a breath, then added a genuine-sounding: 'Sorry...'

There was a lump in Jennifer's throat that she tried to swallow away. Ella's bruise proved nothing but felt ominous. It was getting really hard to blame the police for believing Daniel was involved.

Jennifer was already on her feet when she asked to use the toilet. She didn't need to go, just needed a few minutes to herself. Gary led her back into the hall and pointed to a door near the stairs. He said he'd be in the kitchen, then left her to it.

Jennifer locked the door, though didn't bother to lift the seat as she sat and stared at the wall. There was a cross opposite the mirror, plus some sort of picture that had been made with dried flowers. It had an upmarket hotel smell, with a pile of neat, fluffy towels on a wooden table, next to the sink.

She really needed to sleep, and the idea only escalated when Jennifer looked at herself in the mirror. There were darkening circles under her eyes and faint threads of red in the whites. No wonder Gary had offered her coffee.

Jennifer tried calling Daniel again, largely to see his name on her phone screen. She didn't expect him to answer, and he didn't. Jennifer so desperately wanted to know her son's version of everything that had happened. They could tell the police together. She could talk to Andrew and they would move some money around to hire a really good lawyer. Someone who would know what to do.

She flushed the toilet and ran the taps to at least make it sound as if she hadn't disappeared to give herself a timeout. Jennifer was going to head back into the kitchen to thank Gary for his time and excuse herself – except he was already waiting for her in the hall. Jennifer jumped as she spotted him sitting in the windowsill. He popped up as she emerged and held up his hands, apologising for making her jump.

'I thought you'd want to know,' he said. 'They just said on the radio that there's been a sighting of Daniel.'

TEN

Jennifer was almost at Gary's front door when she realised she had no idea *where* the sighting had been.

Gary seemed to have already read her mind, because he offered his own phone, showing a Facebook post from someone on a local page. Apparently, a row of shops had been surrounded and police were telling people to stay away. Someone was asking whether the chippy – *You Batter Believe It* – would be open at lunchtime.

'I've got to go,' Jennifer told him, handing back his phone. If Daniel was going to be arrested and stuck in a van, the least she could do was be somewhere near to offer a friendly face.

She'd already opened the door when Gary spoke. 'There's a vigil for Ella at six tonight at the United Church in town. Harriet and I are planning to go. You don't have to tell anyone who you are if you wanted to go.' He seemed to catch himself, then added: 'I'm not saying you should, or anything like that. I just figured you might want to know.'

Jennifer thanked him, though it was hard to think too much ahead. For now, she simply wanted to get to that row of shops.

She put the address of the chip shop into the Maps app and

followed it until she reached a police officer standing in the middle of the road, swirling her hand in a circle to indicate drivers should turn around.

Moments later and Jennifer had parked on a side street, then rushed back to where the officer was still directing traffic. The shops were further along the street and, probably unsurprisingly, a small crowd had gathered in the centre of the closed road. Jennifer could see them pointing their phones in the direction of the shops, either filming or live-streaming whatever was happening.

From what Jennifer could tell, it wasn't much.

Officers had massed in front of the rank, with a pair of police vans nestled next to three more cars. Someone in a uniform was vaguely wafting people further back, though making little attempt to actually enforce anything.

Jennifer slotted in behind a parked car and tried calling Daniel again. He wasn't going to answer, but she had to try. She pictured him in a room somewhere at the back of the shops, wondering if he knew there were so many police officers outside. They would have one of those huge metal battering ram things, there'd be shouting, maybe even a flash grenade. It would be terrifying for anyone and she could only see her little boy frightened in the middle of it.

He didn't answer – and his phone still wasn't ringing.

Then she saw the gun.

An officer was carrying a rifle out of a van, the barrel pointing to the ground. Jennifer wasn't sure she'd ever seen police carrying a gun except at an airport. There was a surreal haze, as if she really *was* watching a drama.

Before Jennifer knew what she was doing, she had dashed across the road, heading for the shops before an officer reached for her. It was a man in a uniform, tall and broad, who wrapped an arm across her front and pulled her away.

'You can't go that way,' he said harshly.

Ahead of her, Jennifer watched as the officer with the gun headed into an alley and out of sight around a corner.

'He has a gun,' Jennifer said, unable to get out anything else. She was pushing against the officer, even as he overpowered her, desperate to tell him that they didn't *need* the weapon. That she couldn't stand by and watch her son get shot. There had to be another way.

'You have to move!' he replied, louder now.

The volume got the attention of a second officer, a woman this time, who stepped across and blocked Jennifer's view.

'That officer had a gun!' Jennifer repeated, with a quiver.

'It was a bean bag weapon,' the woman said. 'It's a last resort. I need you to move away.'

Jennifer felt herself go slightly limp as the officer released her. It wasn't a proper rifle that she'd spotted. Daniel wasn't going to be shot.

'It's my son,' she said, quieter now, speaking to the woman.

'Who's your son?'

'Daniel Farley. I'm his mum.'

That got a confused glance between the pair of officers.

'Have you really found him?' Jennifer added.

There was some sort of movement a little out of sight, which sounded like a group of footsteps moving in unison.

'We can't say,' the female officer said. 'But I do need you to move back across the road.'

Jennifer didn't shift. She was trying to peer around the officer, wondering what was going on with all the footsteps. She could see the alley at the back of the shops, likely where there were steps leading up to the flats that sat above. She could see a bin, though not much else.

Jennifer glanced up to the flats. There were lights on inside and one of the windows had a plastic pumpkin in the sill.

'I want him to be safe,' Jennifer said, focusing back on the officer. 'If he's inside, I can talk to him. He'll come out for me.'

She was still picturing the size of the rifle that had been carried around the corner. Bean bag ammunition or not, it would do some damage.

There was another short glance between the officers and then the woman said 'Wait there', before stepping away. She crossed to the front of the chip shop, standing in the doorway and talking into the radio that was pinned to her lapel. She glanced up every few seconds, taking in Jennifer, before continuing the conversation.

It wasn't long until she returned to Jennifer. 'Have you got any way of talking to Daniel?' she asked.

'He's not answering his phone. I have been trying. I drove through the night to be here. I've not slept.'

Jennifer knew she was sounding manic now, which mirrored her thoughts.

Something fizzed on the officer's radio and she pressed a button. It felt as if she was about to speak but then the footsteps were back, clattering in unison up what sounded like steps.

Jennifer angled herself to the side, still trying to peer around the officer – but then they all froze.

Because a clear and crisp gunshot pierced the quiet morning.

ELEVEN

Jennifer lurched ahead. Daniel had been shot and she needed to be at his side. That giant rifle wasn't for bean bags after all.

She had already taken a handful of steps past the officers when the larger man grabbed her again. He wrapped his arms around her, lifting her off her feet, and pulling Jennifer away as she battled against him.

'That was a door,' he said loudly.

Jennifer was struggling to take things, to make sense of his words, her mind a fuzz from the lack of sleep and the endless panic that had been building for twelve hours.

'It was a door,' he repeated, quieter this time, as he put her down. 'They were entering an upstairs flat.'

Jennifer tried to play back what she'd heard. There had been those footsteps, a few moments of quiet, and then a really loud bang.

She was staring at the woman officer, silently asking for confirmation, which came with a soft nod.

'It was a door,' she said.

Jennifer was released a second time, though her knees felt

weak. So much had happened and she needed to rest – except she needed to speak to Daniel more.

The woman officer stepped away and pressed something on her radio, angling her head towards it.

Out of sight, from what sounded like the flats upstairs, there was a series of muffled bangs that might have been more footsteps.

'Nobody's been hurt,' the officer said, as she let go of her radio. She made eye contact with her colleague and then Jennifer. 'He's not here,' she added.

'What do you mean?'

Jennifer got an answer of sorts as a group of heavy-booted officers clumped down the stairs and emerged into sight. They started to mass towards the vans.

'Some sort of misunderstanding,' the officer said. 'There was a sighting but it's not him.' She looked to her colleague again. 'I think we just gave someone the fright of their life. He was on his PlayStation, wearing a headset, and hadn't heard us.'

'It's not Daniel?' Jennifer asked.

'No.'

Jennifer straightened herself as she realised she'd been holding her breath. She was relieved in one way but not entirely. If Daniel had been there, things would have been in motion to find out what happened. As it was, she still had no idea where he was, or what he might have done.

'Are you all right?' the female officer asked.

Jennifer was nodding, although she wasn't sure. What counted as 'all right' when a person's son was wanted for murdering his girlfriend? When he couldn't be found?

'There's not a lot you can do here,' the woman added. 'But you need to contact us if you hear from your son. I'll give you a number.'

The officer produced a business card, plus a pen. She rested on her colleague's back and scribbled something on the card, before handing it over. 'You've got the main number, my desk number, and a mobile there. Any time of day or night is fine. Someone will answer. I'm Nina.'

Jennifer scanned the card, then slipped it into her jacket pocket. Nina Sheridan was a sergeant.

'You should probably go home,' Sheridan added. 'There's not a lot you can do here. Maybe get some sleep somewhere first?'

It wasn't only Jennifer who thought she looked tired, then.

She hovered for a moment, watching as the other officers headed back towards the vans. Someone was talking into a radio, somebody else on a phone. It felt as if they were going to disappear as quickly as possible. Probably try to pretend they hadn't accidentally broken down the wrong door.

'You really should go home,' Sheridan repeated.

Jennifer blinked at her and had to fight away a yawn. She wanted to tell the other woman they had everything wrong. That Daniel wasn't capable of what they thought he was. Then she remembered that giant pile of money in Daniel's locker. She knew she should tell someone about that – but she couldn't. The police would think the worst and it wouldn't get her any closer to finding him.

Jennifer turned and headed back towards the larger crowd. She passed a rakish man who had been leaning on a nearby wall. He was staring at her, though turned away when she looked back.

With the drama over, residents were putting away their phones and heading home. Jennifer pulled her jacket up higher, pushing her hands into the pockets. Now she was away from the shops, she again realised how cold it was. Her fingers were tingling, eyes stinging. Perhaps she would be better off getting some sleep, as Sheridan had suggested?

Jennifer was looking for the car, trying to remember where she'd parked, before realising it was a street over. All the streets looked the same and everything felt hazy. There was an alley which likely served as a shortcut that she must have missed before. It passed along the back of a row of houses and Jennifer slipped into it, trying not to trip on the uneven cobbles.

She was a quarter-way along when she heard the footsteps behind. Jennifer quickened her pace instinctively, checking her shoulder as she hurried. The skinny man who'd been watching from the wall was now following. The collar of his denim coat was up and, as she upped her pace, he did the same.

Jennifer switched her attention back to the front as she tried to walk even faster. The jutting, jagged edges of the cobbles had her wobbling as, from nowhere, the footsteps were suddenly close.

This time, when Jennifer turned, the man was barely a step behind, seemingly reaching for her shoulder. He was young, maybe early twenties, and waspishly thin – but he had the element of surprise. Jennifer stumbled, trying to keep her balance as she grasped at a telegraph pole. Everything had happened so quickly that she wasn't quite sure how to react as she wobbled into a sitting position as the man stood over her. She was in his shadow, barely able to make out his features.

She had never been mugged but perhaps it was an inevitability in life. She should shout, try to get someone's attention. Except she was so tired. So defeated.

And it wasn't a mugging anyway.

The man was sneering, with seethed menace, 'Your son killed my sister.'

TWENTY FOUR YEARS AGO

Heads swivelled at the sound of something solid hitting the ground. The *thunk* echoed around the enclosed space as, momentarily, everyone stopped. That was the thing with a library: there were hushed whispers, the click-clacking of computer keyboards, and not much else.

Jennifer watched as a girl picked up a book from one of the long racks. She quickly shoved it back onto the shelf and then ducked her head before hurrying out of sight.

Natasha was off at the IT desk, trying to get her password reset. She could never remember it. That left Hayley and Jennifer at side-by-side computers typing out their latest essay. The main aim was attempting to make their versions seem different enough that they wouldn't get pinged for copying one another. Copying without making it look like copying was a skill they had largely nailed down during their first year.

The other thing was that, because all the lecturers had reading lists comprising expensive books largely written by themselves, the library was a way of not having to buy everything. Instead, they shared the books between them, taking it in turns to check out the various copies.

Jennifer yawned. She'd been doodling on a notepad as they waited for Natasha to sort out her login. A girl over by the nature books section had been eyeing the computer station next to hers for a good five minutes – even though Jennifer had already told her it was reserved. That wasn't technically, or literally, true. Natasha would be using it if she ever came back.

'I need a wee,' Hayley said suddenly, as she stood and picked up her bag. She said she wouldn't be long, but it left Jennifer trying to hang onto three computers.

She twisted in her seat, trying to glimpse through the bookcases towards the help desk. Somebody in a red top was at the front of the queue, which might be Natasha – although Jennifer couldn't remember what her friend was wearing.

She turned back, returning to doodling on the pad, waiting for one or both of her friends to return. It would really help if she could get her own laptop to save having to sit in the library all the time. That would take money, though.

As she was daydreaming about that, Jennifer's neck prickled as she sensed eyes on her. She expected it to be the girl who'd been eyeing the spare computer except, when she looked up from her notepad, she realised it wasn't a girl at all.

Craig was standing next to the fire door, staring across the floor towards her. He had that same Tesco bag-for-life that he'd carried the first time she saw him. Jennifer wondered how long he'd been watching her but, as soon he realised he'd been spotted, he dipped his head and darted behind the row of sports books. It had happened so quickly that Jennifer had to convince herself it was definitely him. It was only the bag that felt convincing.

She shivered as she continued to watch the area near the fire door, feeling eyes on her, wondering if he was peeping through a gap in the shelf. Was he following her? Or maybe following all of them? Had he trailed them to the library?

'You OK?'

Jennifer jumped as Natasha appeared from nowhere. She dropped herself into the vacant chair and started typing.

'I sorted my password,' she added, not waiting for a reply, and then continuing: 'Where's Hayley?'

Jennifer shifted her attention back to the computer, though the prickling sensation remained. Craig was still watching – and for a reason of which she wasn't quite sure, Jennifer knew instinctively it wasn't the first time he'd been spying on her.

TWELVE

'Your son killed my sister and now you're here?' the man said. He wasn't shouting but there was a dangerous edge to his tone. He was still in shadow, expression hidden. Jennifer was on the ground, the bumpy cobbles poking her backside as she tried to stand.

'I'm trying to find Daniel,' she said. 'I want to help.'

The man had lunged down and Jennifer flinched. It happened so fast that she didn't have time to fight, let alone flee.

Except he wasn't lunging for her. Instead, he stretched and picked up the bag that had somehow slipped her grasp. He stepped to the side and offered it, while Jennifer picked herself up. She kept her eyes on him, not quite sure what had happened. He'd been running at her, hadn't he?

'Didn't mean to scare you,' he said, as Jennifer wondered if she'd misunderstood. Had there been a sneering menace to his voice? Had he been angry? If there was, it was gone. 'I wanted to introduce myself,' he continued, now Jennifer was back on her feet. She took her bag and then he added: 'I'm Callum. Ella's my sister. I heard you talking to the police...'

Jennifer took a small step away from him, still not quite

certain of his intentions. She was so tired that she wasn't sure she trusted her instincts – but she definitely didn't trust him.

'I didn't know Ella had a brother,' Jennifer said. She was a further half-step away, struggling to see how Callum had seemed threatening moments before. He had the build of a person who'd lose a battle with a paper bag. So skinny, his cheeks were triangular.

'Callum,' he repeated with a nod.

'I'm so sorry to hear what happened with Ella,' Jennifer said, unsure how to put it. She *was* sorry – but she was also convinced whatever had occurred wasn't down to Daniel.

'You OK?'

A woman's voice was calling from beyond Callum, a little further along the cobbles.

When Jennifer looked around him, three young women were standing together. She suddenly realised she was rubbing her wrist absent-mindedly, having landed on it.

Callum backed away a fraction, eyes darting between Jennifer and the women.

'I'm fine,' Jennifer called back.

'You sure?'

Jennifer glanced to Callum again, who was angling away, as if about to make a break for it. She wondered if she'd missed something.

'Honestly,' she replied. It was good of the women to check on her. 'Thanks for making sure.'

The trio hovered for a moment more, before deciding they were happy. They turned to head back the way they'd come, leaving Jennifer and Callum alone in the alley. She was still hesitant of him.

'Do you know Daniel?' Jennifer asked.

'Dan? Yeah, I guess.' It didn't sound definitive, more like a person blagging an answer at a job interview. *Yeah, sure I've got five years' experience.*

'Have you heard what they're saying Daniel did?'

It was a dangerous question, though, Jennifer was hesitantly beginning to think he might not be a threat. Callum was so weedy, his tracksuit was hanging off him, like the after photo from a *Weightwatchers* ad. Plus he had the jittery sense of a person suffering from a series of rashes.

'I heard they'd found him. That's why I came down. Dunno what to make of it all.'

Callum was hard to read. At first, Jennifer had thought he was furious that she was Daniel's mother, that she'd dared to be there; now he didn't seem so sure. Jennifer wasn't convinced he was even that affected by what had happened to his sister.

'Are you up to much?' he asked, though it sounded like he was chatting to a mate, rather than as a man whose sister had just been murdered.

'Not really. I was hoping to find Daniel. Maybe try to figure out what's happened.'

He was nodding. 'I might be able to help with that.'

Callum *couldn't* help with finding Daniel. That much was almost immediately clear. He'd led Jennifer around a corner until they reached a pub. It was one of those places that opened at nine for coffee and breakfast, while acting as a borderline community centre, because everywhere else had been shut down.

He had asked if Jennifer was hungry, which she wasn't – though she knew she should probably eat. He looked like he needed a good meal, and with Jennifer seemingly volunteering herself to pay, he ordered himself the all-day breakfast, with a coffee and two cans of Coke.

Jennifer picked at her multigrain toast, accepting that Ella's brother had likely chased her down because he was hoping for this exact scenario. He ate like a hostage who'd spent a year chained to a radiator, hoovering down the food with barely a breath. Jennifer had barely got through a slice of her toast as Callum finished wolfing down the final sausage. He picked up the ramekin of baked beans and upended it into his mouth, slurping like it was an oyster.

'Whew,' he said, to himself, before cracking the can of Coke.

He might have used her for a free meal but, as Jennifer watched him empty at least half the can in one go, she realised she had woken up somewhat.

'Do you want another?' she asked, nodding at the plate.

Callum lowered the can and eyed the remnants of his food rampage. 'If there's one going...'

Jennifer dug around her purse, then passed across a ten-pound note. She knew no change would be forthcoming, despite the breakfast being a four-quid morning special.

He snatched the money with a mumbled 'ta', then hurried off to the bar. As expected, the change was deposited into his pocket before he stumbled back to the table. She was fairly certain he was limping, though it was hard to tell because the crotch of his jogging bottoms was below his knees.

He slurped down the rest of his first Coke can, then opened the second, while checking over his shoulder to see if the second breakfast was on its way.

'You can finish that if you want,' Jennifer said, pushing her second and third slices of toast across the table. He eyed the food and she knew he wasn't entirely onboard with the multigrain nature of the bread. Not that it stopped him.

'Ta,' he repeated. He chewed slowly at first, suspicious of the bread, before apparently deciding it was fine.

Jennifer watched him finish her toast, then check again to see if his second breakfast was coming. He was constantly tugging at his clothes and his crotch, endlessly scratching his head and arms.

'Do you know Daniel well?' Jennifer asked.

It wasn't the most tactful question, considering Daniel was accused of killing Callum's sister, but she had more of a read of him now. She doubted he'd mind – and he seemingly didn't.

'He and Ella were together all the time,' Callum said, still chewing. 'He was all right.'

'Are you close to your sister?'

Jennifer almost winced at the present tense, not that Callum appeared to notice. 'Not really. Older bruvvers aren't supposed to get on with younger sisters, are they?'

'How much older are you?'

Callum counted on his fingers: 'Three years? Four?' He finished the final piece of toast, then continued without prompting. 'Ella's in a band: Pixie something. I think they met through that. Mum reckons they write songs together.'

He pulled his phone from the pocket of his hoody, almost dropped it, then grabbed it again. There were cracks across the screen and all along the back. He fumbled clumsily with it, then turned it around for Jennifer to see.

A video was playing of what looked like the inside of a crowded pub. People were talking but, past them, a girl was singing on a makeshift stage. The sound was tinny and the cracked screen made it hard to see exactly what was going on. Ella had short dark hair and was wearing all-black. She smiled and pointed, then the camera swung around to where Daniel was sitting at the bar. He grinned and raised his drink towards her, before the footage looped back to the beginning.

Jennifer watched the scene play a second time and it was so... nice. So normal. Two young people apparently happy and in love. She could see the adoration in Daniel's eyes as he gazed across the packed bar towards his girlfriend. It was only a few out-of-context moments – but there was no sign of what would happen. Of what he would be accused of.

'When was this?' Jennifer asked.

Callum put the phone back in his hoody. 'A year ago? Summer before last.'

He didn't sound sure, though quite a few of Callum's answers appeared to sound like he was questioning himself. Daniel had spent that summer flitting between his university flat and living at home, so he could see his old school friends.

'Can you send it to me?' Jennifer asked. She craved seeing her son in such a happy place and a part of her wondered if he would ever be like that again.

Callum fiddled with his device, eventually managing to send the video to Jennifer's phone. She watched the first few seconds, making sure it was the same piece, then returned her phone to her bag.

Meanwhile, Callum's attention had been lost to his second breakfast. The server had barely placed it on the table before he had picked off a sausage. He gave a muttered 'Ta', then began the demolition.

Jennifer let him eat in peace and it wasn't a long wait. He slurped the beans from the ramekin once more, as if shooting whisky, then finished off another can of Coke.

Jennifer had to remind herself that his sister had died barely hours before. He didn't seem particularly affected – although she knew grief manifested itself in different ways for different people. Perhaps, for Callum, it meant... hunger?

He was fidgeting again, this time twisting and turning the ring pull on the can.

'When did you last see them?' Jennifer asked.

'Who?'

'Ella and Daniel?'

Callum chewed the inside of his cheek for a moment. 'Maybe a week ago?'

He was avoiding eye contact and it felt like a lie at worst, a guess at best.

Perhaps picking up on her scepticism, he added a quick:

'They were in town, on the high street. I was, um, meeting someone – and they were walking through. We stopped and said hello for a minute or so.'

'Did they seem... OK?'

Callum stopped fiddling with the ring pull momentarily as he caught her eye. It suddenly felt like a dangerous question, as if she wouldn't like the answer.

'They were fine,' he said, dismissively, though it again felt couched. Perhaps not a lie, though not a complete truth.

He was messing with the can once more, until the ring pull popped off. He bent the metal and then dropped it into the can itself.

Jennifer wasn't sure how much more she would get from Callum, and he didn't feel trustworthy anyway. Instead, she picked up her phone again and started watching the video he'd sent once more.

Ella was singing and then she pointed out of shot. The camera swung around to Daniel, who turned away from the person he'd been talking to, then lifted his drink to acknowledge her. On her first few views, Jennifer hadn't noticed that Daniel was speaking to someone.

She paused the video and turned the screen for Callum to see. 'Do you know who that is?' she asked, pointing at Daniel's apparent friend.

Callum squinted. 'That's Ben,' he said.

Jennifer almost dropped the phone, such was her surprise. The driving licence in Daniel's locker had been in the name of a Ben.

'Who's Ben?' she asked.

Callum stared for a moment. 'Ben Davies,' he said. 'He's been missing for ages.'

THIRTEEN

Jennifer twisted the phone back towards her again, taking in the frozen image of Daniel half-turning away from the young man at his side. It was a fraction blurry and she couldn't recall the picture on the driving licence well enough to know if it was the same person. She thought so.

'Daniel's got a friend who's missing?' she asked, surprised that he'd never said.

Callum seemed bemused by her interest. 'No, they hated each other,' he said.

Hate felt like such a strong word. She was obviously biased but couldn't really picture her son hating anyone. 'Why didn't they like each other?' she asked.

'Dunno. I saw them fighting one time. Might've been that night, actually.'

Jennifer was still eyeing the stationary image. She wanted to check the driving licence. It was in her bag but she knew she couldn't while Callum was there. Then she clocked what Callum had actually said.

'You saw them *fighting*?'

A nod.

Jennifer wasn't sure she believed much of what Callum had been saying – but this felt particularly untrue. As far as she knew, Daniel had never been a fighter. It might be naïve but he simply wasn't the type.

'What do you mean "fighting"?' she asked.

'Swinging punches. I think it was at the back of that pub a bit later on. The guy on the door kicked them both out and sent them home. Ella was really upset. I asked what happened and she said to mind my own business.'

Jennifer thought on that for a moment.

Callum was suddenly looking at her, something he'd been avoiding through much of their conversation.

'How long has Ben been missing?' Jennifer asked.

'Dunno. Ages. There were posters up all over for a while.'

'Do the police know Daniel and Ben were fighting?'

Callum was focused back on fiddling with the ring pull of his second can. 'Dunno.'

Jennifer had no way of knowing if the police had linked Daniel to Ben – but it was a bad look if Daniel had been fighting with someone who'd gone missing. Then, months later, his girlfriend was found dead, seemingly in his room. Perhaps it was even worse that Ben's driving licence was in Daniel's locker. Had he stolen it? If so, why not simply get rid of it?

There were so many questions.

'Who is this Ben?' Jennifer asked. 'Is he a student?'

Callum had picked off the second ring pull and dropped it into the can with a tinny *dink*. He rattled it for a moment, then squished the sides.

'Dunno,' he said – which was an even clearer lie than anything else he'd said.

'Are you friends with him?' Jennifer asked.

'No.'

Jennifer figured she was going to have to do some googling once Callum had gone. She was struggling to figure out why

Ella's brother had bothered to approach her. There was the free breakfasts but he can't have assumed he'd get that. She had the sense that she was missing something. He didn't seem distraught in the way a person might expect.

There was a silence between them now: two people with nothing in common, somehow thrown together.

'You look like you haven't eaten in a while,' Jennifer said. It was probably the wrong thing to say in modern times, though it got a shrug.

'The church kitchen is always giving out free stuff,' he replied.

'Do you still live with your mum?'

Jennifer would have put a lot on the answer being 'yes'. He was early twenties, maybe twenty-five at the most, but there was nothing about him that said self-sufficient.

'Sometimes,' he said. 'Depends if she's being a bitch or not.' He waited a moment, then added: 'Police were there this morning, so I went out. Me and them don't really get on.'

There was only one reason why the police would've been at Ella's mum's house that morning.

Jennifer was about to ask about Callum and the police not getting on – but he had other things to talk about. 'They had a big argument the other week.'

'Who?'

'Ella and her mum.' A pause. '...And me, I guess. Dad died a bit back in a car crash. Then Grandma died a few months ago. We didn't know but she had some savings and left everything to Ella. That annoyed Mum, 'cos she thought it should've gone to her.'

Jennifer was making the mental calculations of who was who. In short, it sounded like Ella's grandmother had died and left her – and *only* her – some money.

'How much was it?' Jennifer asked.

'Dunno,' he replied, and it again felt like a lie. Perhaps realising it was unlikely that he wouldn't know, he added: 'Few thousand.'

Jennifer considered her next question. This time, there was definitely something she was missing. 'If your gran left money to Ella, didn't you get any...?'

Callum's gaze shot up, eyes narrow, a barely concealed fury simmering. For a moment, Jennifer thought he might erupt. She still wondered if that's what she'd seen in the alley, when he'd come up behind her.

He bit his lip, though she could see his fingers gripping the table hard. 'I'm adopted, ain't I? Granny don't think I count.'

Callum was clenching his jaw, anger apparent. Jennifer didn't exactly blame him. If he was telling the truth, he'd been screwed over.

That was a big 'if', though.

Callum stood quickly, almost sending his chair flying as he did so. He looked up to the clock on the wall and started scratching his arm. 'I've gotta go,' he said as he patted his pockets. He was holding his phone, so it wasn't that for which he was looking. 'I don't suppose you could, um...?'

Jennifer didn't know what he meant.

He was squirming and quickly expanded: 'I need to put some credit on my phone.'

It sounded like yet another lie.

Jennifer could've pointed out that he'd earlier pocketed the change, though she didn't know if she might need to talk to him again in future. She reached into her purse and pulled out a twenty-pound note.

Callum's greedy gaze shone as she passed it across, where it was quickly dispatched into his pocket. He took a small step away, visibly limping as he muttered another 'Ta'.

'Is your leg all right?' Jennifer asked.

He stopped, looking down to his foot, as if having not noticed there was a problem. It was the first time Jennifer noticed the hole in his trainer, with his sock-covered toe poking out.

'Had a bit of a car crash a while back,' he said, then added: 'It's fine.' He offered another 'Ta', took a step away, hesitated, and then angled back towards her. 'Do you know if Dan has a, uh... like a... locker? Something like that?'

He was avoiding eye contact and Jennifer almost answered with a truthful 'Yes', before stopping herself. It was an oddly specific question that could only have been asked by a person who knew that there was a locker, even if the location was a mystery.

'How do you mean?' Jennifer asked, buying time as she thought. The idea occurred that this was the reason Callum had approached her in the first place. Everything else was a smokescreen.

Callum ticked and scratched. 'Dunno, just maybe a place he might keep things...?'

'What sort of things?'

'Things of Ella's, I guess.'

Of all Callum's possible lies, this was the most obvious. He twisted on the spot and scratched furiously at his forearm.

Jennifer pictured the tens of thousands she'd found in Daniel's locker and wondered if that's what Callum was talking about. It felt likely.

'I assume he keeps things at his house,' she said. 'The police were there earlier.'

'Right...'

There was a sigh and a moment in which it felt as if Callum was trying to figure out what to do next. As it was, he mumbled something Jennifer didn't catch – and then he was gone. Or, he almost was. He misjudged the spinning door and nearly got himself caught in the frame as it closed on him. He practically fell out the other side, back onto the street.

Jennifer watched through the window as he looked both

ways and then darted across the road, weaving between a
slowing car that beeped its horn.

A taller man in a suit was leaning against a lamp post but
straightened as Callum reached him. It happened so quickly, so
well-practised, that Jennifer almost missed it. Callum reached
into his coat pocket and removed something small and palm-
sized, that might have been a bag. He pressed it into the other
man's hand, while accepting what was likely cash, that was
instantly deposited into the pocket of his joggers.

Within a second or three, the deal was done. Callum
ducked his head and bounded towards the nearest alley. The
man in the suit headed in the opposite direction and, barely
moments after they'd concluded what was likely a drug deal,
the pair were gone.

Jennifer wasn't naïve about such things, although she had
little idea which drugs were popular nowadays. She wasn't sure
it mattered, though the thought occurred that she probably
shouldn't have been so open about giving Callum money if he
was a dealer.

From nowhere, Jennifer felt her neck itch. She reached to
scratch, fighting away a shiver. She sensed she was being
watched and turned in a semicircle, wondering if Callum had
somehow looped back around and entered through a different
door.

There was nobody paying her any attention.

And then Jennifer realised there was.

There was a balcony above the ground level and a man was
leaning on the rail, staring directly at her. He was in a long wool
coat, with a smart suit underneath. He might as well have been
wearing fifty-pound notes. His gaze lingered a second too long,
because he wanted her to know he was watching – and then,
with an almost dramatic swish, he turned and walked away.

TWENTY-FOUR YEARS AGO

The bouncer held open the doors as Jennifer, Hayley and Natasha emerged into the night. Jennifer had been dancing for an hour, probably longer, and the cool of the evening was cold against the sweat and grease of her hair. She trembled, half wishing she'd brought a coat – not that she ever did. None of them did. Better to shiver for the twenty minutes it took to walk home than spoil the going-out look.

The trio of girls stood momentarily on the street, getting their bearings, as the muffled music blared from the club behind. A taxi blurred along the street, going too fast and making a lad stumble away from the kerb. He wafted an angry hand and shouted a pointless 'Oi!' He scratched his head, then bumbled across the road, almost walking into a bollard, before ending up in the kebab shop.

'Do you want chips?' Natasha asked.

Hayley was looking slightly green. She had carried on drinking a good hour past the time when Jennifer and Natasha had called it a night. Her dress was too short, heels too high. She could barely stand.

'Let's go home,' she slurred. 'This way.'

Without waiting for the others, she set off towards the alley that ran along the side of the club. It was something of a short-cut, albeit one of which Jennifer was wary. It cut three or four minutes from their journey but there were no lights and plenty of shadows.

Not that Hayley had given them much choice. Jennifer hurried to reach her friend's side and then the three of them walked as quickly as their tipsiness would allow. Natasha was humming to herself, while Hayley had her head down, on a charge. Jennifer was rushing to keep up – and was so focused on her speed that she bumped into the back of Hayley, who'd inexplicably stopped directly in front of her.

But it was explainable. Jennifer stepped around her friend, to find Jo sitting on the ground, her head resting on a giant wheelie bin. Her purple hair was matted to her face, with a large graze above her eye, a blackening welt underneath, and a series of scratches that looked like they could be from fingernails along her arm. The last time Jennifer had seen Jo, she had marched triumphantly up those stairs near the students' union, hand-in-hand with Craig.

'Are you OK?' Natasha asked.

Jo blinked rapidly and winced as she tried to stand. Jennifer crouched to help but Jo shook her head. 'I think I'll stay here for a bit,' she said.

'Did someone do this to you?' Jennifer asked.

Jo stared at her, stared *into* her. She was saying it without needing to.

'Was it Craig?' Jennifer added.

Jo sighed and rubbed her arm. She closed her eyes momentarily, then opened them again. This time, she managed to stand, swaying slightly as she leaned against the bin.

'Can you get me a taxi?' she asked.

'We can share one if you live near us,' Hayley said.

Jo took a step around them, back towards the main road.

'We should call the police,' Jennifer said.

'No,' Jo replied, firmly.

'It was only a month ago he threatened you with a knife. Now he's beaten you up.'

Jo was walking towards the road, though she hesitated a fraction. The other three girls were still next to the bin.

'Not now,' Jo said, over her shoulder. And then: 'You coming?'

Hayley was the first to move, stepping past Jennifer, wobbling a fraction, and then heading after Jo. That left Natasha and Jennifer shivering in the shadows.

'What do we do?' Natasha asked.

'I don't know,' Jennifer replied.

FOURTEEN

Jennifer was still in the pub. She checked her phone, while keeping half an eye on the floor above, in case the suited man returned. That single gaze made it feel as if he knew her, though she had no idea who he was. She wondered how long he'd been watching and whether he'd seen Callum. Perhaps it was Callum he was spying on?

There were so many unanswered questions.

A waitress came by and cleared the table. She gave a quick 'no rush' and then disappeared back towards the kitchen.

Jennifer hadn't received any messages from her husband since that morning, and she wondered if Andrew had gone to work. Whether there was still a car sitting opposite the house? She could ask – but a stubborn part of her wanted him to contact her, rather than the other way around.

She watched the video of Ella and Daniel a few more times, pausing it at various points, mainly to look at her son's face.

There was love in his eyes when he looked across towards his girlfriend on the stage. Jennifer knew what it looked like, even though she hadn't felt it in a while when it came to her husband.

If the video had been filmed a year or so before, she couldn't understand how things would ultimately end the way they had. Ella was dead, apparently in Daniel's room.

Jennifer stopped the footage on Ben's face and then checked the driving licence she'd found in Daniel's locker. As best she could tell, it was the same person – although she was essentially looking at someone white and unremarkable with dark hair.

She typed 'Ashington' and 'Ben Davies' into a search engine, which threw up a handful of news stories.

Ben had disappeared thirteen months before, although there wasn't much in the way of details. The articles said he was twenty-four and that he volunteered at a local food bank. Apparently the people who ran the bank had contacted the police after he failed to turn up. There was a photo of him that was much clearer than the blur of the frozen video – and this face definitely matched the one on the driving licence. The police statement said he was a 'vulnerable' young man who'd not been seen in almost a week. They asked for anyone to contact them with details – but that was it. There was little more indication of who he was, or if there was a connection to Daniel.

Jennifer yawned, tried to force it away, and then yawned again. She knew she needed to sleep but it was barely noon – and, even if she wanted to find a hotel, they wouldn't be letting people check in quite yet. She closed her eyes for a moment, just a blink, but then jolted as her bag started to buzz. She banged her knee on the table as she tried to work out what was going on, wondering if she'd momentarily fallen asleep, before realising her phone was ringing.

Jennifer's thoughts were instantly dark – it definitely wouldn't be good news – and, when she saw the name on the screen, she knew what was to come.

'Hi, Lisa,' she said, fighting away a yawn and still trying to blink herself awake.

'Where are you?' Lisa asked, not bothering with a hello.

Jennifer had forgotten to tell her work that she wouldn't be available. There was a procedure for sick days, or personal time off, and she'd not bothered with any of it. There had been more important things going on.

'You've not replied to any emails,' Lisa added. 'Plus you missed the morning meeting.'

Ah, yes. That daily Zoom call in which Jennifer fought the urge to log off, quit, and never go back. The hour or so of people endlessly talking while not actually doing any work. The Lisa special. She was in her element chairing those meetings.

'Sorry for not calling in,' Jennifer said. 'There's been a few issues with my son at university. I've had to drive up. It's an emergency.'

It was then that a barman took the opportunity to drop a tray. A glass shattered and someone from the far side cheered loudly. Jennifer winced, knowing it would have been heard by Lisa.

There was a chequered few seconds, perhaps as Lisa wondered whether to ask if Jennifer was skiving off in a pub. Jennifer watched as the barman picked up the tray and then fetched a brush and pan from the other side of the bar.

'What's going on at the university?' Lisa asked, as abruptly as ever.

Jennifer might have told her if she wasn't certain that it would be around the office within seconds of the phone call ending. Lisa's biggest gripe with Covid hadn't been people dying, people wearing masks, or the stilted economy. It was that her source for office gossip had withered to nothing. She'd been left telling others on Zoom that she thought one of her neighbours might be spending too much time doing his outside exercise, and that she was considering calling the police.

'It's hard to say,' Jennifer replied, trying to keep it as neutral as possible. 'But I might need some time off.'

The silence lasted a few seconds too long. Lisa might have been more accepting if Jennifer had offered up anything juicy. She'd love a good ol' murder to witter on about. Immediately after the call, she'd have been turning to the person next to her: 'You'll never guess who's dead!'

Instead, she gave a stunted: 'You might need to talk to HR,' she said. 'You're already short on holidays.'

'I'm not *on* holiday. I've got a family emergency.'

'That's why you need to talk to HR. There's something in the handbook about exceptional situations.' She gave it a second, then added: 'If you want to tell me what's happening, I can probably put in a word for you...?'

Jennifer rolled her eyes. 'I didn't catch that,' Jennifer said. 'I think you're cutting out.' That was the benefit of an actual phone call, rather than Zoom.

Lisa repeated herself but Jennifer left a long gap, before replying.

'I didn't hear any of that.'

She pressed the button to hang up and spent a few moments looking at her phone, half expecting it to ring again. There was no way Lisa would let it go, but the least of Jennifer's issues would be a conversation with HR. It was so hard to process what felt like minor work problems when there were far more serious issues at hand.

Even as she thought that, Jennifer realised it would soon be impossible to keep a lid on what was going on. For the moment, Ella's death and Daniel's disappearance was a local news story. At some point in the very near future, it would go wider – and then people in her hometown would know.

Jennifer sighed and rubbed her eyes. She needed to sleep but how could she? Daniel was still out there – and he'd called her.

She checked the local news on her phone, where an article described the unexplained death of Ella Clarkson, whom it described as 'a singer'. It didn't quite say that Daniel had killed her, though it did state that police were looking for her boyfriend, Daniel Farley. That line warning the public not to approach him was repeated and Jennifer found herself struggling to get past it. That made it clear *they* thought he'd killed Ella. How could things have come to this?

Something buzzed and, for a moment, Jennifer assumed she'd received a text – then she realised the phone was in her hand and nothing had appeared. The exhausted fuzz had her yawning, then stretching as she assumed she'd imagined it. Then she remembered there was a second phone. The one she'd found in Daniel's locker. She thought she'd turned it off – but, when she removed it from her bag, there was a new message notification.

Jennifer clicked into it, struggling to get the cracked screen to register her touch before the message appeared.

I can get you out of this

FIFTEEN

Jennifer stared at the text. Somebody knew what was going on with Ella and the police and they were offering to help. Presumably they were offering to help Daniel. The phone had been in his locker, after all. Her thumb hovered over the keyboard, wondering if she should reply, knowing she would. Except she had no idea what to say. It was an anonymous 07 number and she could hardly ask who it was.

Before Jennifer could send anything, another text appeared, offering a time and a place. It was forty-five minutes in the future, with an address that showed as twenty-five minutes' away.

Jennifer stared for a minute, maybe longer, but then she knew what she was going to do.

There was no time to hang around, so Jennifer grabbed her bag, dumped both phones inside, pulled out her car keys, and set off to discover who was texting her son.

Jennifer used her sleeve to wipe the condensation from her windscreen. She checked the address from the text, against the

Maps app on her proper phone, then the scene in front of her. The dewy, cold morning had given way to a misty early afternoon. One of those days where it was sort of raining but not really. Just damp all round and a complete waste of everyone's time.

The address was for a building on the edge of a small park, which housed a crazy golf club rental on one side, with an ice cream place on the other. Both were closed after the end of the season, their metal shutters graffitied by a series of tags, not to mention the customary cock and balls.

Jennifer didn't want to leave the car. She didn't know who'd texted the phone from Daniel's locker, nor what they wanted beyond the 'I can get you out of this'. She was struggling with a guilt that, if the message had been meant for Daniel, then maybe she was getting in the way. She was preventing him from being saved from whatever was going on. If it wasn't that, the police should probably be involved. Anyone but her...

Except it was a bit late now.

She stretched to rub the mist from the windscreen again, then continued staring towards the park hut. A part of her wondered if Daniel *would* turn up. If he'd have got the message somehow anyway.

But nothing important was happening.

Someone was walking a dog on the furthest side of the green, while, past that, two men were on a roof, wrestling with some rusty gutters. It felt unlikely any of them had messaged Daniel.

Jennifer shivered and considered going into her suitcase in the back of the car to find what clothes she'd packed. The night before had been a bit of a blur, though she was fairly sure she'd thrown in a thick jumper or two. She fought with the seat belt and then, as she was twisting, realised there was something reddish on the back seat.

It had been seven weeks back that Andrew had dropped off

Daniel for university. Considering where she currently was, Jennifer's reluctance to visit Ashington now felt bizarre – yet she had opted out of the previous trips. It was only after Andrew got home that he'd realised Daniel had left a hoody in the car. Jennifer had spotted it the next day but, in the passive-aggressive life they had drifted into, they were each too stubborn to take it out. Jennifer wasn't going to crack first: after all, it had been Andrew who'd not checked the back seat when he'd packed their son off for his second year. Presumably Andrew wasn't going to take it out, either.

Jennifer stretched and pulled the hoody into the front. It was from Daniel's secondary school, in its maroon colours, with a small 'Class of…' lettering. Jennifer pulled it over her head and pushed her arms through. She cleared the windscreen again, then sat with her arms folded, at least somewhat warmer than she was.

The man walking the dog had disappeared and the green was empty. Jennifer rechecked the address on the locker phone, then the Maps app. She was definitely in the right place.

And then, as she looked up from the devices, she saw someone tall in a large coat walk quickly along the pavement towards the park hut. They slowed momentarily as they reached the bench to the side of the building, then glanced around the side, presumably looking for someone. The person's hood was up, their hands jammed in their pockets. From the height, it was likely a man, though Jennifer wasn't certain. He walked a few paces back the way he'd come, spun awkwardly in a semicircle, paused, and then started retracing his steps. This time, he was walking a lot slower than he had been.

He was at the corner when Jennifer made her decision. She jumped out of the car, locked it, and then hurried after the man in the coat. The last thing she'd seen was him crossing the road and heading into a narrow alley that passed between a pair of houses. As he rounded the bollard that blocked vehicles from driving through the gap, he checked his shoulder. Jennifer was a fair distance back, though, as she rushed to catch him, she was almost certain he'd spotted her.

But he didn't stop. If anything, he picked up his pace.

Jennifer wondered if this was what he'd planned. He was never going to meet someone in the open, next to that green; he was going to lead them somewhere quieter.

A nurdling voice was whispering to Jennifer, telling her this was a bad idea. If this person was expecting Daniel, they were going to be surprised to find her. Daniel's girlfriend was dead and there was all that cash in his locker. Nothing good could happen.

And yet, a different voice told her she had nothing else to go on. She had no idea what her son was up to, nor where he was. What else could she do?

Jennifer entered the alley as the figure in the coat exited the other end. He ducked around the corner, out of sight as Jennifer's warring voices told her to simultaneously turn around and press on.

She pressed on, the air cold in her lungs, her breath spiralling in front, as she reached an almost jog. She didn't want to lose whoever she was following. Jennifer almost burst from the end of the alley, skidding slightly on the dusty ground as she scanned from side to side to see where the person had gone. There was a car stopped almost directly in front of her and then—

A blur slammed into Jennifer from the side. She was already off balance and had no time to react as she was shunted forward. She was falling, falling... but only towards the car. Jennifer reached to stop her fall, though only succeeded in clipping her elbow on the wing as she slipped to her knees. Someone was directly behind her, clamping one arm under her shoulder, while using the other to open the car boot.

Jennifer knew what was happening a moment before it did

– except the person manhandling her was so much stronger that there was nothing she could do. The world twisted, there was pavement, then sky as Jennifer was flipped off her feet and into the boot. It happened so quickly that she had no time to shout. Instead, the boot slammed shut – and then there was only darkness.

TWENTY-FOUR YEARS AGO

Jennifer was nearly home when she spotted him. Craig was sitting on the wall of a house three doors down from her student digs. He was swinging his feet, staring at the ground. His bumbling, awkward frame was unmistakeable, with every kick of his legs making it look as if he might overbalance.

Jennifer froze, wondering if she could turn and head back the other way before he spotted her. She hadn't seen Craig in almost a month, since that day in the library when she was sure he'd been watching her. That sense of being spied upon had crept up on her in the subsequent weeks, leaving her wondering if it was paranoia, or if he really was somewhere nearby.

As for Jo, Jennifer hadn't seen her since they'd watched her get out of the taxi on the night they had found her outside the club. Jo had insisted that the police shouldn't be called – and that she would handle things. Hayley had been too drunk to argue, while Natasha had seemingly been content enough to leave things there. It was only Jennifer, apparently, who still felt uncomfortable at it all.

And now Craig was *right there*. Jennifer dodged behind a

lamp post and kept as still as she could. It couldn't be a coincidence that he was so close to where they lived.

Breathe...

Jennifer counted to ten. In through the nose, out through the mouth.

She had been on her way back to the house after lectures, and thinking about beans on toast for much of the walk.

Not now.

Jennifer edged out from behind the lamp post and turned to head back the way she'd come – except she had only taken one step when a man's voice stopped her.

Craig was a couple of paces away, looming over her.

'You're Jen, right?' he asked.

Jennifer backed away a fraction, realising it was the first time for sure that she was aware of him knowing her name. The confidence she'd had from the canteen a couple of months before had seemingly evaporated. It felt as if she'd been a different person then.

'What do you want?' she asked.

'Just wanna talk.'

Jennifer glanced towards the other side of the road, hoping there might be someone there who would spot she was in trouble. This was a conversation she didn't want – and they were only a few doors away from her shared house. There was no reason for him to know her name, let alone where she slept. How had he found out? How long had he been following her around?

'What do you want to talk about?' Jennifer asked, looking for time.

Craig was avoiding eye contact. 'Can we go somewhere?' He angled towards her house, as if asking for an invite inside.

'I've got lectures,' Jennifer lied. 'We can talk here. What do you want?'

He didn't answer that, instead saying: 'I heard you lived here...?'

There was a hopefulness to his voice, which wasn't reflected by Jennifer's rising alarm.

'Who told you that?'

'Dunno...'

Jennifer backed away another step, though Craig followed. She was in his shadow.

'We live on Warren Street,' Jennifer said, pointing across the path. Warren Street ran parallel but three or four roads over. 'I was going to the Spar,' she added, nodding past Craig towards the shop on the corner. Not that she could see it: he was still blocking the way. She winced, remembering she'd just told him she had lectures, and now it was the shop.

'Oh,' he replied.

It wasn't much of a response but, as he spoke, Craig hefted that crumpled Tesco bag upwards. He'd been carrying it almost every time Jennifer had seen him and she wondered if the knife was still in the bottom.

At the thought of that, and with seemingly nobody else on the street who might intervene, Jennifer muttered a sharp: 'I have to go.'

She stepped around Craig, half-expecting him to block her way. When he didn't, she hoicked her bag higher and hurried along the road, not looking behind. As she passed her house, she was careful not to look towards it, before continuing – eventually – into the corner shop.

She was well-known there, most of the students were, given they were daily visitors. Jennifer said 'hi' to Vikram behind the counter. He joked that she looked flustered and she almost told him the reason.

'Tell Nattie that her lasagnes are coming in tomorrow,' he added – and it took Jennifer a minute to remember that

Natasha was often clearing out the stock of Weightwatchers ready meals at the back of the shop.

Jennifer said she'd pass on the message – and then went to hide in the crisp aisle. She peeped through the gap between the Monster Munch and Wotsits, watching the door and wondering whether Craig would follow her in. She was struggling to work out what was going on.

Craig had threatened Jo with a knife and Jennifer had put herself between them in what increasingly felt like a moment of madness. After that, they had seemingly got back together, then Jennifer had seen Craig watching her in the library. Most recently, Craig had hit Jo outside a club – and now he was waiting for Jennifer very close to their house. Beyond that, there was that constant sense of unease that she was being watched. He knew her name, he knew more or less where she lived. He'd apparently been asking around about her.

Jennifer gave it a couple of minutes, in which time nobody had entered the store. She grabbed a Twix from the chocolate aisle, then went to the counter. Vikram said something about her sweet tooth which, from what Jennifer had gathered, was a thing he said to everybody who bought anything non-savoury. She went with it, paid, and then headed back outside.

There was nobody waiting for her; no sign of Craig. Jennifer slipped between a pair of parked cars to look both ways along the street. There was a trio of girls walking in the opposite direction, towards the university, but that was it.

To be sure, Jennifer headed away from her house, ducking into an alley and following the cobbles that sat between two long rows of terraces.

Jennifer rarely used the back door of the house, but slowed as she neared the gate. She checked over her shoulder twice and then slipped through the rickety metal gate into their dusty back yard. A pile of coal sat in the corner, which the landlord had once promised to move. Hayley had a row of pot plants against the sodden fence panel, that she had brought from home.

Jennifer waited, only realising she was out of breath as her stomach twisted. She counted to ten, then twenty, then fifty. If someone had followed, then they'd done a decent job of not making it obvious.

Jennifer lifted the third pot, the one Hayley insisted would definitely bloom when the sun appeared. She plucked the key from underneath and let herself into the house, before locking the door behind her.

The warmth of the kitchen was such a relief that Jennifer almost let out a sob. She took a long, deep breath and then filled the kettle. She had never needed a cup of tea more. Natasha might even have a packet of chocolate digestives somewhere. She usually did.

As the kettle boiled, the sound of muffled indie music drifted from somewhere along the hall. Jennifer left the kitchen, following it to Hayley's door. Jennifer and Natasha had bedrooms upstairs, while Hayley had the one on the ground floor. It had been a living room at some point, before the land-lord had converted the house into a trio of flats.

Jennifer knocked and waited for the quick: 'Hello?' that came. Inside and Hayley was in her bed, duvet high under her chin. Her television was playing some sort of cookery daytime show, that she'd muted, with music on the radio instead. Her face was puffy and red and she snorted a long snotty breath, before breaking into something close to a smile. 'I've got a cold,' she said. A beat and then: 'What's wrong?'

'That weird Craig guy was waiting outside,' Jennifer said.

Hayley frowned, or she tried to. Her features were too swollen to make much of a difference. 'Why?'

'I don't know. He knew my name and more or less where we live. He was a few doors down. He said he wanted to talk.'

'What about?'

'That's what I asked but he said he wanted to go somewhere and I didn't trust him enough for that. In the end, I hid in the Spar.' Jennifer thought on that for a moment, then said the thing she really feared. 'I think he was trying to find out the exact house where we live. I told him we were on Warren Street, then snuck in the back door. I don't think he followed.'

Hayley let out a short cough, covering her mouth and groaning slightly. 'Sorry,' she mumbled, as she battled a yawn.

'Shall we call the police?' Jennifer asked. She wanted to talk to someone, to share the urgency she felt.

Hayley partially shrugged from underneath the duvet. 'Dunno,' she said, with another sniff. 'What would we tell them?'

SIXTEEN

As the car started, Jennifer had tried banging hard on the back panel, hoping someone would hear. That notion was quickly dispelled as the vehicle set off, sending her bouncing and rolling around the dark space of the boot. She ended up cradling her head, trying to keep herself in something close to the recovery position. She couldn't see much of anything and was existing in a new world of experiencing her surroundings by bouncing off them. She felt every groan and surge of the engine and came to anticipate the changes in speed. That left her trying to twist herself in a way that would stop her body from bumping off the various corners. Every now and then would come a precious respite, which she assumed was traffic lights.

If it wasn't such a physical workout, Jennifer would be terrified. As it was, she didn't have time for that. She had lost all concept of space. The thought occurred that she'd left her bag in her car when she'd got out in a hurry. It had been on the passenger seat, and contained both phones, her purse, Ben Davies' driving licence, plus the key that had been in Daniel's locker.

Either of those phones might have been useful if she actually had them, plus the time to stop and call 999.

For now, the hum of the engine dimmed as the car slowed. Jennifer wriggled to try to wedge her feet against the inside of the boot, with her shoulders resting on the rear of the seats. She pushed hard as the vehicle took a corner, just about stopping herself from sliding into the harsh metal at the side, before everything righted itself.

If she had to guess, they'd been driving for fifteen minutes, though Jennifer wouldn't have been surprised if it was much less. Her knees were sore from the first corner, in which she'd cannoned into the wheel rim. She'd also taken a bang to the head from being thrown upwards into the top of the boot, plus her palms were sore from trying to grasp onto to a hook she'd found when the lock latched.

As the car again slowed, Jennifer wedged herself back into place, anticipating either a bend, or a rapid acceleration. Except, this time, the humming ended abruptly as the vehicle reached a full halt.

Now there was time to be afraid.

Jennifer scrambled around the small space, hoping to find something she'd missed previously. Anything blunt or sharp. Anything with which she could fight back. If only she'd remembered her bag and the phones.

She felt the driver's car door open and then slam, as a shuddering *thunk* boomed through the back. Jennifer was fumbling for something she knew wasn't there as footsteps pounded on tarmac, closer, closer, until a hand slapped the metal directly above Jennifer's head. She winced, which left her reeling as, from nowhere, light flooded dark. She screwed her eyes closed, gasping at the suddenness of it all. Greeny-pink stars fizzed that were impossible to blink away. Jennifer's eyes were open, though it was hard to make out much of anything. Someone in a dark top or coat, maybe. Someone in a mask, maybe. Or a bala-clava. Maybe.

She winced, covering her head, waiting for whatever was coming.

Except it never did. Instead, there was a man's voice.

'Shit.'

SEVENTEEN

The boot of the car slammed closed once more – and Jennifer was again engulfed by the creeping, encompassing embrace of darkness. She waited, wondering what was happening; fearing the worst. There were the muffled tones of what sounded like a man's voice. The words were impossible to make out, though he was saying something, waiting for a reply, and then talking again. He was likely on the phone – and from the stilted, harsh tone, he was annoyed.

Jennifer strained to listen, partially wondering if she should bang and make a noise. In the few seconds the boot had been open, she'd had no chance to get her bearings, though it felt unlikely they had stopped somewhere public. Making a noise might only annoy the man further.

And he definitely sounded frustrated.

The words had the punchy intonation of someone who was not happy. There was a thump of what sounded like him kicking the bumper or a tyre and then a somewhat clear: 'I don't know who she is!'

Jennifer pressed her ear against the cool metal at the very

back of the car. She knew it would hurt if he thumped again but was desperate to hear more.

From nowhere, she realised what had likely happened. When he had bundled her into the back of the car, he must have thought she was a man. Which was when Jennifer realised she was wearing Daniel's hoody.

The man thought he was abducting… *Daniel?*

The hoody was massive on Jennifer, and she was wearing a woolly hat that largely covered her longer hair. It felt possible that someone had made the mistake. He'd seen her over his shoulder from a distance, then grabbed her the moment she exited the alley.

The thought was barely fully formed when the driver's side door slammed and the engine growled once more. Jennifer tensed, trying to wedge herself into the gap before the vehicle lurched forward.

She spent the next indeterminate amount of time trying to protect her head, while simultaneously anticipating the car's movements. Her body was aching, which gave her mind little time to touch on the darker thoughts.

If the person who'd grabbed her had taken the wrong person, what was he going to do with her now? Nobody knew she had the phone from Daniel's locker, nor that she was following a text that had been received. Apart from the vague notion of her being in Ashington, no one knew where she was. Her phone, with its Find My Friends, had been left in her car, near the green. The driver wouldn't have to go far before they'd be in the leafy country lanes and the miles of woods. If he harmed her, or worse, she would never be found…

Jennifer battled those thoughts, while trying not to be thrown around too much. Time passed, and then the engine faded to a halt. The driver's door opened once more. Jennifer had one final fumble around the enclosed space, hoping to find something – anything – that might help her fight back. She would definitely scream this time, kick, scratch, bite if needed.

Anything.

But then the light flooded her like a blow to the face. It was impossible not to screw her eyes closed, even as she felt someone's hands upon her. She opened her mouth to scream, except a hand clamped across it. She wriggled and kicked, not that it did any good. The man was so much stronger and, while he knew where they were, Jennifer had no idea. Everything happened so quickly. Her plans to bite, shout and fight came to nothing as she was dumped on something hard.

She opened her eyes, still squinting from the bright, searing daylight. Her hip stung from the drop and stars were spinning again.

The man was standing over her, silhouetted, his face covered by a balaclava. The smell of something fruity hung inexplicably, like a strawberry field on a summer afternoon. Jennifer was so baffled by its presence that she momentarily lost any sense of self-preservation.

And then... it was over.

Jennifer had started to crawl away – but the man wasn't interested in her. He turned back to his dark red car and got inside. The fruity smell was replaced by engine fumes as he revved – and then blurred away and out of sight.

Jennifer was sitting on what turned out to be a pavement. She rolled onto her side, rubbed her elbow, and then pushed herself up. She was suddenly full of the things she should've done. Why hadn't she looked for the number plate and memorised it? Why hadn't she shouted for help? Why hadn't she tried to kick her way through the backrest that connected the car boot to the seat? Why hadn't she paid better attention to the person she'd followed into the alley?

Why?

Except, beyond that, Jennifer was safe. *Relatively* safe.

She jumped as something banged and turned to see a woman exiting a house. The person had slammed the front door and was busy digging into a bag, looking for keys.

It was so... *normal*.

Jennifer had pictured abandoned wasteland, or a secluded country park. The sort of places in which it felt as if terrible things might happen. Instead, she was opposite a row of houses. There was a trampoline in one of the front gardens and a carved pumpkin in the window of another.

It took a few moments for Jennifer to realise she was back at the exit of the alley where she had first been grabbed. She wasn't sure how long she'd been gone but she had essentially been taken in a big circle.

The woman who'd slammed her front door had found her key. She locked up, then got into the car on her drive. Jennifer watched as she pulled away, marvelling at the normality of it all. From terrifying to simple domesticity in no time. If it wasn't for her aching hip and elbow, it almost wouldn't feel real.

The light was still disorientating as Jennifer turned to head back through the alley, towards the green and where she'd parked. She realised the car key was in the pocket of Daniel's hoody, which meant it could have been used as a weapon between her fingers if she'd been clear-headed. There were times, usually at night, when she walked with a key in her fist just in case. Her mother had taught her that one.

Now, she was thinking of Craig in the university canteen again. It never felt too far from her thoughts, even though it had been so long ago. That was when she'd felt cool in a crisis. She would have backed herself in most circumstances and Jennifer wondered what had happened to that young woman. Now, she felt out of her depth to the point that she hadn't even remembered to scream. She'd watched those crime dramas and practically screamed at the main characters for forgetting to do the basics. Now she knew why: the terror was too strong, things happened too quickly. Bodies shut down and so did the brain. She couldn't quite believe everything that had happened in the past few minutes.

Jennifer traced along the alley, sticking to the very centre, away from any possible shadows. The air was harsh and cold, the wisps of fog hanging low.

As she reached the car, Jennifer spotted her bag still sitting on the passenger, the top open, both phones on display. In other towns and cities, the window would have been smashed and everything gone.

Jennifer unlocked the driver's door and fell inside, listening for the click of the central locking, and then closing her eyes.

She could finally breathe.

Jennifer was shivering, though it might have been fright, rather than the cold. She could hear her heart thundering, still smell that fruitiness that had thrown her off the second time the car boot had opened. Jennifer had no idea what it might have been, or whether it was there at all.

The clock on the dash of the car said that barely half an hour had passed – and it was all a blitzed haze of what was increasingly feeling like a dream. She was so tired that it almost hurt to think.

Jennifer knew she should call the police. She had been kidnapped – if only temporarily. Except, if she called them, she would have to explain about Daniel's locker and the phone she'd found. If she didn't tell them about all that cash, they would go there and find it themselves.

All of that would mean so many more queries for Daniel, if and when they found him. Probably more trouble, as well.

Which left Jennifer with one, enormous, unanswered question.

What on earth had Daniel got himself involved with?

EIGHTEEN

Jennifer had been asleep within seconds of collapsing onto the hotel bed. She could have spent some time researching reviews and ratings, maybe even checking in with Andrew to see if he had rewards points with one of the various chains. Instead, she'd driven to the Comfort Inn she'd seen a little off the motorway junction, asked the guy on the front desk if she could check in early, slipped him twenty quid when he'd said she'd have to wait until 4 p.m., and then allowed herself to succumb to the tiredness that had been threatening to over-whelm her.

The next time she moved was three and a half hours later. Jennifer jumped, reaching and stretching to where she half expected the sides of that car boot to be. A part of her was still there – and perhaps it always would be.

The hotel room curtains were open; the evening darkness enveloping the room. The only light was a gentle sliver of white from under the door, plus the vague glow of the street lamps surrounding the car park outside her window.

Jennifer had slept on top of the bedcovers, still wearing Daniel's hoody. She yawned as she pushed herself up, then she stretched high until her shoulders clicked and her back crunched.

It was now just after five. The day had barely begun and now it was over. She'd not been right since the clocks went back the weekend before. Governments and the like simply couldn't stop dicking around with stuff.

Jennifer hauled herself up and crossed to the window, where she looked over the bleak scene of a hotel car park, next to a motorway. Someone in an oversized Volvo was struggling to reverse into a space, while the light of their phone screen lit up the side of their face. On the furthest side of the tarmac, the drive-thru Burger King was doing a roaring teatime trade.

Jennifer eyed the boot of the Volvo and found herself picturing being inside. It had been so dark and everything had felt so close. It was surreal that whoever had taken her had simply let her go again. She wondered if she really had been mistaken for her son and whether Daniel would have been released.

She could call the police and tell them what had happened – except surely they'd be as baffled as her? Plus that officer had told her to go home, and Jennifer had ignored her.

On her own phone, there was a message from Andrew, asking how things were going, but little else. Nothing about whether that mystery vehicle was still parked over the road. Nothing from her son.

Her email box was chocked with nonsense from every company she'd ever dealt with advertising their 'Halloween sale'. Then it would be the Fireworks Night sale, then Black Friday, then Christmas, then Boxing Day, then new year, then Valentine's. It never ended. She deleted them all, ignored the one from the council's head of HR, then checked the phone she'd found in Daniel's locker.

There was still only the one message: the one that had drawn her to that hut next to the small park.

I can get you out of this

It really felt as if someone had sent that to Daniel, trying to draw him to them. She was so desperate to ask her son with what he was involved. What had he done?

Jennifer clambered out of his hoody, hung it in the wardrobe, and then took a shower. It took a while for the water to get hot but, when it did, it was steaming. Jennifer couldn't close the curtain all the way because it felt too confined.

At least she was clean.

Once out of the water, she perched on the end of the bed and replied to her husband. She left out the part about the kidnapping and the cash, while telling him that she'd not got much closer to finding Daniel. That would be quite the text to receive: 'Hey, hun, just got kidnapped. All good tho. You OK?'

Jennifer searched her son's name and doom-scrolled through news websites. It seemed as if the police were still keeping many of the details to themselves, except it was out anyway. People were on the local Facebook pages, confidently saying Daniel Farley had murdered his girlfriend with a lamp cord in his bedroom. They named the road and house number. There were photos that people had copied from his Instagram page – all combined with parents asking if it was safe for their children to be outside.

Jennifer couldn't stop looking at the word 'killer'. That's what Daniel was being called by so many people who didn't know him.

Her son was a killer... except she knew he wasn't.

Elsewhere, people were posting about Ella. It was mainly those who said they'd enjoyed her band, but a woman had written that Ella had babysat for her a few years back. There was a link to the page set up for Ella's band, Pixie Dreampeople – and Jennifer clicked into it. She scrolled through hundreds of photos, not entirely sure why. None of it made her feel any better. Every image of Ella singing left Jennifer with an over-whelming feeling of senseless loss. All that life and potential was gone.

But still Jennifer continued scrolling. She only stopped as she reached one Instagram post saying there was to be a memorial that evening. Jennifer had forgotten Gary suggesting she could go until it was in front of her, with the place and time.

There was no way Jennifer could let anyone know she was Daniel's mum, not with everything of which he'd been accused – and yet a large part of her wanted to be there. If nothing else, she wanted to hear what people had to say about Ella and what she meant to them. They had not spent much time together back when Daniel had brought his girlfriend down for Christmas, but Jennifer had liked the young woman.

Jennifer ate the two-pack of Borders biscuits that sat next to the grubby kettle, then raided the Dairy Milk from the minibar. That was six quid she wouldn't get back. She would need to eat properly at some point, plus sleep for more than three hours, but it was enough for now.

She didn't bother unpacking but pulled out the darkest clothes she had in her suitcase and put them on. That niggling voice was still going, telling her it was a terrible idea to attend the memorial of the girl who'd apparently been murdered by her son. But then, in a day of terrible ideas, Jennifer figured what was one more?

NINETEEN

The church was packed as Jennifer slotted in at the back. Wide stone columns towered high to the steepled ceiling above, with light glimmering from the stained-glass windows that lined the sides. The pews were wooden and uncomfortable looking, with many of the rows lined with young people who had turned out in a rainbow of colour. Somebody also in black like Jennifer mumbled something about it being a 'celebration not a memorial', though Jennifer doubted anyone would mind too much.

Parents, maybe former teachers, were pressed along the sides of the church, leaning on pillars and whispering to one another as an underlying rock tune crept from the speakers. Jennifer doubted it was the church's usual fare – but then there wasn't too much usual about any of this.

Jennifer squished herself between a group of adults and tried her best to hide behind a post. She had a view of the front, though a good two-thirds of the people in the church couldn't see her.

And there were *a lot* of people in the church.

More were still filing in, young adults and older, dark

clothes and bright, as people pointed towards their friends, while others shuffled around to make space.

There was a lump in Jennifer's throat. Children weren't supposed to die before their parents, and especially not in such a brutal way. There was grief – but also guilt because it wasn't fair for her, of all people, to be feeling such things. This poor young woman was somebody else's child to grieve, not hers.

Jennifer jumped as someone brushed past her, heading for the aisle. They had already muttered a 'sorry', without looking back. She hadn't been recognised and it was an accident – but the memory of being forced into the back of the car was desperately, devastatingly close. Jennifer crept closer to the pillar. Nobody was going to get her there.

She waited, listening to the murmur of voices around her. When things began, it wasn't a service in any traditional sense. The priest or vicar, whatever he was, wore jeans. He had the vibe of a supply teacher who'd perch on the corner of a table and call everyone 'guys'. He spoke about remembering those who gave to the world and enhanced the lives of those around them. There was no mention of God or Jesus, no religion at all as he said that a loss would only be complete if the memories went as well. That Ella's friends could keep a part of her alive if they listened to her music, shared their recollections of her with one another, and celebrated the life that was.

There was music but no hymns. Instead, it was tracks that Ella liked, all of which were rocky guitar songs, with female vocals.

Jennifer struggled to hold it together. She shrank further behind the pillar until she couldn't see the front. It was almost too much. She ducked her head into the collar of her top, using her sleeve to keep some degree of control on the tears. The lump in her throat never shrank, let alone disappeared.

Everything from the past day or so felt incomprehensible.

A song had finished playing and then somebody new was

speaking. Jennifer peeped around the pillar to where Gary was on stage. He'd been introduced as a church 'elder' and 'chief community outreach officer', whatever that meant. He was in a suit yet somehow looked more comfortable than the vicar as he said that Ella was an important part of his family. He said that she co-tutored his son, Charles, while making no mention of the other co-tutor. It was understandable, though only emphasised to Jennifer how desperate she was to hear from her son.

'... We are obviously devastated to hear what has happened to Ella,' Gary was saying. 'I spoke with the police earlier and they asked me to re-emphasise that everyone in our community should feel safe.'

There were mutterings through the church, likely because a tall white man telling others they should feel safe was easy for him to say when a young woman had been killed. Something subtle shifted in the mood and perhaps Gary felt it too. He seemed far more authoritative in his suit, compared to the fleece of earlier.

'I'd also like to add that if anyone here wants to discuss what happened, even just to have a stranger to dump on, I'll be around afterwards. I'm also happy to give you my card, plus the doors of The Mission are always open.'

As Jennifer was wondering what 'The Mission' was, Gary pressed his fingers into each other, steepling his fingers as if about to pray. He thanked everyone for coming, wished them all a safe journey home, and then stepped away as another song began.

People started to stand, some shuffling for the exits, others grouping to chat. Jennifer overheard someone saying that there was a rock night happening in one of the local pubs – and the general sense was that many of the young people were heading there.

She had no intention of going, but Jennifer followed the masses through the main doors of the church, where they emerged into a courtyard. A pair of trees were whispering in the evening breeze and it somehow felt warmer than it had through the day. There was no sign of the moon, only a whiteish glow creeping through the clouds.

A large group of young adults in bright clothes headed through the gates and disappeared into the night, leaving mainly adults massing on the cobbles. Jennifer slipped into a shadow underneath a large stone obelisk, which gave her a decent view of the courtyard, plus the rest of the shade. She wasn't expecting Daniel to be there, and yet a part of her wondered if he would want to see the turnout for his girlfriend. She was so sure he hadn't killed her, despite everything to the contrary, primary of which was the fact he was missing. His 'It wasn't me' still haunted. He knew Ella was dead and that he would be suspected. He *knew* – and he had called his mum because he wanted her to know it wasn't him.

If that was true, as well as being worried about himself, Daniel would be devastated at what had happened to Ella.

Which was why Jennifer took a slow walk around the courtyard. A trio were smoking a fraction outside the gates, while other small groups chatted on the cobbles. Jennifer kept her head down, not wanting to accidentally be drawn into a conversation about who she was and how she knew Ella. She had completed a lap and was almost back where she'd started when she spotted someone in a dark jacket watching from underneath one of the trees. They were alone, leaning to one side, upper half hidden by the shadows, watching – but they hadn't spotted Jennifer. It could be Daniel... maybe. Although the figure was possibly bigger.

Jennifer kept to the shade, tracing the outer walls of the church until she was in line with the tree. Closer and closer, wondering...

But it wasn't Daniel.

The man was too tall, his smart shoes too shiny. Jennifer

wasn't even sure that Daniel owned a pair of brogues like the ones on the feet of the man next to the tree.

He still hadn't spotted her and, as Jennifer neared, she realised she *had* seen him before. He was the man who had been on the upper level of the pub. The one in the suit and long coat – which he was still wearing. At the time she thought he had been watching her but, as she followed his gaze towards the main part of the courtyard, she realised she had likely been wrong. His stare was fixed on Callum.

Ella's brother was shuffling around the courtyard, also wearing the same clothes from earlier. In his case, it was the loose grey joggers, which didn't feel quite right for his sister's memorial, even if a lot of people her age had turned up in colourful, casual clothes.

Callum was still limping, though it seemed more pronounced than when she'd seen him that morning. Jennifer watched him stop near the middle of the courtyard, then seemingly spot someone he knew. He ambled across to a couple of youngsters who were standing with their backs to the church, next to a statue. They were probably seventeen or eighteen, with blotchy spots on their cheeks that were clear even from a distance. One of them exchanged a similar kind of practised handshake with Callum, before both withdrew their hands into pockets. It was so bleak for a brother to be dealing at his murdered sister's memorial service.

The teenagers turned and darted for the exit as Jennifer returned her attention to the man by the tree. He'd still not noticed her but he had apparently seen enough as he slipped his own hands into his pockets, before striding towards a different exit. Jennifer watched him, wondering who he was and why he was so interested in Callum. She wondered whether he had been at the service itself, watching and waiting for Ella's brother. He could be undercover police, although she figured he was probably too smartly dressed for all that – not to mention the crispness of his suit was anything but undercover. She doubted police salaries covered that level of tailoring.

'I wondered if you'd be here...'

Jennifer jumped as she realised someone had crept up on her. She twisted to see Gary standing a couple of paces away.

He reached to calm her: 'I didn't mean to startle you,' he added quickly. 'Are you OK?'

Jennifer had spun in a semicircle, ending up facing Callum, who must have heard her mild squeak. He eyed her through the gloom for a moment, or perhaps he was looking to Gary. It was hard to tell, although he made no attempt to approach. Instead, he turned and bounded towards the furthest gate, and the night beyond.

Gary let out a long breath that said a lot.

'You know Ella's brother?' Jennifer asked, knowing the answer.

There was a short, contemplative, pause – and then: 'We're acquainted.'

It was a pointed response, which perhaps said more than the sigh. It didn't sound as if there was much love lost between them.

'How are you?' Gary added quickly, moving on.

'I got some sleep,' Jennifer replied, knowing it wasn't an answer.

'The police came back to the house a few hours after you'd left. They wanted to check a couple of things based on what Harriet had told them, but it was mainly dates and times that she didn't know. I don't have any more news for you, I'm afraid.'

It felt a little as if he was fishing to ask whether Jennifer had heard anything else, though she didn't necessarily mind. What was she going to tell him? There was tens of thousands of pounds in Daniel's locker – and she'd been temporarily kidnapped while chasing a message received to the phone that had also been in the locker?

She let the silence sit, then motioned towards the gate behind them. 'Did you see the man in the big coat who went that way?' she asked, fully expecting him to say he hadn't.

Instead, Gary cleared his throat. 'Mr Williams,' he said. 'Lance. He owns a couple of buildings in town. Shops, a pub, flats. That sort of thing.' Gary waited a beat and then added: 'He's, um... *controversial.*'

It sounded ominous and Jennifer looked up to Gary, who was focusing on the gate through which the mysterious Lance Williams had left.

'Why?' Jennifer asked.

Gary let out a small cough, then paused, seemingly thinking of the best way to put things, before settling on: 'I'm not sure I should speak out of turn.'

Before Jennifer could ask any sort of follow-up, he turned back towards the church.

'I'd like to introduce you to my wife, if that's OK? I understand if you say no but Harriet had a proper soft spot for Daniel. She's been a wreck all day. It's hard to believe he could be accused of such a thing.'

Jennifer was still thinking about the word 'controversial', while trying to memorise the name 'Lance Williams'. She would have to look him up.

But then, as she clicked into what Gary had said, it sounded as if he and his wife also believed that Daniel was innocent. She wondered if they'd been telling other people.

'Is she inside?' Jennifer asked.

'She's at The Mission – but it's only a couple of minutes away.'

'What's The Mission?'

'It's a mix of food bank, soup kitchen, shelter and lending library. We have a collection of tools and appliances that people can check out if they need.'

Gary bobbed from one foot to the other as Jennifer remembered he was after an answer. She told him she would be happy to talk to his wife, keeping to herself that she had no idea what they might want to say to one another. A part of her craved it, though she knew she couldn't face hearing about Daniel and what now felt like his old life. He *was* a music tutor, he *was* a student, and Jennifer doubted he ever would be again.

Jennifer followed as Gary led her through the church. He waved and nodded to what felt like every other person, then fist-bumped with someone in a wheelchair, before leading Jennifer through a back door into a small stone room. They passed through a second door, then out into a graveyard. The shadows were long as the wind wittered louder than before. Gravestones stretched from a chain-link fence on one side to a chain-link fence on the other. Small trails led away from the main path, though Gary kept striding at pace, until they reached a large one-storey building at the furthest end of the church grounds.

As they got closer, wisps of meat broth caught on the breeze, making Jennifer's mouth water, and sending her spiralling to the old, old days of Sunday roasts at her nan's house. Almost forty years, but she could still remember sitting on the patchy flowery carpet, playing with Lego as the grown-ups talked in the other room.

Gary used a key to unlock a darkened door at the back of the building – and then held it wide for Jennifer to pass inside. The smell was stronger still as Gary directed her along a corridor towards a door, from which light was seeping around the edges.

They emerged into a large hall, with a serving counter at one end. A couple of dozen people were milling on chairs, with a handful playing board games on a pair of tables near a fire exit. It was warm and bright, a vast contrast from the chilled darkness outside. Jennifer was trying to get her bearings as Gary stepped around her.

'This way,' he said, leading Jennifer towards the counter.

A man was sitting nearby on the floor, eating a hot dog from a paper plate, while wiping greasy fingers on his grotty jeans. Suddenly, the smell wasn't the meaty broth of Jennifer's youth, it was hot dogs of her primary school canteen, and Friday nights with the Girl Guides. She couldn't remember the last time she'd had a hot dog – not that she craved one now.

'This is Harriet,' Gary said, moving to the side and holding a hand out, as if to present the woman behind the counter. She was wearing a hairnet, with a slightly off-white apron that was tied a little too tightly.

Harriet peered up from the metal pan of sausages. Her eyes widened a teeny amount in recognition. It wasn't much but it was enough – and Jennifer suspected she'd done the same thing. Because that was the moment she realised they already knew each other.

TWENTY-FOUR YEARS AGO

Jennifer knew nothing about sport. If that hadn't been clear before, then it certainly had been when the pub quiz team of her and Natasha had been the only ones to not know that Manchester United were the Premier League champions. Natasha thought it might be Leeds, but that was because her dad supported them. It turned out that Leeds weren't even *in* the Premier League, let alone champions. The lad from their course, who'd claimed he was a sporting expert, had ummed and ahhed off every question, before admitting he only knew anything about basketball.

The picture round hadn't gone much better, neither had current affairs or, well, anything. They had finished second-last, defeating only the team who'd left after three rounds because one of their members had drunk so much, he couldn't stand up. Even *he'd* known Manchester United were champions.

Jennifer and Natasha left the pub arm in arm: beaten but not defeated. Jennifer was giddy from the cider; the right side of drunk. It had been two days since Craig had waited for her on the street and she hadn't seen him since. She had spent an hour determined to call the police and then changed her mind,

largely because it felt like such a faff. She didn't know Craig or
Jo's full name, or where either of them lived. When they'd been
in the taxi together after that night at the club, Jo had got off
outside a takeaway and said it was 'close enough'. Jennifer didn't
know if they were students, even though Craig had been in the
library. Apart from her friends, there were no witnesses to the
other incidents – and it was only her who'd seen Craig on the
street. What would she tell the police? She was worried for Jo?
She thought Craig might be following her, even though she'd
only seen him twice?

So she left it. Jennifer went to lectures the next two days,
then to the weekly pub quiz with Natasha. Hayley would
usually be there, too, except she was still full of snot at home.

Jennifer and Natasha click-clacked along the largely
deserted pavements, weaving between parked cars to cross,
until they were on their road. There was nobody sitting on the
wall where Jennifer had seen Craig, even though she now
looked for him every time she peeped out her upstairs window.

At the far end of the street, Vikram was yanking down the
shutters on his shop, the creaking of the metal echoing along the
empty street.

Natasha never took her key, leaving Jennifer to retrieve hers
from her bag. The lock was tricky, not quite fixed in place, and
she battled it open until they bumbled into the hall.

Jennifer was ready for bed... although perhaps there was
one of those microwavable burger things in the fridge and she'd
have that instead. There was nothing quite like—

Something was wrong.

A chilled, fizzing breeze whipped along the lower floor of
the house and, as Natasha followed the cooler temperature into
the kitchen, she stopped and turned, perplexed. 'The back
door's open?' she said, phrasing it as a question.

Jennifer knew. Oh, she knew. Perhaps Natasha did too,
because Jennifer saw her gulp as she moved back from the

kitchen and knocked on Hayley's bedroom door. It should have been closed, it always was, but it hadn't clicked into place, and the door swung inwards with a low, creaking groan.

She was still near the front door, shivering from the cold, her arms folded across her front – but Jennifer saw all she needed to in the way Natasha's face exploded. Her jaw fell, eyebrows arched, head rocked.

'Jen...'

Natasha didn't move, didn't do anything except stare, as Jennifer edged along the hall towards her. There was no way she was going to look into Hayley's room, but she knew she would. Around the door, towards the bed, where the lamp had seemingly been ripped from the wall.

Natasha repeated, 'Jen...' as the two women stood together in the doorway, staring into the horror that had once been their friend's bedroom.

TWENTY

Harriet offered a clipped: 'Nice to meet you' as Jennifer goggled at her.

'Um... you too,' Jennifer managed.

Harriet was avoiding Jennifer's stare, while stirring the hot dog sausages in the pan. When done with that, she restacked the bread rolls, even though she was apparently piling them in the exact way they already were.

Gary was oblivious, explaining that Jennifer had come to the house earlier, while Harriet had been with the police. He'd told Jennifer how Daniel had helped Charles come out of himself – and now he thought Harriet might want to meet Daniel's mother.

He seemingly had no idea they already knew one another.

Jennifer sort of absorbed it, though her thoughts were a long way from the echoing church hall.

For her part, Harriet was nodding along, while generally ignoring Jennifer's presence.

'That's him,' Gary said, catching Jennifer's attention as he pointed across to a small group of boys in the corner. There were four of them, maybe seven or eight, all playing with tablets. 'Charles is in the red top,' Gary added.

Jennifer watched as Charles angled his screen for one of the other boys. They said something she didn't hear, before swapping devices. The yellow and blue guitar on his top was unmistakeable.

'Charles would barely talk to the other boys before he started the tutoring,' Gary said. 'He was always so shy. It was Daniel and Ella who helped bring him out of that.'

He was about to add something else when a woman tapped him on the shoulder and motioned towards a stack of chairs at the back of the room. She asked if she could have a word and then the pair disappeared to the far side of the hall.

Harriet was watching the boys as Jennifer turned back to her. Jennifer waited a moment, wondering if the other woman would state the obvious. Wondering if she should.

'It's been a while,' Jennifer said in the end.

Harriet replied with a whisper that Jennifer didn't catch. Jennifer offered a polite 'Pardon?' – and, this time, the response was hissed and crisp.

'I don't want to do this here,' Harriet said.

Jennifer thought for a moment. 'That's fair,' she said, before peering around to make sure nobody could overhear her. She couldn't leave it there. 'I didn't know Daniel was working for you,' she added. 'He said he was tutoring and things were going well. I didn't realise Charles was your son.'

Harriet's eyes were fixed on the boys, though they were narrow. 'Not *here*,' she repeated, slightly louder.

Jennifer took a step back. This wasn't what she'd expected and it was clearly true for Harriet as well. She was another pace away when Harriet called after her. There was still nobody near enough to overhear.

'Tomorrow,' Harriet said firmly. 'We can meet tomorrow if you want. Are you staying in town?'

'In the Comfort Inn by the motorway,' Jennifer said. 'I came up last night when the police told me what was happening.'

That got the merest nod of acknowledgement.

'I've been trying to find Daniel,' Jennifer added.

'And have you?'

'No.'

If anything, Jennifer felt further away from her goal than she had when she arrived. She'd certainly discovered some things she would rather have not known.

When it was clear no reply was coming, Jennifer added: 'Where do you want to meet?'

It felt as if Harriet had already made these calculations. 'There's a coffee place called Grounded. No one's going to see us there.'

She gave the name as if it was a place in which she'd had numerous meetings where she would rather not have been recognised.

'I'll look it up,' Jennifer said.

'Does ten work for you?' Harriet added. 'Charles will be at school by then. I've got a bit of admin at the shop but shouldn't be late.'

'I'll be there.'

Jennifer hovered for a moment. It had been such a long time since she'd seen the other woman. Natasha was right: with the glasses and without the purple hair, Jo looked completely different – except for the eyes. There was something about the way Jo, about the way *Harriet*, looked over the glasses, her gaze angling up, that had Jennifer back in the alley next to the club. It was the night Craig had hit her, then left her by the bins. The night Jennifer wished she'd called the police – although there was more than one of those nights. She saw the irony that, even now, she was avoiding contacting the police, despite, deep down, knowing she should.

'You look good,' Jennifer said, meaning it. 'I'm glad you're OK.'

Harriet gave a silent, short nod, though immediately turned her attention to a woman who'd just entered through the main doors. She was pulling one of those half shopping bag, half wheeled trolley things behind her, the sort that Jennifer immediately associated with her gran. The woman stopped and blew into her hands, before heading towards the warmth of the food, where the wheels of the trolley clicked rhythmically across the floor. Harriet knew the woman's name and started serving up a plate of food before she'd reached the counter.

Jennifer took that as her cue to leave the other woman be, drifting away to have a nosey at the rest of The Mission. The main area was a large hall, with a wooden floor and high ceiling. It was the sort of place in which she'd had Brownies and Girl Guides when she'd been much younger. Where the boys did knee skids for the annual Cubs and Brownies disco.

As well as the boys playing in the corner and the tables for board games at the back, various chairs were dotted around the space. There was an open cupboard off to one side, packed with blankets and pillows, next to an arrow and sign that pointed towards the bedrooms. Another cupboard nearby had a neatly organised row of various phone chargers, with a note asking people to return them when they were done. There were paperbacks in the same case as the board games, plus the lending library Gary had mentioned. Jennifer had been unsure what he'd meant at first but there was everything from a food mixer to a lawnmower behind a locked mesh door, with a list of the items written on a whiteboard at the side. Most were tools, like an electric drill or power saw – but there was also a slow cooker and food dehydrator for people to borrow.

Opposite that was a separate storage area, filled with canned food. There were signs about 'quiet time', more telling people when the doors would be locked, alongside an emergency phone number. There were multiple posters in which The Mission was asking for volunteers – while Gary was named a lot on the various signs as The Director. With this, the antiques business, being an elder at the church, and being a parent, it felt as if he and Jo had a lot on.

He and *Harriet* had a lot on.

Jennifer found herself wondering about the change of name. The 'why' was obvious enough after everything that had happened. She also realised that, with Harriet being close to her own age, Gary had to be a good fifteen to twenty years older. In the old days – or present-day Hollywood – nobody would have thought anything of it. Except Jennifer couldn't help but feel that something felt slightly *off* about it all, especially given what Harriet had been through.

'Do you fancy a game?'

Jennifer had been lost in her thoughts as she'd drifted towards the back of the hall, where there were people playing board games. A man was looking to her hopefully, indicating the draughts board in front of him. He'd sounded so friendly that, for a moment, Jennifer wondered whether she knew him.

'I don't bite,' he added, with a slightly mischievous smile. He was likely in his seventies; wrinkly and wiry, with fingerless gloves and wild eyebrows.

'I really need to sleep,' Jennifer said with a sigh, before inwardly kicking herself. This man, a stranger to her, didn't need to know she needed sleep.

He shrugged a *suit yourself*, before setting up the board anyway.

Jennifer looked across the room, towards where Harriet was still talking to the woman with the trolley. There was no sign of Gary but Jennifer felt it was time to leave. The last thing she wanted was to be identified by anyone other than Harriet as Daniel's mum. There was little point in continuing to push her luck.

She tried to remember through which door she'd entered, then figured she'd go out the main one. It was colder away from the main room, with a draughty porch, surrounded on both sides by posters advertising various services or events. Jennifer yawned her way towards the exit, and already had one hand on the door before she realised what was *actually* on the poster nearest the rippled glass.

There was a photo of a young man who seemed familiar – though not as recognisable as the name. 'MISSING' was in large letters across the top and then, at the bottom, was the name that matched the driving licence in Jennifer's bag. The one she'd found in Daniel's locker: 'Benjamin Davies'.

TWENTY-ONE

Jennifer allowed the main door to close and then poked a head towards the larger hall, making sure nobody was near. With everything clear, she fished Ben's driving licence from her bag and held it up against the poster.

It was definitely the same person.

That's when she remembered the articles she'd found earlier in the day. They had said that Ben had worked at a local food bank when he went missing – which almost certainly meant this place. Gary had even called The Mission 'a mix of food bank...' when he'd described it.

Jennifer returned the licence to her bag but spent a few seconds more staring at the poster. The page was raggedy, as if it had been up a while. Ben had been missing for a little over a year and, if Callum was to be believed – which he wasn't – Ben and Daniel had fought not too long before.

Before he went missing, Ben likely worked at The Mission, which was run by Gary. Gary said he was 'acquainted' with Ella's brother, Callum. Ella and Daniel were tutors for Gary's son; while Callum knew Ella, Daniel and Ben. Of them all, there was one dead woman and two missing men. One of whom was her son.

There were a lot of links there.

A second missing poster identical to the first was pinned to the opposite wall, so Jennifer carefully pulled one away from its staples, folded it, and put it in her bag. It was a big if – but *if* Jennifer could find the direct connection from Ben to Daniel – she was hoping she could find her son.

Jennifer knew something was wrong as soon as the heavy door to her hotel room swung shut behind her. She stood in the small entranceway, next to the long mirror on the wall, listening. There was the distant hum of the motorway and... *what?* Her skin was tingling, senses on edge, as she pressed steadily into the room. She almost expected someone to be waiting behind the corner, half concealed by the large dresser, though there was nobody there.

'Hello...?'

Jennifer's voice went unanswered as she placed her bag on the counter. She'd been given a twin room and her suitcase was still on one of the beds, lid open, her clothes ruffled and half unpacked. She struggled to remember whether she'd left them this way. She had definitely gone hunting for black clothes but there was far more of a mess than she remembered. Had someone gone through her things? How would anyone know where she was staying, let alone which room?

The net curtain was billowing, and, when Jennifer checked, the window was latched open. It was one of those that couldn't be opened by more than a few centimetres. That meant nobody could have come in from the outside, which felt unlikely anyway, since she was on the second floor.

Except Jennifer didn't remember opening the window. Had

it been warm when she'd checked in? Had room service left it open and she'd not noticed?

The fug from lack of sleep and lack of food sizzled the edges of Jennifer's gaze. Maybe she had opened the window and tossed her clothes around her suitcase?

She checked the bathroom, where the extractor fan hummed, though the room was empty. She looked under the bed, just in case, but there was only cobwebs she would rather have not seen.

Jennifer closed the window and stood, facing the room, wondering what she'd missed. She had been in a rush to leave earlier but should have paid better attention.

She was so tired. What else had she done in the room?

Jennifer headed for the wardrobe. The only thing she definitely remembered doing was hanging up Daniel's hoody. She pulled open the doors, expecting the maroon top to be in front of her... which it wasn't. Jennifer goggled for a moment. Somebody had been in the room while she'd been out. They had gone through her things before finding Daniel's hoody in the wardrobe, which they'd...

The hoody was bunched on the floor, having slipped from the hanger.

Jennifer stared at it, then crouched to pick it up. Perhaps she'd simply not hung it up properly? She held it for a moment, then placed it on the bed, half convinced someone had been in here, while simultaneously knowing she was too tired to remember how she'd left things.

Jennifer checked the door was locked and then clipped the keychain into place. She eyed the empty corridor through the peephole, then returned to the main room, where she grabbed the corner of the dresser and tried to drag it towards the door. If someone was determined to get in, she was going to make it as difficult as possible. There was a squeak of wood on floor as the heavy furniture moved a couple of millimetres.

She stopped, knowing she was never going to be able to drag it so far, certainly not without tearing up the carpet. It was late and had been close to twenty-four hours since Daniel had called. Jennifer was out of breath and couldn't even work out if someone *had* been in the room. She left the dresser where it was and returned to the bed, picking up Daniel's hoody and putting it on the spare pillow next to her head.

Jennifer was lost in a miasma of conflicting thoughts. Her son was a killer but of course he wasn't. He had a good reason for running and hiding but why had he? Jo was Harriet but how? Someone had been in her room but they hadn't.

Everything blurred into a fuzzy, translucent mess, obscured by her total exhaustion. Things might seem different in the morning but, for now, she *really* needed to sleep.

TWENTY-TWO
WEDNESDAY

Grounded was the sort of coffee shop where a super skinny guy with a massive beard would leave his steel bike on the kerb outside, enter, and tap his phone to pay seven quid for a single-origin pour over. It was a far cry from the Nescafé sachets in Jennifer's hotel room.

She'd settled for a latte and found a table near the window as she absorbed the rest of the menu. There was a sliding scale of milk prices. Jennifer had heard of oat milk and almond milk – but *hemp milk?* For a quid a shot? Someone was taking the mick.

Not that she could deny the shop was popular. There was no let-up for any of the servers as the steady line was instantly added to the moment anyone left. Jennifer half watched the queue, half watched the window, waiting for Harriet to arrive.

Jennifer had woken up confused by the mania that had overtaken her the night before. She eventually *had* remembered opening the window, because the extractor fan in the bathroom did a lot of buzzing, without a lot of extracting. As for Daniel's hoody, there was every chance she hadn't placed it on the hanger properly. The idea that she could have moved that solid dresser by herself felt even madder than the other stuff.

It had all seemed so much clearer after a sleep – even if she'd awoken with the vaguest sense that she'd forgotten something from the night before.

Not that anything had changed.

Andrew had messaged a few times overnight, saying that the car he'd seen over the road had gone, to be replaced by another. He was certain the house was being watched – and was probably correct. Jennifer wondered if someone was keeping an eye on her, then realised it was unlikely, seeing as she'd been bundled into the back of a car without anyone intervening. It was probably why that officer Nina Whateverher-namewas had told Jennifer to go home. They didn't want her running around town, getting in the way, possibly finding Daniel first.

As Jennifer sat in the window of the coffee shop, she read the local news – which was full of everything from the day before. Someone had been at the memorial and there were quotes from Ella's friends and bandmates, talking about their shock, and how she would be missed. There were photos taken from the band's website, others from screengrabs of a TikTok account, while people had started leaving flowers outside the pub where Ella's band had their first gig. Jennifer found it so hard to read, yet forced herself to go through it. Her focus was on Daniel, and she genuinely believed he could also be some sort of victim in everything. Except, the other victim could never tell her story.

There was little mention of Daniel in the main pieces, though the police had urged him to turn himself in. There was a phone number to call if anyone saw him, though Jennifer didn't know whether to take solace from the fact that the police also didn't know where he was. There was such a big part of her that wanted him to reveal himself and tell everyone – especially her – what had happened.

She took out her phone and called him, knowing he wouldn't answer, but needing to see his name on the screen. There was a brief pause, then a blip, then the call dropped, having not even connected.

The queue had dwindled in the shop, with a couple hanging around the collection area, while three more waited to be served. Jennifer looked outside, hoping to see Harriet, though there was no sign of her, nor anyone their age. Everyone inside was almost exclusively young twenty-somethings. It was five-past ten and, despite saying she shouldn't be late, Harriet was exactly that.

Jennifer returned to her phone, scrolling past something about an 'epidemic' of car theft in the region, before returning to the article about Ella. She read it a second time, then kept scrolling until she reached the comments. She knew she shouldn't but it was impossible not to take in every remark about how hanging should be brought back.

Quarter-past ten and still no sign of Harriet. They hadn't swapped numbers and Jennifer was doubting the other woman would come. She didn't necessarily blame her as the previous evening had been something of a blindside for both of them.

Jennifer was still battling the nagging idea that she'd forgotten something.

She sipped her coffee, scanned the menu again, once more marvelled that hemp milk existed and cost a pound a shot, then found herself staring through the window.

Then she remembered. Gary had told her the name of the man who'd been watching her and Callum from the upper level of the pub. She had meant to look him up – but got distracted by Harriet, The Mission, Ben's missing poster, and then the idea that someone had been in her hotel room.

She searched 'Lance Williams Ashington' – and immediately found out why Gary had called him 'controversial'.

Williams had been found not guilty of drug trafficking almost two years before. He was described as a 'local businessman' in the articles, which sounded deliberately vague. There were some older pieces about his arrest, which had happened at five in the morning and involved a large battering ram knocking down the door of what looked like a massive house.

It was surely not a good thing that Williams had been keeping an eye on Callum. Jennifer wondered whether Ella's brother knew, though she doubted it. He didn't seem particularly careful while concealing that he was dealing. She'd spotted him doing it twice – including at his own sister's memorial.

Jennifer pictured all that cash in Daniel's locker and it was hard not to wonder if it connected her son to Lance Williams. Was that man in the long coat and shiny shoes somehow responsible for what had happened to Ella? Was Daniel hiding from him?

Half-past ten and still no sign of Harriet.

Jennifer finished her coffee and considered ordering another. There was no queue now, with the servers busy cleaning machines and tables. They never stopped and Jennifer hoped they were getting a decent portion of that seven-quid coffee.

The other option was to leave – which she would – except she had no plan for what to do next. She'd come to the town to find her son and ended up with far more questions than answers. She *needed* Harriet to turn up.

Jennifer was gazing aimlessly through the window when she realised the parallel for the first time. Harriet's boyfriend had murdered Jennifer's housemate twenty-four years before. She probably blamed herself then, and now. No wonder it was so hard for her to acknowledge Natasha and Jennifer so many years later.

Which felt like the position Jennifer might find herself in. Perhaps it was already true? Daniel was accused of doing something unspeakably evil – and, though Jennifer was sure it couldn't be him, what if it was? He would always be a killer, which meant she would always be the *mother* of a killer. The same way Harriet was *always* the girlfriend of a killer. No wonder she'd changed her name.

Jennifer shuddered, suddenly unable to think of anything else.

Mother of a killer, she whispered to herself.

TWENTY-THREE YEARS AGO

Jennifer headed down the long, wide flight of steps outside the court. She hadn't needed to be there, though knew she'd have regretted not seeing the sentencing in person.

Natasha was already at the bottom of the steps, having changed her mind at the last moment about entering the courtroom. Jennifer didn't blame her: it had been hard to watch Craig in the dock after everything that had happened. He'd not even been bold enough to look anywhere other than his feet. Natasha had said she would wait outside, and here she was, sitting on a bench, facing an empty fountain that had the water turned off.

'How long?' Natasha asked, as Jennifer slotted in at her side.

'Life – but one of the lawyers said it might actually be fifteen years.'

Natasha let out a long sigh as she leaned back and stared up at the dazzling blue of the sky. Around them, people in suits were streaming down the steps, dashing towards the car park.

'We won't even be forty when he gets out.'

It felt like such a long way away and yet... not. Somehow a

blink and a lifetime all at the same time. Jennifer thought she and Natasha could be anywhere by the time they were forty. They might be married, they might even have kids. Those were the sorts of thing people had done by that age.

'Was Jo there?' Natasha asked.

'She sat in front of me. Craig didn't look at any of us the whole time.'

'Did she say anything?'

'No – but the prosecution solicitor said in the summing up that she feels a lot of guilt because of everything.'

'It's not her fault.'

Jennifer had told herself the same, and it probably wasn't, but then Jo *had* taken him back after that time in the canteen. Did that make it her fault? Or was that only in Jennifer's mind because she was the person who'd stood up to him back then? If she'd stayed at her table like everyone else, it would never have put her and her friends on Craig's radar.

It had been a little over seven months since Hayley had been killed. Craig had suffocated her with the lamp cord next to her bed, while that supermarket bag he carried everywhere had been found in the room. The prosecution seemed unsure why he'd targeted Hayley. There had been speculation that he might have been looking for Jennifer, though very little of that had made it in front of the jury. Jennifer herself didn't know. It was a question she didn't think would ever be answered.

The two young women sat in silence for a while, listening to the bristling background of the day. 'Did you figure out if you're going to redo the year?' Natasha asked.

Jennifer bit her lip. She had told Natasha in vague, round-about ways that she was considering staying around to retake the year, even though she'd known for a long time that she was going to leave Ashington and never return.

'Are you?' Jennifer asked.

'I already re-enrolled. They've waived all the fees for the

year and said there's a counsellor I can work with if I need it.' She paused and then added: 'You should stay.'

There was hope there, even though Jennifer suspected she knew the truth.

'I can't,' she said.

Natasha sighed again, though didn't ask why. Perhaps she knew that as well. Jennifer wasn't going to get past the idea that Craig had followed her home and watched her enter the house via the back door. She wouldn't forgive herself for failing to raise the alarm after the canteen incident, let alone when she thought he was stalking her, or when he beat up Jo, or when he showed up almost outside their house. There were so many opportunities for her to do something – and Hayley was dead because she hadn't.

It was *her* fault.

Natasha pushed herself up and stretched. 'I have to get off,' she said. 'But if you ever need anything, I'll be around.'

'You too,' Jennifer replied, although neither statement felt real. They'd be going their separate ways to their separate lives.

As Jennifer stood to say goodbye, she stopped to watch Jo head down the steps on the far side. She was talking with one of the prosecution solicitors. It had been a long few weeks for all of them. Jennifer had been in on two days to give evidence, then returned for sentencing. From what she'd heard, Jo had given her evidence against Craig and then turned up for each subsequent day. She'd told the jury that Craig had had an obsession with Jennifer and her friends ever since that moment in the canteen. She herself had gone back to him out of fear. Now she felt responsible for everything that had happened.

She was always going to be the girlfriend of a killer.

Jo's purple hair had almost returned to its natural brown, though there was still a hint of colour that hadn't quite washed out. The remnants of a prior life.

She stepped off the bottom and momentarily cupped her

midriff, before turning to look for what turned out to be a black car. She opened the door, then straightened her dress before climbing inside.

The door had slammed when Natasha next spoke. 'Did you see that?' she asked.

Jennifer didn't need to question what she was talking about. 'I think so,' she replied.

Natasha thought for a moment, re-running what they'd both seen. 'Is Jo... pregnant?'

TWENTY-THREE

Harriet was almost forty-five minutes late when she eventually turned up. She glanced in Jennifer's direction when entering the coffee shop, then nodded towards the menu: 'Do you want something?' she asked.

Jennifer had already ordered a second drink and said she was fine. A minute or so later and Harriet was back at the table, hands cupped around a steaming mug of black coffee. No hemp milk for her. She was dressed well, in a smart skirt suit, with oversized sunglasses that ended up on the table. The memories of that purple hair were a long way gone, with her lacquered brown hair up in a tight bun.

'You look tired,' she said, slotting into the seat opposite Jennifer.

It was so direct that it was borderline rude – which immediately made Jennifer laugh. It was the first time she'd felt anything other than despair in the past day and a half.

'Sorry,' Harriet added. 'I didn't mean it like that.'

It was hard to imagine how she *had* meant it, although Jennifer was hardly going to disagree.

The bustle of the café had slowed in the time Jennifer had

been waiting. A man with patches on the elbows of his cord jacket, plus a moustache waxed to curly points was tapping on a laptop. Except for the computer, it looked like he'd travelled a century through time.

'Do you come here often?' Jennifer asked.

It got a shake of the head. 'Never. That's why I suggested it.'

Jennifer turned away from the guy with the Edwardian moustache and took in the woman she'd barely known, yet with whom she was inexorably entwined.

'Harriet's my middle name,' the other woman said, answering the unasked question. 'I was Joanne Harriet Vickery back then. Nobody calls me Jo now.'

Jennifer didn't need to ask why: Jo would forever be associated with Craig and what he did. Would that be *her* fate? Jennifer Farley would always be associated with Daniel Farley.

'I know what you're thinking,' Harriet added quietly, even though Jennifer doubted it. 'I was in a bad place after Hayley and everything. I sort of found myself going to church, which is where I met Gary.' She waited for Jennifer to catch her eye. 'I know it's a cliché but things changed after that. New name, new me, all that. I'm Harriet Etherington now.'

Jennifer still had that niggling doubt that a man fifteen to twenty years older had taken advantage of someone who'd been enormously vulnerable – but who was she to judge? Her marriage was crumbling, which hardly made her an expert on relationships.

'I wasn't thinking anything negative about you,' Jennifer assured the other woman, even though it wasn't completely true. 'I'm glad you're in a happier place.'

Harriet picked up her drink, sipped it and hid behind the cup momentarily, before lowering it. 'We were so shocked to hear about Ella,' she said quietly. 'She and Daniel had made such a difference with Charles.'

'That's what Gary said.'

Harriet offered a small nod of acknowledgement. 'You used to be Jennifer Benson. I didn't realise there was any connection to Daniel Farley. It's such a coincidence, don't you think?'

The thought had definitely occurred to Jennifer.

'When did you realise?' Jennifer asked.

That got a soft huff of amazement. 'When Gary introduced you last night. I'd been with the police all morning, going over dates and things like that. They wanted to know how long Daniel and Ella had been tutoring. When I got home, Gary said Daniel's mum had dropped over, asking questions – but he didn't realise the connection, either.'

'Did you tell him last night?'

'Briefly. He doesn't like to hear about everything that happened back then, with Craig and everything.'

Harriet stopped and picked up her drink as Jennifer thought on that. It felt like an odd reaction from a husband; certainly not a supportive one. It also occurred to Jennifer that if Harriet had talked to the police the previous morning, chances were they didn't know about the connection from Harriet's past with Jennifer to her present with Daniel.

Perhaps because that was on her mind, too, it was Harriet who spoke next: 'Have you talked to the police?' she asked.

'They came to the house the night before last to ask if I'd seen Daniel. I think that was not long after Ella had been found. I drove through the night to get here.'

A pause and then: 'Why did you come?'

It was a fair question, even though Jennifer had kind of said the night before. It felt strange to say she wanted to find her son, even though that was the truth.

'I was hoping I could help,' Jennifer said instead. In truth, Daniel's 'It wasn't me' still haunted and that was why she'd come. It felt like her little boy crying out for help. 'They said to call if Daniel contacted me.'

'But you've not heard anything?'

'I wouldn't know where to start looking.'

That was broadly true, even though Jennifer thought it sounded like a lie as it came out. It was difficult to explain why she was in town if she had no idea where to look for her son, and had barely had any contact with the police.

Harriet seemed to be thinking on something as she gazed aimlessly through the window, to where a guy in short shorts was fixing a puncture on his bike. 'What would you do if he asked for help?' Harriet asked.

Her attention never switched from the cyclist, as if she couldn't quite face Jennifer for the answer.

'I don't know,' Jennifer replied. 'I suppose it depends on what he'd say, or how he was.'

It was probably the question on which Jennifer had been thinking the most since Daniel had called. Should her loyalty be to her son, or a dead young woman? To her own feelings, or the rule of law? It felt as if every answer would be wrong.

For a moment, it seemed as if Harriet would ask whether Jennifer thought her son could be a murderer. That would be a difficult reply, too, even if Jennifer gave an instant 'no'. She *didn't* think he was capable of such a thing... and yet she couldn't explain why he'd disappeared immediately afterwards.

'Does Daniel know about Hayley?' Harriet asked instead.

Jennifer winced a fraction at the sound of her old friend's name. It was so hard to hear.

'He knows all that,' Jennifer said. 'I didn't want him coming here but this is where he got the offer to do his course. He didn't get the grades for any other university. I've not been back until yesterday. My husband drove him up for his open day and the starts of term.' Her final: 'This town is cursed' was a mumbled thought that she should have probably kept in, not that Harriet reacted.

Jennifer was daydreaming of her son again, wondering

where he was. He'd been missing for a day and half. Was he hiding from the police, or had something happened to him?

It was while she was thinking of Daniel that she remembered the court steps so many years before, when Jo had cupped her midriff just before crouching to get into a car. Now she wasn't so tired and Jennifer's thoughts were clearer, she remembered that Gary had told her his wife had a son in his twenties from a different relationship.

'Your husband said you have an older son...?' Jennifer said, trying not to sound too eager.

It got a nod, though it felt as if Harriet knew where the conversation would go. Perhaps she had even prepared for it.

'I got pregnant the week before everything with Hayley. I didn't know at the time, obviously.'

'So your son is...?'

Jennifer couldn't bring herself to say Craig's name, even as Harriet nodded slowly. 'He's called Nick – but he's nothing like his dad.' A pause. 'I suppose he is in some ways. He's big and tall, which he obviously doesn't get from me. He's clever, though. Works for an insurance company and got a promotion about six months ago. He's been doing really well.'

There felt little point in Jennifer saying that her husband also worked in insurance, especially as Harriet was fiddling with her bag. She pulled out a phone and jabbed at the screen, before turning it around for Jennifer to see.

'That's Nick,' she said.

Jennifer almost gasped. Harriet might have said that Nick was nothing like his father – but there was a definite resemblance from him to the man who'd killed Jennifer's friend so many years before. There was the rounded face and the wide eyes; the broad chest and the clumsy sense of a short person having body-swapped into that of a tall person. Jennifer wondered how it was possible that Harriet couldn't see the resemblance.

Or perhaps she did but she couldn't allow herself to believe it? Nick was her son after all.

Harriet returned her phone to her bag, seemingly oblivious at Jennifer's shock. 'Nick's much closer to Gary than me. They've got a proper father-son thing going on.' She left a gap but quickly closed it, as if realising the accidental implication. 'We do get on. It's not like we're estranged, or anything.'

'Does he know about his dad?'

A nod: 'When he was younger, Gary was there the whole time. We decided to tell him when he was twelve that Gary wasn't his real dad. He had a lot of questions, which were difficult to answer.'

'Did he ever meet his dad?'

There was a gentle wince that Jennifer almost missed. 'Craig died in prison. He killed himself after about eighteen months of being inside.'

Jennifer realised that she *did* know that. Someone from the prison service had contacted her a long time back. It had been a relief to know he would never be getting out. Of course Nick had never met his real father. She wasn't sure why she'd asked. Her mind was such a muddle.

Harriet was still talking: 'He hung himself with a bedsheet. One of the guards got fired for daring him to do it.' She blinked as if travelling through time, before focusing back on Jennifer. 'Long time ago.'

It was – and yet Ella had apparently been killed by a lamp cord around her neck, in the same way Hayley had. Jennifer wondered whether Harriet knew. She'd not read it in any of the reports, and only knew because Daniel's housemate had told her. The parallels were so strong, and that was before Jennifer had seen the photo of Nick. Was he closer in nature to his father than Harriet could possibly know? It was impossible for Jennifer not to think it, even if she couldn't say.

Not explicitly anyway. 'Do you know whether Nick was

friends with Daniel?' Jennifer asked, knowing immediately it was too direct.

Harriet reeled a fraction, blinking, and turning to take in Jennifer. It had been a question out of the blue. 'They've only met a couple of times, so I doubt it.'

There was a curt edge, and Jennifer presumed it was because Harriet had read her new-found suspicions of Nick. That left Jennifer abruptly shifting subjects.

'I saw that you and Gary have an antiques business.'

Harriet had stopped to finish her coffee, so Jennifer did the same. She was wondering how to bring the subject back around to Nick. He looked so much like his father. Could he possibly have followed in his footsteps?

'Gary started trading antiques when he was a teenager,' Harriet said, with the slimmest upturn of her lips. *I know*, she didn't say. 'He didn't even get it from his parents. He was into antiques the way other boys are into football. The business was already successful before he met me. I do a bit of admin behind the scenes but the auction house largely runs itself nowadays.'

'Is it in town?'

Jennifer knew the business was registered to the house that was slightly outside Ashington. It was how she'd found Gary and Harriet in the first place. It didn't seem as if there was any sort of warehouse or actual business there.

'We're down by the docks,' Harriet said. 'Anchor Row. Gary appointed a manager three or four years back, to give him more spare time. He goes on the odd trip to source stock but most of his time is spent at The Mission. That's his passion project.'

She stopped to rub her neck, and there was a notable click.

'You all right?' Jennifer asked.

Harriet let out a gentle groan. 'Got rear-ended while driving a couple of years back. The insurance paid out but the premiums nearly tripled, so we put cameras in our vehicles now. Gary's always complaining about surveillance Britain, with the speed cameras, then he's the one who swaps out the memory cards in both cars every Sunday night. He even has an alarm on his phone to remind him. Can't do anything without it being recorded.' She shrugged a *What can you do?* look, while continuing to massage her shoulders.

Andrew had done something similar by insisting on putting up the dummy cameras at the front of their house.

Jennifer watched Harriet for a moment, still thinking about ways to twist the conversation back to Nick. It would be dangerous ground. Only one of their sons was actually being sought in association with a murder, after all.

Except Harriet had brought up The Mission, in relation to her husband, which meant there was something Jennifer could ask.

'Do you know Ben Davies?'

Harriet's fingers stopped pinching the join of neck to shoulder as she looked up curiously to take in Jennifer. 'Why are you asking?'

Jennifer could hardly say it was because she'd found Ben's driving licence in her son's locker, along with piles of cash. 'I saw the missing poster last night,' she said instead, surprised at her own quick thinking. 'I wondered if it might somehow be connected to everything with Daniel.'

There was a hint of a frown on Harriet's face that might have been confusion. 'He volunteered at The Mission and disappeared about a year ago – but I don't think any of it's connected to Daniel.'

'I heard Ben and Daniel had some sort of fight not long before Ben disappeared...?'

The frown deepened. 'Who told you that?'

There seemed little point in lying. 'Ella's brother. I ran into him yesterday.'

Harriet's knowing nod was almost identical to the one her

husband had given the night before, when telling Jennifer that he and Callum were 'acquainted'.

'That explains it,' Harriet said. 'Ben came to The Mission as a runaway. He'd fallen out with his parents, something like that, so we gave him a bed. He helped around the place, then Gary gave him a bit of work at the auction house. Mainly moving heavy things, unloading, that sort of thing. I didn't really know him. The Mission is Gary's thing, I just help out here and there. He's there most evenings.' She paused to think for a moment, then added: 'I think it was Gary who reported Ben as missing – but I might be wrong.'

'Did Daniel ever volunteer at The Mission? Maybe tutored there? Something like that?' Jennifer was stretching, looking for a link from Daniel to Ben, to Nick, to anyone who might have been the person to kill Ella. Maybe there was a jealous ex-boyfriend? Or someone who liked Ella and couldn't take rejection? Anything? Anyone other than her son?

'I don't think so,' Harriet said. 'You could ask Gary. He'd know more than me.' She sighed again. 'As for Callum, he's trouble. I wouldn't trust a word he says. Gary said he was dealing outside the church last night. He was banned from The Mission for doing that but he'll never learn. It's amazing he and Ella are brother and sister. They're so different. I didn't know they were related until Ella said one time.'

'He told me he was in a car crash.'

'He says a lot of things.'

'He also said there was an inheritance from a grandmother that was given only to Ella. He was furious about that.'

Harriet had been picking at a fingernail but stopped to take in Jennifer properly. 'He said that yesterday?'

'He said he's adopted. His dad died and Ella's mum isn't related to him by blood. That's why their grandmother left everything to Ella, not him.'

A pause. 'How much?'

'He said a "few thousand" but I don't know how much that means.'

Harriet considered that a moment and it felt as if she knew something Jennifer didn't. She certainly seemed to believe this part of Callum's tall tales.

'His grandmother sounds like she has the right idea,' Harriet said, ominously. 'That boy is a danger to everyone around him.'

TWENTY-FOUR

There was a steely edge to Harriet's tone, but Jennifer couldn't let it lie.

'Why shouldn't Callum have any money?' she asked.

Another sigh. 'A lot of the people who come through The Mission are there because they don't have any money. They're homeless, or they lost their job, or they fell out with partners, or parents. That sort of thing. We give them somewhere to sleep, to shower, to charge their phones. All that. Gary will pay them cash in exchange for various jobs, either at The Mission, or the auction house. But there are a few that you definitely can't give money to. It'll end up going in their arms, or up their nose. You'd kill them by giving them actual money.'

She spoke so matter-of-factly that Jennifer didn't doubt it. Except she also remembered the cash that she had directly given to Callum. She wondered if it had gone up his nose, or into his arms.

'Gary gave Callum a second chance a few months back,' Harriet said. 'It was a favour to Ella, although she made us promise not to tell him.'

'What happened?'

'We had to ban him from The Mission for stealing. He took someone's phone but wasn't very smart about it. They had that tracking thing turned on – and it was in Callum's back pocket when it started beeping. He was trying to say he didn't know how it got there.'

She spoke regretfully, though firmly – and he was another person about whom Jennifer had her suspicions. If that inheritance money was no longer going to Ella, would it end up with him? Jennifer wondered whether he was on the police's radar.

'He and Nick were friends for a while,' Harriet said, as if it had just occurred to her. 'I think they met through Gary, or maybe at The Mission. They looked so ridiculous together because Nick's big and broad, while Callum's, well... the opposite. I don't think they're friends any more but it's not the sort of thing Nick and I would talk about. Nick doesn't live at home anymore.'

Jennifer had been looking for a way to get the conversation back to Harriet's son – and now they were there. Except, perhaps because she sensed further questions, Harriet squeaked back her chair and stood.

'I've got to go,' she said, glancing to the clock near the whiteboard. They'd been talking for the best part of an hour. 'I didn't realise what time it was. I hope things work out with Daniel. I just... don't know what to make of it all. That's what I told the police.'

That made two of them with little clue as to what had gone on.

Harriet cleared her cup away to the plastic bowl near the door that had a 'please leave dirty dishes here' sign above. Jennifer copied and then they were outside, passing the guy who was still trying to fix a bike puncture, as Harriet pointed to a shiny black Audi. 'This is me,' she said, waiting by the driver's door, perhaps figuring out how they should leave things.

Jennifer felt it, too. They had never been friends and yet they were forever connected – now even more so.

'It was good seeing you again,' Harriet said, although it seemed like one of those things people just say. Telling someone on holiday that you must get together back in the UK, when actually meaning there was no chance you would ever see them again.

Jennifer and Harriet could have easily gone through the rest of their lives never being in the same place, yet they'd been drawn back together. It *wasn't* good to see each other again – and they both knew it.

'You too,' Jennifer lied.

Harriet opened the car door and leaned on it, still not getting in. 'Do you want to swap numbers?' she asked, although she sounded somewhat reluctant. 'If I hear anything from the police, I can let you know...?'

Jennifer agreed, so they sent each other texts and then Harriet reversed her car out of the space and headed off around the corner. And Jennifer was left with one thought.

Nick.

Now that she'd seen the photo of him, Jennifer couldn't stop thinking about Harriet's son. About *Craig's* son. She wasn't sure she believed in nature over nurture, that the son of a killer had to be a killer, but there wasn't too much more to go on. Did the police know there could be a link? Had they looked for an alibi? Or were they so focused on Daniel that they weren't searching elsewhere?

Jennifer returned to her own car and sat inside. Apart from the morning check-in with her husband, she'd had no calls or texts of note. She tried calling Daniel, knowing he wouldn't answer, but was still disappointed when he didn't. She figured she would head back to the hotel to get on the Wi-Fi and do some proper online stalking of Nick. The first step would be to find out if his last name was Etherington, his mum's married name; Vickery, Harriet's maiden name; or Smart – which was Craig's.

She was lost in those thoughts about Craig and his adult son, barely half a mile from the hotel, when the engine began to sputter. The vehicle jolted forward, as if trying to drive itself. Jennifer jumped back into the moment, braking on instinct, and getting beeped at from the car behind, which swerved around her and disappeared into the distance.

Jennifer had never been particularly interested in cars. Turn the key, put it in gear, get on with your business. Anything more than that felt like far too much work. Even as she idled on the side of the road, the engine was coughing and heaving, so Jennifer turned it off and got out. She was trying to remember if they'd renewed the RAC subscription, thinking this was something she could definitely do without. This town was definitely cursed.

She was on the edge of an industrial estate, with a large stack of shipping containers towering ominously on one side, plus a series of signs pointing lorry drivers towards various businesses. Across the road was a row of warehouses and ramshackle buildings that looked as if they'd not changed since Thatcher was in power. The nearest was some sort of industrial cleaning place, with piles of sheets or something similar being unloaded from the back of a white van, into a loading bay. The next had tyres stacked high near an open entrance, as a man in grubby overalls chatted to a bloke by a dark blue Transit.

Jenifer took out her phone again, wondering if she should call Andrew, or search her emails to see if they had roadside coverage. When she looked up, she realised the Transit had gone and the man in the overalls was on the edge of the forecourt.

'You all right, love?' he called across.

He had one of those faces that made it look like he could fix a leaking sink. Two weeks in Magaluf every summer, come home as red as a lobster. Bosh.

Jennifer called across to say that the car had started spluttering and had barely finished the sentence before he was across the road, wiping his hands on his overalls.

'When did you last fill it up?' he asked.

It was like the time a year before when Jennifer had asked her husband if he'd seen her reading glasses, only to be told they were on her head. As soon as the mechanic spoke, Jennifer knew she hadn't put in any petrol since leaving home.

He saw it too and nodded back towards the tyre place. 'I can put enough in to get you to the nearest petrol station. There's one about a mile that way.' He pointed back the way she'd come, then added: 'I can give it a look over if you want to make sure everything else is OK?'

Jennifer told him that sounded good, even though she remained in the process of wishing the ground would swallow her. She was going to be one of those stories he told people about the stupid woman who'd tried driving with no petrol. Not that the man treated her with anything other than kindness. He told her to steer towards the garage, as he gave the vehicle a push.

Moments later and the car was in a bay surrounded by tyres. The mechanic said she could get a drink in the office and he left her in a musty side room that smelled of instant coffee and cigarettes. The radiator burned hot as Jennifer chose the only chair that didn't have foam spilling from the sides.

Jennifer was filled with a sense of defeat so overwhelming that she couldn't even be bothered to check her phone. She had been fighting it ever since Daniel had called but was so tired. Even the yawn that overcame her felt like too much trouble. She closed her eyes, opened them, rubbed them with her knuckles, closed them again, yawned...

'You all right?'

Jennifer jolted as she realised the mechanic was standing over her. She blinked herself awake, wondering how long she'd been asleep. She fought away a yawn and figured there was little chance of trying to claim she hadn't been out of it.

'Didn't sleep much last night,' she said with a smile, trying to make it a joke.

He wasn't laughing, though. Instead, he nodded her towards the main garage, saying there was something she should see.

Jennifer pulled herself up and followed, passing through a connecting door and for the first time feeling a sense of vulnerability. She was alone in the middle of nowhere with a man she didn't know. The fact he wanted her to see something sounded ominous by itself. She didn't have the time, let alone the energy, to deal with a broken car.

As they reached her vehicle, the mechanic crouched and fumbled under the bumper before standing and offering her what looked like an old mobile phone. It was black, boxy, and a third the size of a brick.

'I found this,' he said, as if it should mean something.

'What is it?' Jennifer asked.

His features were grave: 'It's a GPS tracker.'

TWENTY-FIVE

Jennifer took the tracker and turned it over in her hands. Given its size, it was lighter than she thought. Probably about the same weight as a TV remote.

'It's magnetic,' the mechanic said. 'It was attached to your back bumper.'

Jennifer flipped it around, looking for some sort of blinking light, or aerial. Anything that looked like a comic-book cliché tracker. There was nothing.

'How do you know what it is?' she asked.

'There's a make and model number underneath. I googled it.'

Jennifer looked at the underside, where she had to squint to see what he was talking about. There was a receded push-button, too.

'It's turned on,' he told her. 'I can turn it off for you, or it's that button you're looking at. You'll need a paperclip.'

He was already holding one, seemingly a step ahead. She passed him the device and he prodded the needled end of the paperclip inside, before passing her back the box. This time, the push-button was level with the edge of the casing.

'I've never seen one in person,' he said. 'I've heard about them. Jealous husbands and all that...'

He let it sit, a quality bit of fishing, though Jennifer didn't reply. She wasn't quite sure what to say. The chances of Andrew having placed it on at home were zero, meaning it had happened since she'd reached Ashington. Her first thought was that someone could've tampered with her vehicle while she was in that mysterious car boot. Or maybe Callum had gone to her car after he'd left the pub the day before? Jennifer had given him a good ten-minute head-start before leaving. Then there was the ninety minutes or so she had stopped by the church the night before. Possibly even earlier this morning, while she'd been talking to Harriet? So many opportunities for someone to leave the tracker.

It had to be someone who knew she was Daniel's mum.

Did that mean that person thought she might know where he was – and they were hoping she'd lead them to him?

If that was true, it also meant there was likely someone else looking for Daniel, who wasn't her and wasn't the police. It felt dangerous, except Jennifer had already been bundled into a car boot and driven around while terrified. Was this worse?

'You can wait here if you're worried,' the mechanic said, as if reading her thoughts. 'We can call the police, or a friend? Whoever you want. You're safe here.'

Jennifer was back in the moment. The man had genuine concern on his face and had made an effort to step away and give her space.

'There's a landline,' he added, pointing towards a counter at the back of the workshop. 'In case you don't want to use your own phone...'

It was thoughtful and Jennifer appreciated it – but she also didn't want to make it seem like a big deal. She'd not yet told him her last name and, if there was paperwork and the like, the mechanic might associate it with Daniel, whose name was high up on the news. She didn't want these questions.

'It's fine,' she told him. 'I knew it was there. My husband uses it to track mileage.'

The mechanic frowned, not believing the obvious lie, for which she didn't blame him. He wasn't going to challenge her, though.

'Right...' he said. 'Well, the rest of it is done. I inflated your front tyres, topped up the washer fluid and oil, plus put in enough petrol to get you down the road. I started the engine and it sounded OK. If there's been any proper damage, you'll know not long after you get off the forecourt. Hopefully, it will be all right.'

Jennifer passed the tracker from one hand to the other, running a thumb along the smooth edges. She was desperate to know who'd put it under her bumper.

'How much?' she asked.

The mechanic gave a shake of the head. 'It's fine.' He waited a beat and then tried again: 'Are you sure you're OK?'

'I'm fine. Thank you.'

He waited a moment longer but they both knew he couldn't ask again.

Jennifer got into her car, placed the tracker on the passenger seat, and then eased away from the garage. She tensed, waiting for the engine to sputter again. When it didn't, she risked the accelerator – and followed the mechanic's instructions back the way she'd come. It was only a couple of minutes later that she was on the BP forecourt, trying to get the chip-and-PIN machine to accept her card.

She wondered if someone out there had noticed the tracker had been switched off.

After she'd filled the car, Jennifer pulled off to the side and typed the name and model number of the device into her phone. The top link was for Amazon, which advertised a magnetic car tracker. It was only forty quid and, according to the listing, connected to an app, where the target could be seen. The listing claimed the device could be used to keep an eye on nervous new drivers or first-time passers – even though everybody knew it would only be used for more nefarious reasons.

Jennifer picked up the box from the passenger seat and turned it over, to where the button had been switched off. Her thoughts were dangerous, she knew that, but she didn't have a better way to find out what was happening with Daniel.

She reached into the door well, knowing there was a hair-clip in there somewhere and soon finding one. It was easy to open up the hairclip and use it to gently press the button on the device. A red light blinked.

Let them watch.

TWENTY-SIX

Jennifer was back near the docks, close to the stretch where she had met Natasha the previous day. The breakfast van had gone, leaving an empty moss-ridden car park and a trio of seagulls fighting over some remnants. Jennifer was sitting on a bench close to the water's edge, which, if she twisted, gave her a view of her parked car through a gap in the trees.

She sensed the danger, could almost smell it, yet, for a reason of which she wasn't quite sure, didn't feel frightened. Her son was out there and the last thing he'd done before disappearing was tell her that he hadn't killed his girlfriend. Nobody else might believe that – but Jennifer did, even if a teeny, tiny voice continued to whisper that she could be wrong. That Daniel had a secret life that involved cash and burner phones and drug dealers.

Each time those thoughts appeared, Jennifer shoved them away. It was her exhaustion speaking and she didn't want to hear it.

Jennifer had deliberately parked in a place that *could* be a meeting point. She was outside the centre of town, but not outside the boundaries of town itself. It was maybe walking distance to the car dealerships, but nobody was going to walk to a place like this. A secluded car park, hidden from the road by a row of damp trees: The sort of spot she could imagine cheating couples organising affairs. If someone was closely watching a tracking device, it *might* be a location for a mother to meet her missing son.

Jennifer was wearing her own coat this time; Daniel's hoody back in her hotel room. She hoped to be able to return it to him one day, when his name was clear. That was her driving motivation – to prove her son's innocence – every time that niggly voice told her this was a crazy idea.

Because this *was* a crazy idea.

Someone was tracking her and, in an act she knew was madness, she was now trying to track them.

Jennifer looked up from her phone, returning her attention to her car through the gap in the trees. There was nobody anywhere near, and she considered how long she might wait. If the person who placed the tracker wasn't baited by her location, then maybe they would be because the device had been turned off, then on. Perhaps they would come to see if something was wrong.

The phone in Jennifer's hand began to ring. It was work again and she knew she'd have to pick up. One way or another, she had a real life away from Ashington and whatever was happening here.

She answered, expecting it to be her boss, Lisa – but instead it was Caroline from HR. Caroline's first week in the job had involved her going around the office sticking Post-it notes on anything that was a violation of the staff manual. Anything she considered to be 'clutter' – including family photos, charging cables, even someone's asthma inhaler, had to be tidied away by diktat. She was someone else for whom working from home had spoiled her fun. When everyone had to inevitably return to the office full-time, it would be because of people like Caroline. Office work was the only way anyone would ever talk to her.

'Jennifer,' she began, rattling off the name like she was scolding a naughty puppy. 'We need to have a conversation about unsanctioned days off.'

Jennifer let out a sigh, mainly for the other woman's benefit. She was facing backwards on the bench, watching her car, willing someone to approach.

'I'm in the middle of a family emergency,' Jennifer said.

'I understand that but we have a strict policy whereby you *must* phone in before nine to report absences.'

Whereby. Of course Caroline from HR used the word 'whereby' unironically.

'I don't have time to talk,' Jennifer replied.

That got a *harrumph*, followed by: 'I'm going to need something more specific than "family emergency" for the report.'

This was *so* Caroline from HR. She obviously wrote a report for every part of her day. What else did she actually do?

There was still nobody near Jennifer's car.

'Fine,' Jennifer said, with a deliberate huff. 'My son has been accused of murdering his girlfriend and he's currently missing. Is that enough of an emergency for you?'

There had been tapping in the background, fingers on a keyboard, but that stopped immediately, replaced by a long pause.

'Did you say "*murder*"?' Caroline asked.

'Yes. You should probably mark me down as not being in for the rest of the week.'

There was a silence for a couple of seconds.

'Right,' Caroline said. 'I guess that does, um, count as an emergency. I'll, uh... add that to your file.'

She mumbled something Jennifer didn't catch, then said bye, before hanging up.

Jennifer put down her phone, knowing she'd made a

mistake. She'd given herself around thirty seconds of enjoyment at hearing the confusion in Caroline's voice – but that was as good as it got. She could picture her work file, with 'Son a murderer?' written in it. Worse yet, everyone in her office would know the news within twenty minutes. As if she didn't have enough to deal with...

Jennifer started tapping out a message to tell her husband that he'd likely be getting questions over text. A woman at her work was married to someone whose brother worked with Andrew. She wasn't sure who, if anyone, her husband had told about what was going on – but it wouldn't be long until a police officer spying on the house would be the least of his worries.

Jennifer would have been *so* annoyed had things been the other way around – and she knew it. This double standard was the type of thing she and Andrew fought about. Or, worse, they couldn't be bothered to argue about any longer.

She was so lost in thoughts of her failing relationship that she almost didn't notice the person walking across the secluded car park. She had been halfway through writing a text message when she glanced up to see the man in a hoody walking along the tree line. He was vaping with one hand, holding his phone with the other.

It was the first person Jennifer had seen in half an hour – and she didn't hang about. She was immediately on her feet, striding back towards her vehicle, still hidden by the trees as she watched the man slow when he reached the car. He had his back to her, likely still on his phone.

Any fear was gone now as Jennifer hurried through the trees and onto the crumbling tarmac. She was a step behind the man when he turned to take her in. He jumped back in surprise, something dropping to the ground with a crunch as he stared towards her.

He clearly knew who she was – and, perhaps more surprising to her, Jennifer *definitely* knew him.

She gasped in shock, just about holding back anything louder. Because the man was the spitting image of his murderous father. The young man Jennifer had seen in a photograph that morning. Harriet's son.

It was Nick.

TWENTY-SEVEN

'Are you all right?' Jennifer asked. Every part of her was struggling to stop herself screaming that she knew who he was. 'This is my car,' she added, nodding at the vehicle. It was by itself in a car park, with no reason for anyone but her to be next to it.

Nick goggled at her for a good couple of seconds before straightening himself. He stooped to pick up what turned out to be a vape device that he'd dropped.

He held it up and mumbled, 'Dropped this', as if that was the reason he'd stopped next to her car. His eyebrow was jumping with jittery panic as Jennifer couldn't help but remember the time in the distant past when Nick's father had ambushed her on the street, close to her house.

They looked *so* similar. The wide ears, the slightly set-back eyes, that broad build and general sense that they'd only just learned how to walk.

'I'm, uh... on my way back to work,' he added.

'OK.'

Jennifer waited, wondering if he would say or do something. There was a map on his phone screen that he realised was showing, so he clicked a button to lock the screen. They were standing a couple of paces apart, both apparently knowing something about the other while pretending they didn't. There was no way he could be where he was through coincidence – he had to have come for the tracker.

'Do we know each other?' Jennifer asked, feeling a sudden sense of boldness. 'You look like someone I used to know.'

His stare deepened, though it was more confusion than danger. 'Don't think so,' he said, and then: 'I've gotta go.'

He stepped to the side and moved around her – before bounding quickly back the way he'd come.

Jennifer froze.

There had been a moment when he passed in which they'd been within touching distance. He'd been slightly off-balance and dipped closer, which had been the same time as Jennifer had been breathing in.

She was back in the car boot from the day before, blinking and battling with the darkness, temporarily overwhelmed by the fruity smell that had come and gone from nowhere.

Jennifer knew what it was now.

It was the scent of Nick's vape.

The person who'd bundled her into that car boot was the son of the man who'd murdered her friend.

TWENTY-EIGHT

The tracker had been turned off and dispatched into the bin at the front of the Sainsbury's. Jennifer's boldness had disappeared the moment she'd smelled that fruity tang. She was sitting in her car in front of a supermarket, where a constant string of people were heading in and out. Nothing was going to happen to her here – but she had been so reckless, not once but twice. First, she'd followed that burner phone text, where Nick had stuffed her in a car boot. Then she'd drawn him to a secluded car park, where it was only them, and anything could have happened.

His father had killed her friend in her own room – and now she worried he'd done the same. Ella was dead, murdered in the same way Hayley had been.

Jennifer needed to call the police and tell them what she knew. They'd have those old files about Craig and someone would see the link.

Except... if that was true, why hadn't they found it already?

Jennifer knew, of course. They had no reason to think Ella had been killed by anyone other than her boyfriend.

Jennifer was trying to find out anything remotely incriminating or interesting about Nick – but she'd been avoiding using her phone because of the sheer number of messages popping through. Caroline from HR had obviously told everyone in a half-mile radius what was going on, as Jennifer knew she would. That left Jennifer being inundated with messages from people asking how she was, fishing for information, or both. Some were from genuine friends, others from people she barely spoke to, even when she was sitting in the same office. She had a missed call from Andrew that she'd known was coming. They should have talked before she'd told other people quite so publicly – and he deserved an explanation or apology – except she couldn't bring herself to call him quite yet.

That smell...

Those fake, artificial, vapes turned her stomach at the best of times and she knew this one would never leave her. Even the tiniest future whiff would send her spiralling back to the confused dizziness of that car boot.

Jennifer swiped away all the messages and looked up 'Craig Smart'. Everything with Hayley had happened so long ago that there were barely any traces on the internet. Everything on the web made it seem as if history only began in the mid-2000s, or so, when people finally drifted away from those awful Geocities and Lycos pages. Ask your Mum, and all that. Jennifer had been at university a little before that, when the internet existed – but most people her age accessed it through the university's library. It definitely wasn't on their phones.

It took some very specific searching but Jennifer eventually discovered that, as Harriet had said, Craig hanged himself with a bedsheet while in prison. It had happened a little under two years after Jennifer had come down those court steps to talk to Natasha. Much of the information came from a report about a tribunal after a warden at the prison had been fired for negligence in leaving Craig unattended. Harriet said that he'd dared Craig to do it, though that wasn't in the report.

Either way, Craig was definitely gone. He was a villain but he wasn't a Marvel villain who came back from the dead.

That was one thing. A part of Jennifer had wondered if, somehow, Craig had been released without anyone telling her. She'd been told years back that he'd died but couldn't bring herself to check the details.

But his son was out there, looking just like him, walking like him. Jennifer's mind was racing. Had Nick somehow found out the identity of the person tutoring his younger brother? He blamed Jennifer for what happened with his father and decided to take his revenge on Daniel's girlfriend? In doing that, had he framed Daniel?

It felt unlikely, even as Jennifer worked through what little she knew.

And yet... Nick must've thought Daniel had that burner phone and would follow the text to that park hut. When that had failed, he'd put the tracker on Jennifer's car, thinking she knew where her son was. There was little other reason why she'd have had that phone, after all. It could even explain why he'd let her go the day before. If he'd been some murderous psycho, he could've simply killed her and dumped her in the woods. But he was smarter than that, figuring she would lead him to Daniel.

It still felt unlikely.

Another message came through from someone who'd shared a yoga class with Jennifer almost three years ago. They'd swapped numbers and had a coffee once but that had been the extent of their relationship. Now the woman was 'checking in' to 'make sure you're OK'. She might well have been genuine, and probably was, but the more worrying thing was that the formerly localised news story about Daniel had now gone a lot wider.

Jennifer knew she *should* make two phone calls, first to

Andrew to apologise for leaking it without telling him. Second, and more importantly, to the police.

She also knew she wouldn't make either call. Talking to Andrew would mean proper contrition, and to explain she'd been annoyed by Caroline in HR. A conversation with the police would mean telling them about Daniel's locker and all the cash.

Not only that, if she talked to the police, she'd struggle to offer anything in the way of evidence. The tracker was in a bin now, with no proof it had ever been on a car, let alone hers. Everything else, apart from the locker, was either circumstantial, or had been witnessed only by her. Plus who had more reason to want to clear Daniel than his own mother?

Her bag was on the passenger seat and Jennifer picked out the driving licence she'd found in Daniel's locker. She still didn't know too much about the mysterious Ben Davies, other than that he worked at The Mission and had been missing for a year or so. The burner phone had been switched off since the previous day, as she figured it was more trouble than it was worth. Assuming it was Nick who had been texting, he now knew Daniel didn't have the phone.

That left the key.

It was the item in which she'd been least interested the previous day, largely because it was impossible to know what it was for. It was a traditional flat Yale-style key, which meant it could be for *any* door. Probably a lot of padlocks, too. If it was for Daniel's house, she didn't know why he'd have left it in a locker.

Jennifer twisted and turned the key in her hand, which was when she spotted the entwined 'ID' lettering imprinted on one side of the square part. It looked like some sort of stylised logo, although Jennifer had no idea for what. It could even be the brand of uncut key, though Google didn't throw up any suggestions. She didn't know enough about Daniel's university life to make a guess – except she realised she knew someone who might.

The Red Lion pub had been called something different when Jennifer had been at university. She had vague memories of heading up a tight staircase at the back for a karaoke night in an upstairs room. It might have been something themed because she remembered sand on the floor and servers in grass skirts. There might have even been girls in coconut bras. Different times, and all that.

A couple of decades on and it had been remodelled as a sports bar. Jennifer was sitting in an innocuous spot close to a pool table – and, without turning, she could see five different televisions. Each was showing a different sport, all while an indie song played over the speakers. Posters for a weekly pub quiz had Jennifer spiralling back to the evening she and Natasha had found Hayley. There'd been a pub quiz that night, too.

She was sure Daniel's housemate, Mark, said he worked afternoons at this pub. It had been the Red... something – and there was only one bar in town that had 'Red' in the name. Jennifer had ordered a coffee, which wasn't something she could've done in her day, and then sat scrolling through the messages she'd received. There were so many from anonymous 07 numbers: people she must've known at some point and then deleted from her contacts. News about Daniel had well and truly gone around her home town. It would have happened at some point anyway, but Caroline from HR starting things would've led to someone's Facebook post – and that would've been that.

There hadn't been any further calls from her husband, though Jennifer knew it was on her to contact him.

Before that, she wanted to talk to Daniel's housemate again.

Mark had found Ella's body – his housemate, his friend, suddenly dead in her room. Jennifer knew what that felt like.

Even if he was due on shift, she wasn't sure Mark would show up. A normal life felt like an impossibility after something like that.

She knew about that, too.

And Mark had seemed certain Daniel killed Ella. He'd described how he'd found her. Would he even want to speak to the mother of the person he believed to be a murderer?

But a warm pub with people milling around playing pool and the quiz machine did mean she was safe from Nick, for now at least.

Jennifer finished one coffee and ordered another. She was settling back into her chair when the door popped open and closed, with Mark bristling into the main part of the pub. He rubbed his eyes and lowered his hood, before blinking in the room.

He froze when he saw Jennifer.

She could tell from a distance that he hadn't slept much. Girls might know enough about make-up to hide those bags, but that wasn't true for many young men. Even as he stared, Mark wafted away a yawn, before heading towards the bar. He said something to the man behind, who gave a clear 'no problem', before Mark turned and headed across to where Jennifer was sitting.

'I'm on shift in twenty-five minutes,' he said, slotting into the seat across from her. He'd not even bothered to ask whether she was there for him – although perhaps it was too obvious.

'I've not found Daniel,' Jennifer said. 'Neither have the police. I'm worried for him.'

Mark started scratching his head and then sighed. He was staring at one of the big screens, although it didn't feel as if he was properly watching the on-screen snooker.

'I can't imagine him doing this,' Jennifer added.

She expected pushback, partly because Mark had seemed so sure with his 'Daniel killed Ella' when they'd first spoke. This time he slumped slightly. 'Me either,' he said. 'I told the police that.'

Jennifer was open-mouthed at first. She'd not expected the change of heart and, somehow, it helped. He'd found Ella and was presumably the key witness. If he didn't think his friend was a killer... surely that meant something?

'What did they say?' Jennifer asked.

'I don't know. It was all a blur. I think they find it hard to believe it wasn't Dan. He disappeared right after...'

Jennifer understood that. It was partly why she wasn't answering any of the texts she'd received, even the ones from friends offering genuine concern. What was she supposed to say? The fact he had disappeared made Daniel *look* guilty – even to her.

'How have you been?' she asked.

Mark was picking the beds around his nails, even though they were already red raw. 'Not great,' he said, sounding surprised she'd asked. As if nobody else had. 'I slept on a mate's floor the last two nights. The police said we'll be allowed back in the house later today but I won't know for sure until I'm done here.'

'Is there anything I can do?'

He looked up to her, likely wondering if it was a genuine offer, or perhaps whether she had ulterior motives. 'I don't think so,' he replied.

'How are your other housemates?'

'We're dotted around town, sleeping on different floors. Nobody's been to lectures since – but I need the money from this.'

Jennifer's generation had been the first to properly *need* jobs at university. The days of grants had gone not long before she'd started. Things had got so much harder for young people since.

'I don't suppose you've heard anything from Daniel?' Jennifer asked.

Mark's eyes narrowed a fraction, as if he couldn't quite believe she was asking. It was fair enough.

'Sorry,' she added quickly. 'I just... I don't know what to do.'

She moved quickly, wanting to shift the subject slightly, and pulled out the key from her bag. She handed it to Mark.

'Do you recognise this?' she asked. 'I thought it might be for your front door...?'

Mark turned it over in his palm but was shaking his head. 'Our door has a different type of key but the logo seems familiar.'

Jennifer felt her heart tickle. 'What's it for?'

He scowled a small amount, wrinkle lines appearing on his head. 'No idea but it seems familiar. Where did you get it?'

Jennifer took the key back, and dropped it into her bag. 'It's Daniel's,' she said, even though it didn't answer the question. She wasn't sure what else to say. 'Do you know if Daniel had a friend named Nick?' she added.

The rat-a-tat of questions had Mark looking to her, somewhat confused.

'Who?'

'Nick? Maybe Nicholas? He's sort of big and walks like he's constantly going downstairs.'

Mark's head was shaking again. 'I don't know anyone named Nick. If Dan does, I don't think I met him.'

There was frustration now. Jennifer realised how much she'd been hoping for something far more definitive about either the key, or Nick.

Perhaps sensing her disappointment, Mark added: 'The only person who ever came round was Ella.'

He pulled his phone from his pocket and started swiping, before passing it across for Jennifer to see. On the screen was a photo taken in what looked like a living room. There were seven or eight people sitting with coloured paper hats on their heads. Daniel was off to the side, an arm draped around Ella, who was clutching it. Everyone was smiling as fairy lights twinkled in the background.

'We had a mini Christmas party before everyone went home last year,' Mark said. 'Everyone brought something to eat and we had a buffet in the living room, while we watched *The Muppet Christmas Carol*. I'd never seen it before but it was Ella's favourite.'

He went through the names of everyone in the picture. It was Daniel, his three housemates, a boyfriend of one, a girl-friend of another, then Ella.

Mark returned the phone to his pocket and then stared into the distance. 'We said we should do something like that every month or so. It was such a laugh – but it never happened. Everyone was either working, or busy...'

Jennifer felt the same pangs as when she'd seen Callum's video of Daniel watching Ella sing in the pub. A young couple, happily in those early stages of love, trying to navigate work and lectures and... life.

Such loss.

Mark felt it too as Jennifer saw the lump being gulped back.

'Did you know her well?' Jennifer asked.

'Not really, only through Dan. I went to see her band with everyone a few times. She was so good. She and Dan would sit in his room and play the same few notes over and over when they were writing songs.' His features slipped a fraction as he allowed himself a smile. 'It was actually quite annoying.'

Jennifer laughed at that. When Ella and Daniel had visited for Christmas, they'd spent plenty of time in his room – and large parts of that had been accompanied by the same chords on endless repeat.

It felt such a long time ago – and it was hard to ignore the sadness that those days would never happen again. She gulped away her own lump from the throat. Jennifer had hoped Mark might be able to tell her something about either Nick or the key – but this was definite catharsis.

'Do you know Ella's brother?' Jennifer asked.

It got a bemused shake of the head. 'I don't think so.'

Jennifer didn't have a picture of Nick, though she'd found one of Callum while online stalking him the previous day. She pulled it up on her phone screen and turned it for Mark to see.

He winced a little. 'That's Ella's brother?'

'They look *very* different.'

That got a nod. 'I think I saw him yesterday outside the house. I didn't know who he was.'

'What was he doing?'

'I don't know. Quite a few people came down yesterday. Some left flowers but others just wanted to film videos, like it's some celebrity hangout. Someone was live-streaming it.'

He spoke with a clenched jaw. Jennifer could understand the anger. She wasn't one of those people who thought everything was better in her day... but it really *was* better when every terrible thing didn't have to be documented to feed some egomaniac's main character syndrome.

'I saw him yesterday as well,' Jennifer said. 'He knew I was Daniel's mum. We had a bit of a misunderstanding but he ended up telling me he was annoyed about an inheritance Ella was getting that he'd been cut out of.'

She let that hang, though Mark didn't take long to answer what she hadn't asked. 'I haven't heard anything about an inheritance,' he said.

Jennifer pictured Daniel's locker and thought she would chance it: 'Do you know if Daniel keeps cash around the house?'

It was a question too far: 'Why would he do that? Nobody uses cash.'

The 'nobody' was probably a bit of an over-exaggeration but Mark had a point.

'Just something Callum said,' Jennifer replied, hoping she didn't have to elaborate. She wondered whether she should tell Mark that Callum was a drug dealer. She didn't *know* he was for certain. Would it do any good?

Mark held up a finger as if something had just occurred to him. 'There was someone else who used to come round,' he said. 'Dan would be out tutoring and he'd get dropped home after by this guy in a posh car. Something to do with the church.'

'Gary?'

'That's him. I saw him quite a lot but he'd never come in. Sometimes he and Dan would sit outside talking in his car for a while. He was really old.'

Really old was another stretch – although Jennifer could understand why a twenty-something might think a person in their late-fifties with grey hair was on the brink of keeling over at any moment. Up until the age of about thirty, everyone older seemed so ancient. Then a person's back would twinge for the first time and they'd realise it wasn't so old, after all.

There was a cough from the man behind the bar and Mark nodded towards him.

'I've gotta start my shift,' he said. He half stood and hovered over Jennifer. For a moment, his mouth was open and it seemed as if he was going to say something more. Then he closed it and stood properly. 'See y'around,' he added – although they both knew he wouldn't.

'Thanks for the chat,' Jennifer told him – and then she watched as he lifted the hatch to get behind the bar and disappeared through a back door.

Since she'd heard about Nick that morning, Jennifer hadn't

been thinking too much about Gary, but Harriet had told her that Nick and Gary were close. It was another strand to pull at.

Her coffee was cold but Jennifer finished it anyway and then was about to hoist up her bag when something started buzzing. There was a moment in which she thought it might be the nearby fruit machine paying out, but there was nobody there. By the time she realised it was her phone, she figured it was likely one of her friends or, worse, acquaintances, checking in on her. She absolutely did not want that conversation – except the name on the screen read 'POLICE'.

The thought was instant: Daniel had been found, Why else would they be calling? There was still a mess to figure out but at least he'd be able to tell his side. At least he was safe.

Jennifer took a breath and pressed the button. *Please, let this be some answers.*

TWENTY-NINE

Jennifer was sitting in a waiting room that would be cramped, were there anyone else in it. She was re-running the brief phone conversation she'd had forty-five minutes before, in which Sergeant Sheridan had assured her that nobody had been hurt, and that Daniel *hadn't* been found, but specifically asked her to attend the police station.

It felt menacing.

Had the police found out about the money in Daniel's locker? Did they pull the security footage and watch Jennifer open it? She'd be in trouble for withholding evidence.

Or, perhaps it was nothing to do with that and they'd found something significantly worse?

Jennifer had rushed to the station, only to be left waiting while the person behind the counter sent an underling away to find Sergeant Sheridan. It wasn't as if Jennifer had expected a welcoming party – but Sheridan had a serious edge to her voice on the phone that made it sound as if it was something urgent. Something grave.

But now Jennifer was waiting.

The walls around her were layered with various posters

telling people to beware thieves, or counterfeits and the like. There were a few about car thefts, which had Jennifer remembering the article about the 'epidemic' of stolen vehicles in the area. Natasha had mentioned that, too.

In the meantime, she had ignored many more messages from people at home, either asking about Daniel, or checking to see how she was. *How do you think I am?* she wanted to reply, though knew she wouldn't. People meant well. She'd have to do one of those Facebook status updates, thanking people for their concern. Then there'd be a new avalanche. *U OK hun?* and all that.

Her daydreams disappeared as a door clicked open at the far end of the waiting area, revealing Sergeant Sheridan. The officer managed a smile that didn't feel too welcoming and then strode across the room like an Olympic race-walker.

'Thanks for coming,' she said.

'Is Daniel...?'

Jennifer had been told on the phone that he'd not been found but a part of her was still hoping.

'We don't know where he is,' Sheridan said. 'Do you want to come this way? I've got us a private room.'

That felt ominous, too. Something so bad had happened that Jennifer had to be informed in a *private* setting. Not on the phone and not in a waiting room.

Sheridan scanned her lanyard to reopen the door and then held it as Jennifer passed inside. They bounded along a series of corridors as Jennifer struggled to keep up, while making small talk about the weather, which felt like such a British thing. Sure, your son is missing and accused of murder – but it was a bit foggy out yesterday, wasn't it?

Moments later and Sheridan was unlocking another door. Inside, there was a pair of sofas in an L-shape. The walls were covered with colourful posters of cartoon characters and there was something of a primary school classroom vibe.

'This is where we interview vulnerable witnesses,' Sheridan said, taking a seat on one of the sofas and offering Jennifer the other. 'I figured this was better than one of the formal interview rooms.'

She didn't leave a gap for Jennifer to ask if she was supposedly vulnerable.

'I called your house,' Sheridan continued. 'I spoke to your husband, who gave me your phone number.'

Jennifer first wondered why Andrew hadn't told her – then remembered that he *had* called. She'd been the one who hadn't called him back.

'We were wondering if you might go on camera and ask Daniel to give himself up,' Sheridan added. 'We thought it would have a greater impact if it came from you.'

Jennifer had been blindsided. She'd expected some sort of news, likely bad. Either that, or to be cornered by the police asking why she hadn't told them about the money from Daniel's locker. Maybe even someone demanding why she was still in the area, when she'd been told to go home. She didn't think they'd be asking for help.

'We'd come up with a script if that's what you wanted,' Sheridan said. 'You would have more or less full approval and wouldn't be saying anything you didn't want. We'd post it on our social channels and it's likely news sites would pick it up. The goal is obviously for Daniel to see it.'

Jennifer thought for a moment. Her instinct was to say no. If anyone was hunting her son, it felt as if they should be her enemy. Except, maybe, they wanted the same thing – which was for Daniel to be found safe and explain what was going on.

'I could do it,' Jennifer said, still not sure. 'I suppose I want to know what's *actually* going on. I've read the news reports but it doesn't sound like very much has been released. Everyone on Facebook is saying different things...'

She expected pushback but Sheridan was already ahead of

her. 'I thought you'd ask,' she said. 'We've held back certain details for normal reasons that surround any investigation. There's also an autopsy and the results aren't yet confirmed. I can tell you that Daniel's girlfriend was found dead in his bedroom by a housemate. Ella had been strangled with a lamp cord and—'

'The thing is, I came to this university twenty years ago.' It all came out in one rush. 'I was a student and my friend was killed by a boy who was stalking us. She was strangled with a lamp cord, too. I gave evidence against him and he went to prison. I know what you're saying about Daniel, what you think he did, but he knows everything that happened to me. He wouldn't have done this.'

There was a pause that went for too long. Jennifer assumed, probably naïvely, that she was telling them new information. In a way she was – not about the similarity in how the two young women had been killed, but about herself. She hadn't intended to interrupt and blurt things out... it had just sort of... happened.

Sheridan was staring: 'Are you saying you knew Craig Smart?' she asked.

'I didn't *know* him. He murdered *my* friend in *our* house.'

Sheridan took a breath. 'You're Jen Benson?'

'I was.'

The officer muttered something under her breath that Jennifer didn't catch.

'Craig's girlfriend from back then is the person who hired Daniel as a tutor,' Jennifer added. A part of her had been desperate to explain the links to someone.

'Harriet Etherington hired your son...?'

'She used to be called Joanne. Harriet's her middle name. I don't think she knew that Daniel was my son until after she'd spoken to you.'

Sheridan had seemed calm and assured the entire time – but now she was chewing the inside of her mouth and hadn't stopped staring. There was another long pause and then a hurried: 'I'll be right back.'

Without waiting for a reply, Sheridan was swiftly on her feet and out the door, leaving Jennifer alone to wonder what else she should tell them. Clearly, the police hadn't figured out any of these links on their own.

Her suspicions around Nick seemed most important. Should she say he'd stuffed her in a car boot because, presumably, he thought she was Daniel? If she did that, she would have to explain why she was at that park hut in the first place, which would lead back to Daniel's locker and all that cash. She couldn't prove any of that had happened, outside of the idea that Nick's choice of vape had been present in both places. Plus they'd want to know why she hadn't told them before.

A minute or two passed and Jennifer took out her phone, figuring she could be waiting some time. She had been wondering why her husband had only called once to tell her about the police contacting him – but, as soon as she checked properly, Jennifer realised he'd messaged as well. In ignoring all the messages from friends and acquaintances asking how she was, she'd missed the one from Andrew.

Police called, wanting your no. Think they want u to do an appeal for Daniel. What do u think? I'm here if u want to talk. Hope you're ok. Car over the road gone btw

Jennifer had been so consumed with their ongoing marital issues, their borderline contempt for one another, that she'd somehow missed that her husband was struggling. It wasn't only *her* son missing and accused of murder, it was *their* son. Andrew was trying to help, partly by being at home in case something happened, partly because she'd told him to.

He answered on the second ring, with an eager: 'Jen?'

There was a moment, a teeny instance, in which she drifted

back to those ancient days when she truly loved the way he said her name. After everything at university, she'd always corrected the people who called her 'Jen'. 'I prefer Jennifer,' she'd say. But then Andrew had come along and it felt safe again.

'I'm with the police,' she said. 'They've asked if I can do the appeal for Daniel to turn himself in.'

'What do you think?'

She bit her lip, not sure. 'What do *you* think?'

She sensed him taking a breath, perhaps uncertain, but maybe worried this would start an argument. They'd had plenty of those in which one person had asked the other to give an opinion, before jumping on them for having one. Even over things like what food to order in. *How about sushi? / You know it gives me a bad stomach? / Why ask then? / Because I thought you'd pick something we both could eat. / What do you want then? / Not sushi.*

And so on.

After Daniel had moved out, they had quickly reached the point where they had stopped asking.

'I think you should do it,' Andrew said. There might have been the gentlest quiver of nervousness, though it was hard to tell.

'I think so too.'

'I can come up if they want both of us...?'

Sheridan hadn't mentioned that. It would probably take too long to get Andrew up there, even if Sheridan wanted it.

'I don't know,' Jennifer replied.

There was a short pause. Andrew had likely figured out himself that the police wanted to move quickly. 'What will you say?' he asked.

'I don't know. They said we'll come up with a script I can approve.' She left a gap, wondering if he might have any ideas. If he did, he didn't say. 'Have you heard anything?' she asked.

'I've been getting lots of calls and messages from people

who've heard what's happened. Kate from next door came over with a Victoria sponge. I don't think she knew what else to do.'

Jennifer smiled at that. Kate from next door saw everything in life, comedy, tragedy, or drama, as an opportunity to make someone a cake. Everyone needed a neighbour like Kate.

'How have you been?' he asked.

It was a big question. Jennifer didn't want to tell him about the cash she'd found without some sort of context, even though she knew she might never understand what she'd discovered. She didn't want to tell him about the car boot, either.

'Just tired,' she said – which was true, at least. 'I spoke to a couple of old friends but I'm not really sure what I'm doing. I don't think I'm any closer to finding Daniel.'

'At least you'll be there when he's found. It'll be you he wants.'

Jennifer opened her mouth to reply but couldn't because the lump in her throat was too large. It was probably the nicest thing Andrew had said to her in years. Not that all their problems were on him.

'Do you want me to come up?' he asked again.

A big part of Jennifer wanted to say 'yes', simply because she was desperate for someone to be near. She didn't trust anyone. Except it felt like her story to finish. She was the person who'd first come to Ashington all those years before. She was the one who had jumped in front of Craig back in the university canteen. She was so convinced that everything now was connected to everything then. She was there at the beginning and it needed to be her at the end.

'I don't think so,' Jennifer said.

Andrew hesitated a moment and she wondered if he *wanted* to be with her.

'I'll leave it with you about the appeal,' he said. 'I'll back whatever you decide. You can always call if you need me, day or night.'

Jennifer bit her lip, still trying to swallow the lump in her throat. There really had been a time in which they had investment in one another's life. It was such a long time ago but maybe a nugget of that remained.

'I've got to go,' Jennifer managed. 'I'll message you later.'

'OK.'

They each waited, perhaps anticipating the other saying those three words neither of them had meant in years. It still wouldn't be true, even if one of them cracked. They both knew it.

'Bye,' Jennifer said – and then she hung up.

THIRTY

Time passed. Jennifer waited on the sofa for five minutes. Fifteen. She was beginning to wonder whether she'd been forgotten when there was a gentle knock on the door. Sergeant Sheridan entered without waiting for any sort of reply. In contrast to how calm she'd seemed before, there was now a harried, hurried briskness about her.

She wasted no time as she sank onto the sofa across from Jennifer. 'We were wondering when you found out about the connection from yourself to Ms Etherington...?'

'Last night. There was a memorial for Ella at the church. I knew her a tiny bit and wanted to pay my respects. While I was there, Gary was talking to me about how Daniel and Ella had tutored for him. He introduced me to his wife in The Mission part at the back. That's when we recognised each other. We had coffee this morning.'

Sheridan wasn't making *actual* notes, though it felt like she was keeping track of everything.

'Were you friends back then?'

'Not really. There was a time when I was in town and we found her in an alley. Craig had beaten her up and we shared a taxi to make sure she was safe. The next time I saw her after that was in court – and then yesterday.'

Sheridan was nodding along as if she'd expected as much. Jennifer assumed she'd read the old file at some point in the past couple of days. She might have even skimmed it when she'd been out the room.

'They have a son,' Jennifer said, trying to make it sound like a natural part of the conversation, not as if she was throwing suspicion that way.

'Who?'

'Harriet and Craig. He got her pregnant a week or two before Hayley was killed.'

The frown told Jennifer that Sheridan had no idea this was true. It didn't necessarily mean anything – a killer's child wasn't born a killer – yet Sheridan seemed the sort of person who liked to be in the know.

'I realise I didn't call you in for this,' the officer said. 'But we'd like to do a recorded interview with you. It's mainly to get on record the things you've just told me. It might all be nothing.'

Jennifer knew it was dangerous to get herself into such a formal situation. She'd have to omit details about the locker and the money. She didn't want to talk about the car boot, or the tracker – but she did want them to be looking at Nick. Was omitting information *technically* lying to the police? Was that perjury, or did that apply only to things that happened in a court? Either way, it didn't feel as if she could say no.

'I understand your reluctance,' Sheridan said, although she didn't know the half of it. 'There's no reason for you to trust us, so I will share some more things with you that haven't been revealed to the public. First, Daniel and Ella had an argument the night before she was killed. One of Ella's bandmates heard them shouting and then Daniel left. Immediately afterwards, there was a cut above Ella's eye.'

Sheridan had switched topics so quickly that Jennifer barely had time to take it in. 'You're saying Daniel hit her?'

'We don't know. The argument happened when it was just the two of them in a room. Right afterwards, she was bleeding.'

Jennifer simply could not picture her son hitting anyone, let alone Ella. She'd seen the video of him watching her adoringly while Ella sang in the pub. There were the photos from his house of them gathering for Christmas, Daniel's arm draped across Ella, while she clutched onto him.

'What were they arguing about?' Jennifer asked.

'We don't know – but it's obviously important that we find out and why we need him to hand himself in.'

Jennifer knew that. Daniel *looked* guilty, even to her.

'I realise you want to protect your son but, mother to mother, I really think the best way to do that is for him to come to us. The quicker he does that, the quicker we can find out what happened to Ella.'

It was the first time that Jennifer felt unsure about Sheridan. She'd seemed largely trustworthy before but the 'mother to mother' line stung in a manipulative way Jennifer didn't appreciate. A part of her was also wondering why she hadn't been questioned before. It felt like someone had been watching the house at the other end of the country, and, maybe, the police at this end had been keeping half an eye on her, too. Perhaps someone *had* been in her hotel room? The police had checked her credit card to see where she was staying and had wondered if she was sheltering Daniel. They hadn't questioned her because they wanted to see if Daniel would come to either her or his dad first.

Hmm...

Daniel's housemate, Mark, had also told Jennifer that, when he spoke to the police, he'd said he didn't think Daniel was a murderer – but Sheridan hadn't revealed that. What else was she holding back?

'Have you heard much about Ella's brother?' Jennifer asked. 'Callum?'

'I met him yesterday. He seemed very angry about an inheritance Ella was getting that he wasn't.'

Sheridan's eye twitched a fraction. If Jennifer hadn't been looking for it, she wouldn't have seen it. She knew about the inheritance and it was another thing she'd decided not to mention.

'Their mother told us about that,' Sheridan said, as if she'd meant to reveal it all along. 'Callum *is* known to us but he has an alibi for the time his sister was killed.'

Huh. That meant they had at least checked. She wondered what 'known to us' implied. They knew he dealt drugs?

Jennifer had one more thing to ask, though it felt more delicate than the rest. Harder to weave into a conversation. In the end, she decided to go for it: 'Who's Lance Williams?' she asked.

Sheridan was watching Jennifer carefully, eyes narrowing, weighing up the answer.

'Why are you asking?'

'I met him at the memorial last night. He seemed very interested in Callum.'

It was broadly true, although the 'met him' part was pushing it. Jennifer saw him standing near a tree, wearing a long coat and shiny shoes. She'd also seen him on the upstairs level of the pub when she'd been with Callum.

Sheridan thought for a moment longer and then: 'Off the record, Lance Williams is a drugs trafficker,' Sheridan said. 'Obviously, if we could prove that, we would have done.' She paused. 'Do you think there's a link from him to Daniel?'

'Why would there be?'

It felt as if they each knew something they didn't want to reveal to the other. For Jennifer, it was about the cash in Daniel's locker.

Sheridan broke first: 'There are rumours that Williams lost a lot of money about a year ago.'

Jennifer's neck began to prickle: 'How much is a lot?'

'Around half a million in cash.'

'I'm guessing he didn't report it to you...?'

That got a glimmer of a smile. 'He definitely didn't.'

'How do you know, then?'

'I can't tell you that.'

There was another impasse. Jennifer wasn't sure what she'd discovered. There was a lot of money in Daniel's locker – but not half a million. It felt so unbelievably unlikely that he'd somehow stolen it from a supposed drugs trafficker, and yet there might be something there.

'How was the money taken?' Jennifer asked. She didn't expect a reply, though she got one.

'Williams apparently kept it in a car that was stolen.'

'Who keeps that much in a car?'

'You'd be surprised what people transport up and down the country in vehicles. Keep to the speed limit and you're unlikely to be stopped.'

'Thanks for the tip.'

Jennifer gave a smile that was returned. They eyed one another for a moment and Jennifer wasn't sure if she'd done the right thing in introducing Lance into their conversation. She had no real reason to know who he was.

Sheridan spoke next: 'I can look into whether we have anything that might connect Mr Williams to your son, to Ella, to her brother. I'm sure that, if we did, it would already have come up – but I understand why you might be keen. In the meantime, is there anything else you would like to ask?'

It felt like an honest moment. Jennifer *had* been fishing for information and the officer had let it go.

When Jennifer shook her head, Sheridan picked up again. 'I

was thinking we could maybe put together the appeal for Daniel right now.'

'Do you want my husband to come up?'

'It's up to you – but there's a media officer down the corridor, or you can work directly with me if you prefer. We can get something onto our social channels within ninety minutes or so – the sooner, the better – and then we can sit you down for a formal statement about Craig Smart and everything else. How does that sound?'

The sudden haste felt odd but it didn't seem as if Jennifer could say no, even though a part of her wanted to. Perhaps the bigger part. Ultimately, she wanted her son to be safe.

'That sounds good,' Jennifer said.

THIRTY-ONE

Jennifer's voice sounded so much lower in the recording than it did to her at any other time.

By the time she'd left the police station, her appeal for Daniel to turn himself in was already on YouTube, Facebook, and all sorts of other places. The police's media manager said it would be on the local news broadcasts that evening. She'd told Jennifer there was a chance people might recognise her if she was in Ashington, which was something that hadn't occurred to her.

But her voice really *was* low in the video. Did she always talk like that? Was it her equivalent of a phone voice, because she knew she was being filmed? Her mother always had a phone voice. One moment, she'd be gossiping with her friend in the kitchen, accents and slang in full force, then she'd pick up the phone and sound like a personal assistant to the queen.

Either way, her video was live and Jennifer wasn't sure whether she'd done the right thing. If Daniel wanted to come forward, he surely would have done? Would this make it seem as if she was taking the police's side over his? That she didn't believe him? Cooperating felt like both the right and wrong thing to do.

But it was done now.

The formal interview had gone over much of what she'd already told Sergeant Sheridan, though Jennifer was careful with everything said on camera. She didn't tell them about the money in the locker, nor that she suspected Nick had mistaken her for Daniel while abducting her. She had made sure to bring him up twice as being Craig's son, hoping they might look into him.

It was the evening and, as ever in October, night came early. In the hours Jennifer had been away from the hotel, someone had stuck half-a-dozen carved pumpkins around the various counters. There was stringed cotton wool lining a couple of the doors, with a wonky 'Happy Halloween' sign above reception and an orange tub of lollies next to the key drop box. The fact it would be Halloween the next day had largely passed Jennifer by.

The girl behind reception gave Jennifer a curious look, though it was hard to tell if she was wondering whether Jennifer was worth challenging as a guest, or because she'd seen the video with Jennifer asking Daniel to turn himself in. Now the media manager had mentioned the prospect of Jennifer being recognised, she knew she would be looking at everyone in a slightly different way.

Up in the lift and the 'do not disturb' hanger was still on Jennifer's door. She let herself inside, half expecting her things to have been moved – but it was all as she'd left it. She had placed a ball of socks on top of the bathroom door, thinking herself a genius because, if anyone entered, the socks would fall and she'd know someone had been in the room. It felt like less of a clever idea hours later – and, either way, they were still on top of the door. Daniel's hoody was untouched in the wardrobe, too.

Jennifer called her husband and they talked about the video. Andrew had seen it too and insisted she'd done great, that he was sure it would bring Daniel into the open if he saw it. She was less certain, though wasn't going to say so.

She told him about the apparent argument between Daniel and Ella the night before she was killed. The police thought it might be something but Andrew seemed less sure, which was what she thought, too. Daniel wasn't violent. She believed it and *had* to believe it. He told her that there was no sign of a mystery vehicle over the road. If the police had been watching the house, it seemed as if they'd given up – at least temporarily.

They said goodnight, even though it was barely half-past seven, and then Jennifer decided to have a shower. That quickly morphed into having a bath, even though the tub was smaller than the one at home. She was so tired that the idea of lying in the water for a bit, before slipping under the bedsheets and willing the exhaustion to take her was almost unfightable. Jennifer's thoughts felt sluggish and maybe something better would come the next morning, when she'd rested.

She also didn't want to be recognised if she went back out.

Instead, Jennifer sat in bed and replied to some of the messages she'd received. She thanked her friends for their various concerns and said she'd let them know when there was news. There were so many more, including those from numbers she didn't have stored. Maybe people she'd met once and deleted as contacts. Perhaps there were other reporters who knew her phone number. There'd been that one the day before.

Jennifer scrolled through, deleting anything to which she couldn't bring herself to reply. She'd contacted Andrew and her actual friends and that would have to do.

Except there was a message from an 07 number not in her contacts, which wasn't like the others. It had arrived an hour or so before, at roughly the time she'd been leaving the police station. The appeal video had gone up while she'd been getting interviewed, which meant it had been live at the time the message was sent.

She stared at it, frozen on the edge of the bed, not quite believing it was real.

It's me, Mum

THIRTY-TWO

The phone number wasn't Daniel's, but then Jennifer was almost certain his proper phone had been turned off. It might have even been thrown away. If her son was going to message, it would come from a different number that the police didn't know about.

It *could* be Daniel... but then it could be anyone with access to a SIM card who knew her number.

Jennifer clicked into the anonymous contact and pressed to FaceTime. If Daniel answered, she would see his face and know it was truly him. Her phone rang as she stared at her own face, noticing the darkness under her eyes and how grey she suddenly seemed. Either the lights in the room were doing her no favours, or it had been the longest two days of her life.

Daniel didn't answer.

Jennifer was wondering what to do when another message arrived from the same number.

Camera broken. Can't talk

Jennifer knew it was a scam. The message was so obviously

fake. Someone had found her number and, within minutes, they'd be saying they were in trouble. If only she could transfer ten grand to some random bank account, everything would be fine.

Obviously a scam.

But what if it wasn't?

Why not?

Jennifer's reply didn't get a response, and she wasn't sure she expected one. Certainly not without an accompanying message extolling how brilliant Western Union was. It was a scam and she had to stop responding.

Saw your video but I didn't do it

Yeah, I didn't do it... but I need help. If you could transfer some money to this PayPal account...

Jennifer told herself not to reply. Nothing good would come, she knew that. She was an intelligent person who read those consumer advice pages about how to avoid being scammed.

Who killed Ella?

They'd say they didn't know – but if she could just send over lots of Amazon gift cards, then that would be a lot of help. Delete the message, block the number, and move on.

But then the reply arrived. One word.

Gary

THIRTY-THREE

After the single-word bombshell, Jennifer replied to ask 'Why?', 'How?' and then 'Why can't you hand yourself in?' but no further texts arrived. She even tried 'How do I know it's you?' but that didn't get an answer, either.

Jennifer told herself it wasn't Daniel – but then the person messaging *hadn't* asked for money. If it was a scam, then where was the request? Why would they want her to think Gary had killed Ella if that wasn't true?

That single word was read and re-read so many times that Jennifer's eyes started to blur. She found herself wondering if a scammer could have guessed someone named Gary was involved? Or if there were two Garys. Then she went into the months of messages she'd exchanged with Daniel from his regular number. He was a lot like his father in that, aside from the odd 'RU' and the like, he tended to spell things out fully in his messages. It might only be for her, not his friends, but she couldn't see a lot of shortening. The messages she'd received from the 07 number had been similar.

Jennifer's hopes of an early night and refreshed mind were long gone as she spent the rest of the evening constantly checking her phone. She tried calling the number, though it wasn't answered. She sent another text – 'Can you please reply?' – but that got nothing.

Then she slipped into full paranoia mode that the police had set this up to try to entrap her. She was supposed to report any contact to them but she was sitting on this. She certainly didn't trust Sergeant Sheridan.

Jennifer lay on the bed and closed her eyes, hoping for sleep, but the pull of the phone was stronger. Still no reply – just that singular 'Gary'.

And what if it *was* Harriet's husband who had killed Ella?

When Jennifer had spoken to Mark, Daniel's housemate, about any visitors he'd seen at the house, he'd only mentioned Ella and Gary. He'd said that Daniel and Gary sometimes spent time talking in a car outside the property. If Gary dropped Daniel home after tutoring sessions, there was a likelihood he did the same for Ella. Neither Daniel nor Ella could drive.

And by Harriet's admission, Gary had been the last person to see Ben before he disappeared a year before. Plus she said Gary and Nick had a father-son relationship, even though they weren't related by blood. Perhaps it was Gary who'd put Nick up to following Jennifer's car? Who'd had him place that tracker? Both things had only happened *after* she'd visited his house, asking questions about Daniel and Ella.

Jennifer checked her phone again but there was still no reply. She tried calling the 07 number but Daniel didn't answer.

No, *not* Daniel. The *scammer* didn't answer. She had to tell herself that. If it was truly her son, he would answer the phone.

But maybe he *was* in trouble. Someone had grabbed the phone from him and he was in danger.

Jennifer was out of bed again, halfway through getting dressed before she realised she had no idea where she might be going. That mania from the previous night, when she was convinced her room had been broken into, was building once more.

She needed to sleep.

Back undressed, Jennifer returned to bed, plugged in her phone to charge, and closed her eyes. She should turn it off. But what if Daniel *did* call? What if she *should* call the police? What if, what if, what if...

... From nowhere there was light in the room. Jennifer jolted awake, scrambling for her phone instinctively, before hearing the clunk as she rolled. Somehow, the phone had been on her chest and she'd bounced it onto the floor. She had slept, though must have woken at least once in the night to check the phone, before falling asleep again. She had vague memories of the bright blueish light dazzling through the darkness.

It was morning now.

The 07 number hadn't messaged, or called. The clock next to the television said it was almost quarter past seven, which meant Jennifer had more or less slept for six hours. That was more than she'd managed in the previous two days put together.

The crazed irrational thoughts from the night before had largely dimmed, though she still didn't know whether she believed the person texting her was Daniel, or a scammer.

How do I know this is you?

Jennifer sent a repeat message, desperate for an answer. A part of her was convinced Gary actually *had* killed Ella, mainly because it let her believe Daniel was innocent. Another part, perhaps the most rational one, was saying that whoever was texting her simply wanted her to *think* it was Gary. If she was looking at him, then she wouldn't be focused elsewhere.

No reply came.

'What do you want from me?' Jennifer asked the empty room.

There was no reply from that, either.

She yawned and kicked herself out of the covers. It had been so dark the night before that Jennifer hadn't bothered to close the curtains. She stood at the window watching the banality of people driving on the motorway. In the hotel car park, a man was sitting in his car, having an irate phone conversation with someone. Some woman over by the main services was walking around in shorts. The maniac.

Jennifer wondered if there was a car out there somewhere, with somebody inside watching the hotel. *Had* the police been in her room the night before? *Were* they watching her now?

The delusions were obliterated as Jennifer's phone started to buzz. She practically dived across the room to grab it. There was an o7 number on the screen and it had to be her son. He'd tell her what Gary had done and why. They'd come up with a plan to clear Daniel's name.

But it wasn't Daniel. It wasn't even the same o7 number. It was a different person not in her contacts, and a woman's voice.

'Is that Jennifer?' she asked.

Jennifer was a little off-guard. This wasn't what she'd expected. 'Yes.'

'I'm sorry for calling so early – but I've been up all night thinking about you. My name's Michelle. I'm Ella's mum and I was wondering if you wanted to meet...?'

THIRTY-FOUR

THURSDAY

A boy no older than eight or nine was racing a mini motorbike around a car park. The engine howled like a rusty lawnmower as he stood high on the footrests, while blasting over a kerb towards an archway. Jennifer watched him in her rear-view mirror as she took in the block where Ella's mum lived. It was an area of town Jennifer had never visited, despite the time she'd spent in Ashington. She had lived more or less in the middle but, as well as the posh bit at one end, where Gary and Harriet lived, there was the run-down part at the other. She vaguely remembered a story of someone from her course being stabbed when they got lost on the way home – and always associated the incident with this part of town, even though she wasn't sure where it actually happened.

All she had known then was that it was best avoiding the gloomy, blackened tower blocks that dominated the skyline. Years later, she realised how prejudiced that all was.

Middle-class angst or no, Jennifer still didn't feel quite right as she locked her car and stepped out on the wide parking area that sat between three towering slabs of concrete. She was surrounded by balconies with swaying washing getting even wetter from the cloying drizzle that stuck to the air.

Jennifer pulled her coat tighter, rechecked the car was locked, and then headed for the stairwell of Collier Tower. The entrance had a watered-down urine stench, while the sound of a woman trying to reverse a pram out of a creaking lift echoed around the stony space.

'Have you seen a boy on a motorbike out there?' the woman asked, as the pram was finally extricated from the elevator.

'I think he went that way,' Jennifer said, pointing towards the arch on the furthest side of the car park.

'I knew it!' the woman said, angrily backing out of the main doors as Jennifer held them for her. As soon as she got outside, she screeched a piercing 'Mason!' to the skies.

Jennifer stepped into the lift, though it crunched and groaned even as she stood still – which left her figuring the stairs were a better option.

Or they were for the first two flights. By the time Jennifer reached floor eleven, she was huffing and had to hold onto the banister to give herself a few moments of recovery.

She checked the message Michelle had sent, then continued along the hardened walkway, blinking into the blistering breeze, until knocking on the front door of Ella's mother's flat.

Michelle opened the door with a weary smile. Her eyes were ringed red, her nose swollen and sore. 'You came,' she said, sounding slightly surprised.

'Of course.'

Michelle held the door, allowing Jennifer to enter the furnace of her flat. A searing inferno of a radiator was next to the front door, surrounded by peeling wallpaper, with long-dry underwear draped over the edges.

'Just through there,' Michelle said, sending Jennifer into a homely living room. There were two sofas pointing at a large

TV, with various framed posters around the walls, saying things like 'Dream Big' and 'Your Only Limit Is You'. 'Sorry for the mess,' Michelle said, even though Jennifer hadn't noticed any. 'I just boiled the kettle if you want a tea...?'

'Only if you don't mind.'

They went through the milk-sugar ritual and then Michelle disappeared through a net curtain into what must have been the kitchen, leaving Jennifer alone in the living room.

The moment Jennifer spotted the photo of Ella, she started to doubt it was a good idea to come. She was drawn to the picture pinned to the wall, never ceasing to be amazed at how school photos had been the same for forty years. Ella was sitting side-on, twisting to grin at the cameraman. She was maybe nine or ten, in pigtails, with a grey blazer and red tie. Aside from the colour of the uniform, there was a near identical photo of Jennifer from when she would have been the same age.

There were pictures of Ella on every wall of the room, each stage of her life documented with loving testament. Even the images themselves felt loved: the ones over the radiator speckled by browned, curling corners. There was another near the television on which someone had drawn a pair of fake glasses over Ella's face with a felt-tip. Some sort of long-forgotten in-joke.

As Jennifer took in the room itself, the warmth and the memories, the flat felt lived in and Ella felt adored.

The poor girl.

Jennifer was gulping away a lump in her throat again as she picked up a Polaroid from the unit on which the television sat. Ella and Daniel's faces were smushed into one, with Ella's arm partially in shot as she held the instant camera. It must have been recent: a modern-day selfie with tech that had been around since before Jennifer was born. She stared into their faces, wishing she'd known more of their relationship before everything had happened. Her son had been in love for the first time and she'd been told so little about it.

'That was a birthday present,' Michelle said.

Jennifer jumped a fraction, having not heard the other woman re-enter the room.

Michelle placed two mugs of tea on a small serving table that sat between the sofas.

'The photo?' Jennifer asked.

A shake of the head. 'Daniel bought El a Polaroid camera for her birthday last month. I laughed for about ten minutes when she showed me. I can't believe they're back again. She was going around the estate, taking photos of things, then rushing up to show me the photos. I was like, "We had them when I was younger than you". She couldn't believe you could press a button and hold the photo right after.'

Michelle bit her lip, then picked up her tea as Jennifer slotted onto the other sofa.

'How have you been?' Jennifer asked, not quite knowing what to say. What *could* she say?

A shrug. 'Not great. I saw you on the news last night, and it was all over Facebook. Have you heard anything?'

'Nothing.'

It was a lie, maybe, considering those texts apparently from Daniel. Jennifer didn't know for sure it was him.

Michelle was still holding her mug, fingers looped through the handle. 'Do you think Daniel did it?' she asked.

Jennifer couldn't hide the gasp. Of all the questions she'd expected, of all the reasons for asking to meet, she hadn't considered this. The fact the 'it' meant 'murdered my daughter' was almost too much to handle. Jennifer found herself staring at the other woman, mouth open.

'I didn't mean it like that,' Michelle added. It was probably only a second later but felt like so much longer. 'Daniel was always so sweet. He'd come for tea on Sundays and I'd cook for us all. Ella's been vegetarian for about ten years, so I'd make a load of roast potatoes. If there was anything left, Daniel would put them in a tub to take back to his house, then he'd return the tub the next week.'

She smiled kindly, sadly, and Jennifer still couldn't speak. That definitely sounded like her son.

'I'm so sorry,' she managed.

Michelle waved it off. 'He was the best thing that could have happened to Ella. Before that, she spent way too much time with her brother.'

'Callum?'

Michelle met Jennifer's eyes. 'Have you met him?'

A nod – and the silent second between them said plenty, as Jennifer realised that with all the photos of Ella around the living room, she'd not seen a single one of Callum.

'I bought him lunch,' Jennifer said. 'I was trying to find out what was going on and thought he might know.'

That got an exasperated laugh. 'You must be the only person ever who thought Callum might know more than you.' Michelle took a breath and sighed to herself. 'Ella's dad, Bryan, was married with a stepson – Callum – before I met him. When Callum's mum died, Bryan adopted him. Poor kid was only five and had lost his mum. Bryan could've put him into care – but that's not who he was. Bryan and I married about eighteen months later – and Callum was furious about that, even as a child. I tried to be his mum but he didn't want me.' A shrug. 'I mean, I get it. He was young and had lost his own mum. He wanted her back, not some stand-in, but I couldn't help things either.'

Jennifer was still trying to work out the complications of the family relationship. Neither of Callum's blood parents were the same as Ella's.

'Bryan and I had Ella not too long after,' Michelle added. 'Callum was furious about that, too. We really tried with him – but he was off the rails from the age of about nine or ten. He ended up being banned from all the shops around here because he wouldn't stop stealing. One time, a shopkeeper locked him in the back room and called the police. I think that was the first time he was arrested, so he was probably only eleven. He punched a teacher and got expelled from school, then we couldn't get him into any others, even though the council was threatening to take us to court because he wasn't in education. We couldn't figure out what to do.'

Michelle stopped for a drink of her tea. It sounded like hell. Jennifer had heard the odd story of tearaway children but Daniel had been the opposite. He was happy to quietly sit in his room, or head to a friend's house. She would struggle to come up with a single time he'd been in trouble for anything other than getting home a bit late.

'Callum never took his GCSEs,' Michelle continued. 'We could not get him to go to school, no matter what we said or did. When someone from the council came round to tell us about court dates for us not sending him, we'd ask, "What do you want us to do?" and they never really had an answer. For the most part, Ella was separate from that – but then, when she was about fifteen, Callum got her into smoking. Then we found out he was dealing cocaine and ketamine around the estate.'

Jennifer let out a largely accidental sigh, which got a 'Right?!' from Michelle.

'Then Ella met Daniel,' Michelle continued. 'She'd been in a few bands but kept getting thrown out. She'd be hanging around with Callum and miss practices, that sort of thing. But Daniel encouraged her to keep it up. They started writing songs and tutoring kids. She was talking about doing her teacher training and I just—'

Jennifer had gone. She'd felt things building, with the lump in her throat and the stress of everything from the past few days. She was somehow still holding the Polaroid – and couldn't stop staring at her son and his girlfriend with their grinning faces pressed into one another. She felt even worse when Michelle picked up a box of tissues and passed them across. It was the other woman who'd lost her daughter, and Jennifer was making it about herself.

She blew her nose and tried to wipe away the tears from her eyes. 'I didn't know any of that,' Jennifer managed.

Michelle waited, stoic and strong in a way she shouldn't have to be. Jennifer wanted to hear the rest – and said as much. She blew her nose again before Michelle continued.

'When the police came round to say what Daniel had done... I just... didn't believe it,' Ella's mum said. 'I told them I didn't believe it. Why would he?'

Jennifer couldn't speak. It was validation for everything she'd been telling herself for two and a half days. Not only that, it was coming from the person who, above anyone, *could* have hatred for her son.

There was a simmering silence between them, punctured only by the rattling clicks of the central heating pipes. Until that moment, neither had known quite how much they were on the same page.

Jennifer needed another moment, but then managed a snotty: 'Do you know anyone else who might have...?' She couldn't quite add: 'killed Ella'.

Michelle's lips were pressed tight, like she was carefully thinking about her choice of words. 'I'm not saying it's Callum,' she began. 'I mean, he's done a *lot* of things in the past – but this would be awful, even for him. Except Bryan's mum died recently. She left about four thousand pounds for Ella – and Callum was furious it wasn't going to be split with him.' She stopped to have a drink of her tea, swilling it around her mouth, almost chewing. 'Maybe it should have been,' she added. 'But it's not my money to divvy up. Also, if he got half, it would be gone like that.' She clicked her fingers.

Michelle's words echoed what Harriet had told Jennifer the day before.

'He'd end up dead,' Michelle added. 'I'm serious. I don't know what he's addicted to now but he'd smoke it, inject it, snort it, whatever.'

Jennifer was feeling even more guilty about the money she'd given him, wondering what habit it might be funding. 'He told me he'd been in a car crash recently,' she said.

That got a wide-eyed look of bemusement in return. 'Really? I know he's been limping around but it's hard to know with him what's true and what isn't. Either way, when he found out that money was all Ella's, he was *so* angry.' She poked a thumb towards the kitchen: 'He smashed a window out there because he threw a can of beans at me when I said I couldn't do anything about it. I kicked him out about a week ago and have only seen him briefly since. He came by when the police were here. I told him that Ella was dead and he took off.'

Jennifer figured she must have encountered him not long after that, considering Callum had told her the police were with his mum.

'He's got gambling debts,' Michelle added. 'As if everything else wasn't already enough. He has one of those personalities that becomes addicted to anything and everything. He bets on his phone and plays those terminal things in the betting shops. I keep telling him that people never really win long-term – but then, whenever he *did* win something, he'd come round to tell me. He never mentioned the losses and I don't know how much he owes.' She nodded past the front window, towards the estate. 'One of my friends has a son about Callum's age and she reckons Callum owes thousands. I don't even know who to.'

She sounded exhausted and it was hard to blame her. There was the sense that she could talk for endless hours about the grief through which Callum had put her over the years.

'What happened to Bryan?' Jennifer asked.

'Died on the railways a few years back. Irony was that he was a big union man. He was shop steward – and it was a workplace accident that killed him. Ella didn't take it too well – which was the other reason Daniel was so good for her. It's not like she forgot her dad but he helped her get over it.'

Jennifer hadn't heard about any of this from Daniel but then he was the sort to modestly go about his life. He didn't talk about himself that much.

'Ella must've got all that from her dad,' Michelle said, from nothing.

'All what?'

'She started helping out at the church.'

Jennifer had been thinking of Daniel, but something suddenly clicked. 'At The Mission?'

Michelle nodded. 'That's the one. She would be there serving food, or running the food bank once or twice a week. That's how she and Daniel got their first tutoring gig. They met someone there...'

'Gary?'

A click of the fingers: 'That's him.'

Jennifer felt the weight of that text that might have come from Daniel. The single-word accusation.

'I never met him,' Michelle added. 'He dropped her off last weekend, before all this happened. I think she and Daniel had been tutoring for him and it had run late.'

Jennifer was trying to remember the things she'd been told in recent days. Everything had meshed together, except Ben's driving licence was still in Jennifer's bag.

'Do you know the name "Ben Davies"?' Jennifer asked.

Michelle thought for a moment and then: 'Is he missing?'

'I think so. Do you know if he was friends with Ella, Daniel, or Callum?'

Michelle took a few seconds to think again. 'I'm not sure. I know Callum would spend time at The Mission because of the free food. Ella did some days there when she was in her full Robin Hood stage.'

'What do you mean by that?'

Michelle laughed: 'That rob from the rich stage that most teenagers seem to go through. She organised a car wash on the estate last summer, then gave all the money to a homeless charity. Things like that.'

Jennifer wasn't sure what that meant, if anything. There still wasn't any obvious reason for Daniel to have Ben's driving licence.

'When you saw Ella at the weekend, was there a cut above her eye?'

Michelle looked up to acknowledge Jennifer's question. Given everything Jennifer had been told by Sergeant Sheridan, about a potentially violent argument between the pair, she was almost worried to hear an answer.

'The police asked about that,' Michelle said. 'Did they talk to you as well?'

A nod: 'Yesterday. They said Daniel might've done it.'

Michelle grimaced a fraction: 'Did someone see what happened?'

'I don't think so.'

The other woman considered things for a moment and then: 'I asked El about it and she said it was nothing. I assumed she'd caught it on a door, something like that. She didn't seem bothered.' Michelle took a breath and then, from nowhere, the grief took her. She covered her face and pulled her knees to her chest. 'I just can't believe I'm not going to see her again,' she sobbed through her hands.

Jennifer didn't know what to do. She felt it too and it wasn't even her daughter.

'She was sort of living here, sort of living with Daniel,' Michelle said. 'She'd text if she was going to be home for tea and I'd cook, even if it was just fish fingers. I check my phone every afternoon, expecting her to have messaged to ask "What's for tea?"'

Jennifer passed Michelle the tissues, just as she'd been handed them not long before. 'Is there anything I can do?' she asked. 'I can pick up food? Take you somewhere...?'

That got a teary shake of the head. 'Find Daniel,' she said. 'Find out what happened.'

THIRTY-FIVE

Jennifer was sitting in her car when another text arrived from the 07 number. She'd heard nothing since receiving 'Gary' the night before, though the thread was filled with her begging for a response.

Have you gone home yet?

The text was so simple, yet baffling at the same time. It felt like she'd missed an entire conversation in which she'd said she was leaving – except the topic of her getting out of Ashington hadn't come up.

Jennifer replied with a simple 'Why?' Because she had been waiting so long since the previous evening, she didn't expect a response. She got one almost instantly.

Cos they'll use you to find me

Jennifer was so desperate to believe it was Daniel at the other end of a phone keyboard. Why else would someone want her to leave? If it was a scam, then what was it?

There was obvious truth to the message. Someone *had* texted that burner phone, presumably hoping to lure Daniel to the park hut. Someone *had* put a tracker on her car, likely hoping she'd lead them to Daniel. She was almost certain that person was Nick.

Jennifer was also struggling with the newly added pressure. It wasn't Michelle's fault, and Jennifer certainly didn't blame her, but she was now determined to find Daniel for a cause greater than her own. Michelle was relying on her, too.

Where are you?

Jennifer had barely sent that text, when she followed it with another:

Who's "they"?

She pictured her son hiding somewhere dark and cold, panicked by every noise and movement in case it was either the police or the mysterious 'they'.

This time there was no instant reply, but Jennifer was hesitant to start her car, in case it might jinx things. She'd been on such a roll of getting answers and she willed another message to appear.

The skies had darkened since Jennifer had left Collier Tower. The drizzle had become a heavier shower and the wind was fizzing around the blocks. Jennifer could feel her car gently rocking and checked over her shoulder to make sure there was nobody there. It was a downcast day anyway but the blocks towered high above, swallowing her in gloom.

Then a reply popped through.

I cab't say

Jennifer stared at it, seeing the typo, wondering if the texter was answering her first, or second question. Maybe both. She shouldn't have sent them back-to-back, but was so desperate to hear anything that might help get her son out of all this.

And then the answer to her second question arrived:

Gary – but please just go

It had to be Daniel who was contacting her. *Had* to be. He was saying that Gary had killed Ella – and that he'd use Jennifer to find him. There was no how or why but Jennifer was so desperate to believe it.

Was this enough to take to the police? Was it real? Could they protect her from Gary? Could they protect Daniel? A part of her thought she should follow the request and go home – but she knew she wouldn't. There was something rotten with Gary, Nick, possibly Callum, and likely The Mission.

Jennifer sent another message asking 'Where are you?' She waited for a reply that didn't come, though didn't want to risk putting down the phone. In the moment, she was connected to Daniel and didn't want to break that.

Instead, she messaged her husband, saying she'd spoken to Ella's mum, who was also convinced Daniel was innocent. She hoped for an instant reply, in which Andrew would tell her he was certain as well, but that never came, either.

Jennifer was running out of people who might be able to help. It had been cathartic to talk to Michelle – but there had been no clues for where Daniel might have gone, or what had happened. She had now been in Ashington for fifty-something hours and couldn't think of a single clue she'd found about her son's whereabouts.

She looked up, through the windscreen, to where the rain was beginning to pool in a cratered pothole near the middle of the car park. Someone's off-leash spaniel took a running leap at it and began splashing as the impatient owner bellowed 'Pixie' from the far side of the quadrant.

Hmm...

Jennifer's mind felt sluggish, as it had for days. What was the name of Ella's band? Sergeant Sheridan had said she'd been told about the cut above Ella's eye by someone in her band.

Jennifer searched back through her phone's history until she found the band page for Pixie Dreampeople. She had already scrolled through hundreds of photos taken of them performing, with Ella front and centre for almost all. Jennifer went through them again, not sure what she was looking for, but knowing it wasn't there.

She thought for a moment, then clicked through to an Instagram page. The top post was an RIP for Ella, with some paragraphs from the band, saying they were heartbroken. The content on the rest of the page was different than the first. There were still pictures from their gigs but often in a more natural, casual setting. As well as Ella, there were three young men in the band – and there were numerous photos of the group sitting around talking, or playing, when it looked like they didn't know they were being photographed. Jennifer wondered whether it was Daniel who'd taken some of the photos.

She continued through the images, towards the ones that had been posted at the beginning of the year. There was a picture of Daniel and Ella sitting on breeze blocks while the drummer tapped away nearby. A large battered rug was on the floor – and the photo had been taken from the end of a driveway.

They practised in a garage.

It didn't take long for Jennifer to find a general area. The various band members all had their own personal pages and, within minutes, Jennifer had the name of the road on which the bassist lived. He'd put up a photo almost two years before labelled 'new practice space' that matched the picture Jennifer had seen. She found him mentioning a certain road on an even older post.

When Jennifer next glanced to the dashboard clock, twenty-five minutes had passed and there hadn't been any further messages from Daniel. She finally put down her phone. For whatever reason, he was only communicating in short bursts.

Jennifer looked up, ready to start the car and head out to see if she could find a band member who might talk to her. She was desperate for any sort of clue and they'd seen Daniel more recently than she had.

It had to be him, she told herself again, wishing she knew for sure.

Her finger was on the car's ignition key as Jennifer spotted the figure standing in the rain, barely ten metres away. He was near the doors that led into Collier Tower, where the woman who'd raised him lived.

Callum was staring at Jennifer, even as the rain washed over his face. He was talking on his phone, lips moving, his eyes never leaving her vehicle. Jennifer wondered if he could see her through the reflection of the glass, then figured she didn't want to find out.

Moments later and she'd started the engine and pulled off the estate, hoping she'd never have to come back.

THIRTY-SIX

Pixie Dreampeople's practice garage was next to a semi-detached house on the corner plot at the end of a row of houses.

It was bin day on the road, with rows of emptied black wheelie bins upside down and on their sides, as if a freak tornado had blown through. The rain near the tower blocks had largely gone, leaving a silver sky and whispering wind.

Jennifer stood to take in the scene for a moment, wondering where to try first. The garage door was closed and someone had scratched 'no entry' into the peeling brown paintwork. Meanwhile, there was no sign of anyone in the house, with all lights off and the driveway clear of vehicles. Jennifer checked the old Instagram photo once more, knowing it was the right house, and marvelling at how much of their lives people put online. She was hardly a digital expert but she'd found this place with ease.

She didn't expect anyone to answer but Jennifer knocked on the front door anyway. It was old and wooden, slightly squishy from years of wind and rain. There was still darkness in the windows but a clear 'hang on!' sounded from inside. She waited, pressed close to the brickwork as the squall howled behind, before there was a clunk, a click, and then the door swung inwards.

A guy with straggly black hair that was dripping wet stood holding a towel, while still wriggling to try to get an arm into a T-shirt. He was probably twenty or so, skinny, though not gaunt. The sort who could put away a Viennetta and not need to loosen the belt.

'Oh,' he said, 'I thought you were the Amazon guy. I was in the shower.'

Jennifer apologised and then: 'It might be the wrong house but I was hoping to talk to someone from Pixie Dreampeople...?'

He started to close the door: 'We already said we're not talking to reporters.'

'I'm Daniel's mum.'

The door was almost shut but it stopped with an inch or so to go – and then reopened a fraction.

'Oh,' came the reply.

Jennifer could sense the man thinking as the door wavered. Not quite closed, not quite open. But then it *was* open.

He eyed her curiously, rubbing the bridge of his nose.

'I'm Pickle,' he said, somewhat bafflingly, before opening the door wider and stepping to the side. 'D'you wanna come in?'

'If you don't mind.'

Jennifer stepped into a dark hallway, where she looked up to see there was no light bulb in the holder.

'Living room's there,' Pickle said, nodding behind Jennifer as he added that he was going to get changed. He bounded up the stairs as Jennifer followed the nod into what turned out to be a confusingly normal living room. Given the darkness, his name, and the run-down state of the outside, she'd anticipated something closer to a bomb site compared to the neat rows of vinyl records that greeted her. There was no TV but there were speakers and a record player, plus four plastic white garden chairs.

Clumping footsteps boomed from above as Jennifer walked around the room, scanning the record sleeves. From a cursory glance, there was everything from Johnny Cash in the 1950s right up to Arcade Fire – something she'd heard of, and which sounded like a band, although she wouldn't have gambled too much on it. Arcade Fire could be a bloke for all she knew.

She was holding an Elvis record with a battered sleeve when there were footsteps from behind. Jennifer held it up for Pickle to see. 'My dad used to have this record,' she said. Records had been one of her father's few interests. He didn't have a passion for collecting, but would listen to the same half-a-dozen Elvis records over and over.

'Think I found that at a boot sale last summer,' Pickle said. He was now wearing ripped jeans, with a T-shirt that said 'Kenny Omega' on the front. Jennifer wondered if that was another singer she'd never heard of. 'Half of these are my dad's,' he added. 'He goes to all the boot sales, plus stays up late to bid on eBay at the last second. Mum told him she wanted it out of the house, so he asked if I could keep it here.'

'Is this your house?'

Jennifer tried not to sound surprised, although she didn't know many people in their young twenties who owned – or rented – entire houses.

'Used to be gran's,' he said. 'She left it to Mum in the will and I'm renting it from her.'

He said it with a hint of a smirk, although Jennifer couldn't tell if that meant he was fine, or annoyed, with the arrangement. She'd had to pay rent to her mum for living in her own room once she'd turned eighteen – and had been completely furious about it.

'Sorry to ask,' Jennifer said. 'I don't mean to be rude but did you say your name was Pickle?'

That got a bigger smirk. 'Mum and Dad called me Gordon, which doesn't sound much like a rock star's name, does it?'

Jennifer laughed at that, even though she wasn't sure that 'Pickle' sounded like a rock star's name, either. Still, she didn't know whether Arcade Fire were a band or a bloke; nor who Kenny Omega was.

'You're Daniel's mum...?' Pickle said. A question but not. What he really meant was 'Why are you here?'

Before she could answer, he added: 'Have they found him?'

'I don't think so. I was hoping to find him myself – or at least make sure he's safe.'

Jennifer couldn't read Pickle's expression. He didn't seem angry and there were still images of Daniel in some of the old posts on the band page. They hadn't tried to erase him from history and maybe that meant something.

'The police told me there was an argument between Ella and Daniel the night before she died,' Jennifer said. 'They reckoned it was in front of her band, something like that. I was hoping somebody knew what happened...?'

Pickle was still staring, now frowning.

'Sorry for intruding,' Jennifer added.

Pickle's brows dipped and he seemed somewhat confused. 'I told the police it *wasn't* an argument. Dan and El were writing a song and there was a minor disagreement about lyrics. *Definitely* not an argument. I don't know why they said that.'

Jennifer had an idea. It was the same one she'd had ever since the police had turned up on her doorstep. They were convinced Daniel had killed Ella and, because he was missing, weren't even considering any other theories. She'd felt those pangs of manipulation when Sergeant Sheridan had mentioned 'mother to mother'.

'They said she had a cut over her eye...'

Pickle snorted with a mix of what seemed like confusion and derision. He stretched to pick up a drumstick that had been sitting on a pile of records. 'She was trying to do this,' he said, before expertly walking the drumstick in one direction along his knuckles, then back the other way. 'She poked herself in the eye and Dan laughed so hard there was Coke coming out of his nose.' He waited a moment, then clarified: '*Coca-Cola*. I told the police all this.'

Jennifer was suddenly regretting the appeal video she had put out. Sheridan's manipulation felt apparent and calculated. With all the people she'd spoken to, as the mother of the apparent main suspect, she had expected to be turned away. But nobody from Ella's mother, to Daniel's housemate, to Ella's brother had been aggressive at all. None of them appeared to have any great suspicion or resentment for Daniel.

Pickle had slumped into one of the white garden chairs and Jennifer took another. He was staring at the floor and she felt the shift to melancholy. 'I just can't believe she's never gonna sing for the band again,' he said. 'We'd known each other forever 'cos we were in the same year at school. We even had music together, although I don't think we really talked back then. It was my band in the beginning – but that was mainly 'cos I had a drum kit and bass. Ollie had a guitar and his brother wanted a go at drumming. Ollie was well into stuff like the Stones because his granddad reckons he used to manage them, or something like that. We were just mucking around back then – until Ella joined.' He looked up with a shrug. 'She sort of made it *her* band but none of us really minded because nobody was coming to see us before she joined.'

'How long ago was that?'

Pickle puffed out a long, defeated breath. 'A few years. She was a bit, um... unreliable then. She'd miss practice and a few gigs. Then she left the band, then re-joined. We talked about splitting up properly, or finding a new singer. Than El got together with Dan and everything settled. I don't think she ever missed another day after that. Plus she and Dan started writing songs for us. I kept trying to get Dan to join the band, mainly 'cos he was better at playing than any of us, but he was happy writing and watching.'

That sounded like the Daniel that Jennifer knew. When she'd asked him why he was so interested in music as a career, but not in joining a band, he laughed that all the money was in the writing. She didn't think he was serious, nor that money particularly drove him. He liked being in the background.

'I called him "The Roadie",' Pickle said with a mischievous smile.

'Daniel?'

'Right. He'd help load our gear in and out, so he was The Roadie. He and El were a proper team. She was so much happier after he'd come along. We didn't make much from the pubs but she'd give her share away anyway.'

'Who to?'

'Homeless people, usually. She'd hand them cash, or pay for them to get into the hostel for the night. She was talking about us doing a mini charity one-day festival next summer, with some of the other local bands. I think she'd already worked out a space in a beer garden at the back of The Griffin.' A pause. 'Daniel really changed her.'

Jennifer took a breath, realising he was saying this for her benefit. The more she heard about Daniel and Ella as a couple, the more they seemed to bring out the best in one another. It felt borderline obscene that he'd been accused of killing her.

They sat for a moment, Pickle staring into nothingness, his lips pursed into an O, thinking.

'Can I tell you something?' he asked.

'Of course.'

'I didn't want to tell the police.'

'Tell them what?'

He took another breath and then he was staring at her. 'I think they found something.'

'Daniel and Ella?'

A nod. 'It's hard to explain unless you knew them. I mean, I know you *knew* them but—'

'I get it.'

And Jennifer did. A person was many things to many people. Friends could describe them one way; family another; workmates something else entirely.

'El and Dan came up with a chorus,' Pickle said. 'A couplet really. They were working on it last weekend when she cut herself. Something like, "You can't take what's been taken".' He screwed up his lips and then picked up his phone. After a moment of scrolling, he passed it to Jennifer.

There was a paused video and she pressed to play. It was dim but, from what she could see, Daniel and Ella were sitting in the corner of the practice garage, so close their knees were touching. Daniel was holding an acoustic guitar and he looked up as the person filming said 'Play us what you've got'. Daniel and Ella made momentary eye contact and then he started strumming. Ella waited a beat and then started to sing. She was tapping her foot, keeping time. Jennifer had to play the footage three times until she was almost certain she had the lyrics.

She recited them back to Pickle: 'You can't take what's been taken. You left it there, wasn't no break-in.'

'I think that's it,' he nodded. 'It felt real, like something they were actually going through. I don't know how to describe it, 'cos it was just a song. They wrote all kinds of things and I didn't think much about those but this time...'

Jennifer watched the video once more, before passing Pickle back his phone. She wanted to say she felt the same, that there was something authentic about the couplet, but it simply felt like a song to her. Except, she'd never seen her son and his girlfriend sitting in a corner working on lyrics or chords. A part of her yearned for Daniel. To see the young man he'd become while away from her.

'Do you have any idea what they might have found?' Jennifer asked.

A shake of the head. 'No idea. I don't even know if they found anything. Just that's the song they were working on the night before El died.'

'How long had they been working on that chorus?' Jennifer asked.

'Maybe a week? I don't know because they usually begin with something themselves and then bring it to the band when they're ready to hear if we can add anything. It might have been longer.'

Jennifer wished she could add more but it wasn't as if Daniel had been texting her every day to say what he was up to. 'Apart from the tutoring and band, can you think of anything else they used to do together?'

'Something to do with the church,' Pickle said. 'I think it's called The Mission.'

THIRTY-SEVEN

Jennifer was back sitting in her car, as she'd done so many times in the past few days. She was on the road outside Pickle's place, re-watching the video he'd sent. One part of her was convinced Daniel and Ella had found something, as Pickle had suggested, the other couldn't see it. Lyrics didn't have to mean something: John Lennon wasn't an Eggman, after all.

But maybe Pickle was right?

You can't take what's been taken. You left it there, wasn't no break-in.

They could've been singing about the cash that was in Daniel's locker. They'd found money that had been *left*? And then had written a song about it? It felt wildly unlikely. Who left that much cash lying around? But then Sergeant Sheridan had said Lance Williams had lost half a million that he'd left in a car which had been stolen. Was it *that* money?

Jennifer re-read the messages from the person she thought to be Daniel, although the longer she went without a reply, the less convinced she was about the identity. If it *was* Daniel, he hadn't given her a single piece of information to prove it was him. Perhaps somebody *wanted* her to think it was Gary who'd killed Ella?

She started the car and drove without any particular plan of where to go. Jennifer had a lot of puzzle pieces but didn't know what the main image was supposed to be. Pickle had mentioned The Mission and Jennifer considered returning. Though it felt as if something was off about the place, it could also be more to do with the people than the physical place. Besides, she'd already been there once and had no legitimate reason to return.

She suddenly remembered those missing posters of Ben Davies – and his connection to The Mission. Harriet had told Jennifer that Ben worked at their auction house. Jennifer hadn't been able to work out how or why Ben was connected to everything. He was the forgotten man in it all.

Before she knew it, Jennifer was driving around the narrow, winding roads that surrounded the docks. She'd somehow failed to notice before but everything was named after the ocean. There was Maritime Way and Sloop Drive. Port Place and… Anchor Row. Harriet had mentioned the auction house part of their business was based somewhere nearby. She was in an area with rows of looming warehouses on one side, plus stacked shipping containers behind a large fence on the other. Jennifer passed a lumber yard and then saw a sign for Etherington's Auctions that was pointing towards another warehouse.

Inside the warehouse and it was like a daytime TV show. Jennifer thought a lot of what she'd seen from auction houses might have been put on for the cameras but, if anything, the droning rat-a-tat of the guy at the front with the gavel was a walking, talking cliché. She watched for a few minutes as groups of men in heavy jackets nodded to signal bids on what appeared to be junk.

The auctioneer continued burbling at the front, while Jennifer mooched around the back of the draughty warehouse, looking for anything of interest. There was some sort of licensing document on the wall, with Gary's name, but – other than that – very little sign he was involved in the business. Harriet had said something about a manager running things while Gary focused on The Mission.

The auction continued as Jennifer wandered towards a row of shelves in front of a forklift. From everything she could see, it seemed as if a selection of landfill was being bought and sold. There was certainly no sign of anything that could help her find Daniel. No sense he had ever even been to this place. Nothing to do with the missing Ben Davies, either.

It had been a long shot.

Jennifer stepped back outside, though she didn't fancy driving so aimlessly again. Instead, she decided to walk aimlessly. She was on the far side of the water from where she'd set the trap with the tracker for Nick.

The familiar groan of cranes lifting containers seared through the otherwise stillness of the afternoon. She had never spent any time on this side of the water – and the same had been true of the housing estate that morning. It was amazing how a person could live in a town that wasn't that big and yet somehow only inhabit a small part of it.

Creeeeeeeeaaaaakkk.

Jennifer squinted up to the towering crane and could just about make out the dot of a man in a cabin.

She was following a different fence, realising she likely couldn't reach the water because the chain link ringed the entirety of the shipping area. Jennifer turned, trying to get her bearings, when she realised she was at the back of the auction house. She started to head back the way she'd come when she stopped to stare at the far smaller warehouse which backed onto the shipping yard. It was made of metal and probably the size of around three shipping containers. There were shutters at the front and Jennifer would have ignored it if not for the logo painted across the front.

She'd seen it before – and it took her a moment to realise where.

It was etched into the key she'd found in Daniel's locker.

THIRTY-EIGHT

Jennifer had to put her bag on the floor to properly hunt through it. There were receipts for lunches she'd bought years ago, which she had inexplicably kept. Somehow, the key she'd found in Daniel's locker had become buried at the very bottom, hidden under a brush and a small packet of tissues that had likely been there for a good decade.

The 'ID' logo was stencilled onto the centre of the warehouse shutters, with the letters stylised into one another. The square part of the key had the exact same emblem.

Jennifer repacked her bag, holding onto the key as she turned in a full circle, making sure nobody was watching. There was no one at ground level, though the crane soared on the other side of the fence. The man would still be in the cabin above, but she doubted he was too bothered with a single woman and a single building outside the shipping yard.

She strode across the crumbling tarmac towards the ID warehouse. The shutters were clamped to the floor with three massive padlocks – and Jennifer knew her key was the wrong shape to unlock those. The actual door was around to the side, hidden from the crane and whoever might be in it.

Her heart was thundering once more as Jennifer slipped the key into the lock. She half expected to be wrong, that the lock wouldn't turn – but there was no resistance. The key turned easily and then the door popped inwards. There was no light inside and, even from Jennifer's first echoing steps on a hard floor, the space felt empty.

Jennifer was blinking, trying to get her bearings, as the door clicked closed behind her, leaving her in a chasm of darkness.

'Daniel...?'

Jennifer had felt drawn here. This was what she'd expected when returning to Ashington. She had wanted to find her son, even though all she had was gut feeling. She'd craved this moment and – finally – it had come.

He was here.

'Daniel...?'

Jennifer's voice echoed around the solid floor and metal walls. It felt even colder than outside.

She'd taken a few steps, though stopped when her toe touched something solid.

'Daniel...?'

He wasn't answering – but surely he had to be hiding here? It was the perfect place: hidden from sight, where very few people would seemingly ever go?

Jennifer backed away from whatever she'd touched, returning to the door, where she fumbled around the nearby wall. She was looking for a light switch. Instead, there was a pulley like the one that used to be in the bathroom when Jennifer was growing up. She didn't know when they'd gone out of fashion.

She yanked it and dim yellow light flooded from above, leaving Jennifer again blinking to try to get her bearings. She was expecting to see her son in front of her, arms open, asking how she'd found him, except...

It was a car on which Jennifer had clipped her toe. An

expensive car. Jennifer didn't know much about models but it was a sleek BMW that looked more or less new. It felt so out of place given she was standing in a rusting building sandwiched between a fence and a larger warehouse. She could almost have believed it was an unusual parking space if not for the second vehicle on the other side. That was a glossy silver, some sort of SUV that also looked close to new.

Jennifer walked around the cars, neither of which had numberplates. There was nothing else in the enclosed space, and certainly not Daniel. Why would someone be storing expensive vehicles in such a run-down, anonymous building?

And then it seemed so obvious. There had been the posters at the police station, articles on the news website, and even Natasha had said it. The area was in the midst of a wave of car thefts.

She was looking at *stolen* vehicles.

Jennifer shivered slightly, suddenly feeling vulnerable, unsure why she'd been so certain Daniel would be here.

Why would her son have a key to this place? Was he involved with stealing cars? It felt so unlikely, mainly because he couldn't drive. He had shown no particular desire to learn, nor any real interest in vehicles. It had been football when he was much younger and then music as he found himself. Never cars or engines.

Jennifer walked a lap of the room, though the echoing rigidity now felt dangerous. The sort of people who'd steal cars were likely the sort who would not appreciate her having a key to their storage unit, let alone walking around it. She turned off the lights and quickly headed back outside, making sure the door clicked closed behind her. Jennifer needed to get away before someone saw her.

Except it was too late for that. Because, affixed to the building in front was a security camera pointing directly at her.

THIRTY-NINE

Jennifer froze. She wondered whether the camera was recording and someone would see her at a later time, or if it was live-streaming and somebody had already been alerted. Were people already on their way? She was going to have to call the police and explain everything, including Daniel's locker and the cash, if only to keep herself safe. She had to—

—It wasn't a real camera.

Jennifer moved closer until she was standing directly underneath, where she could see that there were no wires or connection points. It was the identical model to the one Andrew had attached above their front door. She'd been scornful of it then, probably still was, but it meant she knew a fake camera when she saw one.

Jennifer stopped and scanned for anything else that could have been watching – but there was nothing, no other cameras, not even any other fake ones. There was nobody around – which was precisely why it was such a good spot to hide stolen vehicles.

This time, Jennifer didn't hang about. She rushed around to the front of the storage unit and kept following the fence with her head down. She dashed past the pile of scrap metal and furniture, almost bursting back onto the pavement that ran next to Etherington's Auctions. She had parked a little past the auction house and was reaching into her bag, fumbling for yet more keys, when she looked up to see somebody all too familiar leaning against her driver's door.

Nick lowered his vape as Jennifer stopped a pace away. 'We need to talk,' he said.

FORTY

Jennifer was back in the car boot again, disorientated by the switch from dark to light, overwhelmed by the stench of fruity vape. The smell hung on Nick.

'I've got to get back,' Jennifer stumbled, desperately trying to think of a better excuse. 'Someone's waiting for me.'

Nick's expression didn't flinch. He returned the vape to a pocket and then hooked a hand underneath Jennifer's armpit to turn her around. It occurred so quickly that she almost didn't realise it had happened until she found herself facing the opposite direction.

Jennifer felt paralysed, partly from that lingering smell but also because it was impossible to distinguish Nick from his father who'd killed her friend.

'I need to go,' Jennifer found herself saying.

'Just walk,' Nick told her.

And Jennifer did, though it was hard to say why. She could try running for it, though doubted she would outpace him. She could shout for help, but, before that idea had come to her, she was already in an alley that threaded around the far side of Etherington's Auctions. Nick was walking almost to her side, perhaps half-a-pace behind, and though he was no longer touching her, Jennifer felt the weight of his presence. That day in the university canteen with Craig and the knife felt so close, even though she was a different person then. She wondered where her confidence had gone because it felt a long way off.

Jennifer was looking for someone, anyone. She would catch their eye, maybe even ask for help outright, but there was nobody in sight. Jennifer couldn't hear anything over the whining groan of the cranes.

She realised as they walked that, if she'd headed around the other side of the auction house, it would have been a short walk to the water. She would have never found those stolen vehicles – but she'd have found the view of the town for which she was searching.

Not that she could appreciate it now.

The town soared on the far side of the water and Jennifer could almost make out the area where she'd had her last meeting with Nick. They were on another tight path that clung to a narrow wall which traced the water's edge.

Nick clutched Jennifer under the armpit once more, grumbling a terse 'here' as she stopped and pulled away. Her chance to run for it had gone, given it was a minute or so back to the auction house – and there was nothing else of note in sight. No dog walkers, no joggers, no anyone: just her and Nick, standing alone in the searing wind as a nearby crane groaned.

'Where's Daniel?' Nick asked, firmly.

Jennifer stared at Nick, though she was really staring at his father. Nick was now around the same age that Craig had been when he'd ambushed Jennifer near her house. That was why she felt so helpless around him. She'd stumbled through time and was facing the monster who stole her friend's life. This was her nightmare and she was now living it.

'I know you know,' he added.

Jennifer tried to answer but her throat was dry and the words a croak: 'Why do you want him?'

'You don't need to know that. I know you have Ben's phone, so Daniel *must* have given it to you. So where is he?'

Jennifer needed a moment to take it all in. Nick had obviously known about the phone, because he had trapped her near that park hut. But it was *Ben's* phone? The guy who'd been missing for a year? That meant Jennifer had the missing man's phone *and* driving licence.

It also meant Nick had no idea about Daniel's locker.

Jennifer flicked a glance over Nick's shoulder, checking for a sign that anyone might be coming to help. Nobody was.

'How do you know I have that phone?' she asked. It was still in the bag she was carrying, though Nick made no motion to look for it.

Instead, he stared and Jennifer was back on that street, near her house, trying to hide from Nick's father behind the lamp post.

He wasn't going to say it, so Jennifer did: 'I know you're the one who put me in the car boot. You thought I was Daniel because I was wearing his hoody.'

Nick's eyebrow twitched a fraction, though he didn't seem particularly surprised she had figured it out. He certainly didn't deny any of it.

'Why do you want him?' Jennifer repeated, sounding far bolder than she felt.

'He'll know why – so where is he?'

Jennifer tried to stare Nick down, though knew he must be able to hear her stomach growling, maybe even her heart beating.

'I don't know,' Jennifer said – and it was the truth.

Nick stepped towards her and Jennifer moved back – but the only way to go was towards the water. He was so big there was no way around him. She peeped backwards to the rippling black of the water beyond. It was a fair drop and there were rocks directly below.

'Last chance,' Nick said, still advancing.

The back of Jennifer's heels were pressed to the wall, with only the rocks and the filthy water beyond.

'I hope you can swim,' he said.

FORTY-ONE

Nick's pudgy fingers were already pressing into Jennifer's shoulder. She could feel the pinch. The *squeeze*.

Jennifer screamed as best she could, though it was caught somewhere in her throat. She tensed and readied herself, knowing there was little she could do except anticipate the fall. She wondered whether the rocks would hurt, or if she'd miss them and hit the water. Would that hurt more? Would she break something? Would she keep consciousness? Would someone hear her shouting? Would she wake up somewhere out to sea? Would it kill her? Would it be instant? Or—

Nick froze and then his grip loosened. For a moment, Jennifer thought it was because of her gargled scream... except there were footsteps that boomed even over the now distant creak of a crane.

Suddenly, Nick had released her and stepped away, leaving a space in which Jennifer could see the shape of a man with his hands in the pockets of a long coat. Jennifer had seen him before – first when he was upstairs in the pub, then when he was watching Callum outside the church. This was the third time Lance Williams had been unruffled by the scene playing out in front of him.

He was focused on Jennifer and she noticed the deepness of his brown eyes as he held her within them.

'Are you OK?' he asked, in a deep, calming voice.

'Um... yes.'

Nick had taken another couple of steps away, apparently cowed by the other man, who stooped and picked up Jennifer's bag. It was splayed on the ground, though she didn't remember dropping it.

'I think this is yours,' he said.

Jennifer took it, though could barely grip the handles because she was shaking. She hadn't noticed that, either.

'Are you sure you're all right?' he asked.

'I don't know.'

That got a nod from Lance, and it seemed like he'd witnessed everything that had just happened.

'Jennifer, isn't it?' His voice was composure personified.

She almost replied 'I don't know' to that, too, but managed a croaked 'Yes.' She was trying to remember what Sergeant Sheridan had said about him but everything was a fuzz. She looped her bag onto her arm and then gripped one hand with the other, trying to stop it shaking.

Nick had been backing away but stopped when Lance's gaze found him. 'This one owes me money,' Lance said.

That was it.

Sheridan had told Jennifer that Lance's car had been stolen a year back and that it had half a million inside. He was a drugs trafficker, albeit Sheridan said she couldn't prove it. Jennifer tried to remember the makes of the cars she'd seen minutes before in the lock-up behind the auction house. Perhaps one of them was his?

'What are you talking about?' Nick said, although it felt like he was choosing a careful tone. There was no threat or spite in his voice.

'I know you're the one who stole my car,' Lance told him. 'We can even forget that – but I want what was in the back.'

Jennifer looked between the two men. They were more or less the same height and build and yet there was almost an illusion that made Lance seem both bigger and taller. There was no question who was in charge.

Nick took a pace back but Lance followed.

'That wasn't me,' Nick said. 'There's this guy, Callum—'

'Oh, I've been watching him, too. Don't you worry about that. It took a long time to crack onto him. He might be good at nicking cars – but he's not clever enough to have stolen from me and kept his mouth shut. If he'd taken what you did, he wouldn't be asking strangers for cash, or dealing Adderall to idiots.'

Jennifer winced a fraction. She was one of those strangers. Plus, Callum was a car thief... but he hadn't taken Lance's? That was, presumably, why Lance had been watching him. He'd been wondering if Ella's brother was busy spending the half a million.

'It wasn't me,' Nick said – and Jessica shivered at his tone. Daniel had told her those identical words on the phone but they had felt real from him. This was more in fear.

'Yes it was,' came the unconvinced reply – and Lance spoke so forcefully that Jennifer believed him, even though she had no idea whether it was true. Lance certainly thought it was. She wondered how he knew. 'I want back what you took,' Lance added. 'And, if I don't get it by this time tomorrow, I won't be so polite next time.'

There was a momentary stare-off, though Nick broke it almost instantly. Lance shifted his weight and then stepped back, apparently ready to head back to wherever he'd come from.

'Do you know my son?' Jennifer surprised herself by managing to speak. She was still holding hands with herself, trying to stop trembling.

Lance's gaze rolled across her and Jennifer felt herself wilting. There was such steel in him. 'You keep popping up,' he said.

'I'm looking for my son, Daniel. They say he killed his girl-friend and he's been missing since Monday. Do you know him?'

Lance glanced to Nick and then back to Jennifer. She felt so certain he was going to say yes, that she readied herself to hear something she probably didn't want to know. There was all that money in Daniel's locker, after all.

'I don't know your son,' he said – and it was both a relief and a crushing disappointment. Jennifer didn't want Daniel to be mixed up in whatever this was, yet she was so hoping Lance was going to say he knew Daniel – and where he was. 'The first time I heard his name was on the news the other morning.'

He stepped away, licked his lips and then turned back to Nick, thinking.

'Don't let me see you within a hundred yards of this woman again,' he said. 'Do you hear me?'

Nick gave a meek nod, though didn't make eye contact with anything other than the floor. Given the fear Jennifer had felt not long before, Nick now seemed so pathetic. A threat to nobody, certainly not her, regardless of who his father was.

'Don't forget what I said,' Lance added. 'One day. You know where to find me, don't you?'

Nick nodded again but was like a cowed puppy that had just been kicked.

Lance gave one final glance between the pair of them – and then spun and strode off into the distance.

FORTY-TWO

Jennifer was in her car again. She'd driven away sharpish from the auction house and found a quiet spot at the back of a car park near a supermarket. Her car had become a primary living space in the time since she'd left home in that mad panic, determined to find out what was going on with her son.

She had to remind herself that Lance Williams was apparently a bad guy.

But he had definitely saved her. Not only that, when Jennifer had mustered up the will to head back to her car, when she'd forced her legs to work, Nick hadn't followed. Lance had warned him to stay away from her and she was certain he would.

She wondered if Nick truly had stolen Lance's car, and the money contained within. Even if he hadn't, Lance definitely thought he had – and that felt like a dangerous situation for Nick to be in.

'He's a baddie,' Jennifer told herself, out loud this time, although he didn't feel like it. If it wasn't for Lance Williams, Jennifer could have been killed.

She wondered if that money in Daniel's locker actually

belonged to Lance Williams. If it did, then how had it ended up with her son?

Daniel.

Jennifer had arrived in Ashington more than two days before and still had no idea where her son was. The only thing that made her feel even marginally better was that the police hadn't found him either. From nowhere, she remembered when he'd been five or six, desperate for entertainment. They'd been at home and she'd told him to hide, before giving a long count to a hundred while she got on with cleaning the kitchen. Eventually, she had set off to look for him, assuming he'd be in a cupboard, or under a bed, giggling to himself.

He was nowhere. She had taken forty-five minutes to not find him, before shouting that she gave up. He eventually unfurled himself from an inconceivably small space within the sofa where he had somehow hid himself.

That memory had been a long time gone but it was suddenly back as she figured he was always good at hiding.

Too good.

Jennifer checked her phone once more, first looking at her old messages from Daniel's actual number, wondering if he might have mentioned somewhere he liked spending time. She'd already checked more than once – and this time was no different. There was nothing.

That left her looking at the exchanges with the o7 number, where she wavered from being convinced it was her son, to telling herself it definitely wasn't.

She read back the entire thread from the initial 'It's me, Mum', through to the most recent reply, in which she'd been asked to leave town. Nothing had come through since, no matter how many times Jennifer had asked where he was.

Was it Daniel? If it was, he'd said that 'they' would try to hurt her to find him and, if not for Lance, that's what would have happened.

It had to be him. Didn't it?

Jennifer yawned and looked over the steering wheel towards a woman who was hurrying away from the supermarket towards her car. In one hand, she was holding a shopping bag, in the other she was clutching a young boy, who couldn't be older than four or five. Jennifer remembered those days but they felt so far away now.

Why wouldn't Daniel simply tell her where he was?

Jennifer re-read the texts once more, battling another yawn. She didn't know what to do next. Didn't know if it was worth staying in town.

And then she saw it. It was right there in his messages, hidden in the plainest of plain sights.

He *had* told her where he was.

FORTY-THREE

Jennifer waited until it was dark, forgetting that the streets would be full of trick-or-treating children. She was parked on a side street, not too far from where Daniel lived, watching as groups trotted up and down, filling buckets with sweets. Costumes ranged from Marvel to Disney characters, from shop-bought, a simple hat, to – very occasionally – something in which someone had invested a lot of time.

She didn't think she had been followed and doubted Nick would dare, given the fear in his eyes when Lance had told him to leave her alone. Even so, Jennifer still did three long, slow laps of the surrounding streets, stopping behind walls to check nobody was following, and once taking five minutes to slip into a corner shop and wait to see if anyone trailed her inside.

It wasn't as if she was an expert, and Jennifer figured she wasn't going to spot some specialist tracker anyway, but there was nobody obvious. And there were so many children around that she felt safe among them.

Jennifer was shivering by the time she reached the place to which she'd been heading the very long way around. The night was cold, the sky clear, moon bright. She passed the 'keep out' signs and kept following the fence until she reached a corner where one panel met another. At one time, there would have likely been some sort of clamp joining them together but Jennifer quickly realised they were simply leaning one against the other. Her hands were trembling, from the cold this time, as she shifted the corners apart, allowing a space for her to squeeze inside.

The moon was so bright that Jennifer was temporarily exposed, as if it was the middle of the day. She darted across the rubble-strewn land, hurrying to a space near a skip where shadows stretched long.

Then she waited.

Jennifer hunched low, hiding in shadows, watching the gap in the fence through which she had squished herself. After the encounter with Nick at the docks, she knew for sure he had been trailing her in an attempt to find her son – and there was no way she could let that happen now.

She waited some more, until her face was so cold that her jaw ached. Her hands were jammed deep into her pockets, though her fingers burned from the chill. How was it so cold in October?

Jennifer risked a glance at her phone, letting it light up her face momentarily to see that she'd been watching the corner of the fencing for almost twenty minutes.

Nobody came. She'd not been followed.

Jennifer edged out from her spot next to the skip, slipping on a crumbling brick and rolling her ankle sideways. She gasped to herself, covering her mouth and returning to her spot. Jennifer tested her weight on the ankle, feeling gentle twinges of pain but not enough to stop her walking.

This time, she avoided the pile of bricks, following the building, looking for a way in. She saw it within seconds. An old fire escape door had been boarded up but, from up close, it was easy to see that the boards were now leaning against the frame.

Jennifer gave herself a moment and checked the text one more time, even though she'd looked at it probably a hundred times since her revelation outside the supermarket.

I cab't say

Jennifer had assumed it was a typo – 'b' was next to 'n' on a keyboard, after all. Except Daniel was far cleverer than that. He would have been concerned about the police or someone seeing those messages and didn't want to give himself away. They would have seen a typo, too, except it wasn't.

Because, when Jennifer was a first-year student, she'd lived in Cabot Halls – one of six blocks that were due for demolition. All were fenced off, out of bounds, and, within weeks, would be piles of bricks.

Daniel had always known where she'd lived when she'd been a student – and he'd told her where he was.

I cab't say

Jennifer slipped into the remnants of her youth, eking the boards back into place and dousing herself in darkness. There was a gritty, dusty smell in the clogged air and she gave her eyes a few seconds to adjust to the gloom. She knew this place.

There were bedrooms on five or six floors above, but there was a large rec room on the ground. She was standing in it again, for the first time in twenty-five years, drinking in the blinkered memories of who she once was.

There used to be a pool table, its baize dotted with cigarette burns – but that was seemingly long gone. So were the sofas on which drunken couples shared their late-night/early-morning snogs and who knew what more. Instead, there was a hollowed-out shell of a space, littered with dust, a shattered table or three, and what looked like a pile of a dozen or so ripped-out shower units.

Shreds of moonlight crept through the boarded-up windows as Jennifer gazed across the building site. There was a whispering silence, in which she could hear only her own breathing... and then a skittering titter. A minuscule squeak. Jennifer sensed movement, though saw nothing, which was when her mind began to wander.

Rats.

A place like this was bound to be home to some sort of rodent. She grimaced at the thought and then blew into her hands, trying to get some degree of warmth into herself.

'Hello...?'

Jennifer flashed back to earlier in the day and another darkened space in which she'd called out. There had been almost new cars there but no sign of life. Here felt different.

'Hello...?'

Her voice echoed around the space and, as her eyes continued to adjust, Jennifer noticed the twisted, crumpled bedframes and chairs. Someone had dumped a load of broken furniture at one end of the old rec room, back where the sink and fridge used to be. Jennifer could still picture the bin that was constantly overflowing with beer cans, even though it was also gone.

The light from Jennifer's phone barely penetrated farther than her feet. There were charcoaled embers in a ring, close to a chair leg, that looked as if someone had tried to start a fire at some point.

Creeeeeeeeeeakkkk.

The sound echoed through the cluttered room, stretching from the hall beyond. Jennifer knew it was an entranceway, where their mailboxes had once been, along with various passive-aggressive notes about people not wiping their feet and clumping mud through the hall. There were stairs leading up to the bedrooms, and would always be someone playing music too loudly. There was always one. There would always be one.

They were ghosts of the past, though the chittering scuttle of what sounded like tiny feet definitely wasn't ethereal.

Jennifer continued slowly across the rec room, following the creak. The mailboxes were still where they used to be, though the locking plate at the front was gone, leaving only a series of pigeonholes. She stared towards them, suddenly doubting herself.

What if the text actually *had* been a typo? What if it had not even been from Daniel?

There was another groan of movement, though the feet weren't tiny this time.

Jennifer turned, too late, because someone was upon her. She flashed back to the street, when Nick had bundled her into the boot, holding up her arms to protect herself, while screeching a small cry of alarm.

Except this person didn't grab for her. There was no smell of fruity vape, only ingrained cigarettes that sent her spiralling back to the days when her mum would lean out the kitchen window to smoke.

A man was standing near where the stairs were. He had a tatty beard, with overgrown eyebrows, and was wearing heavy boots, with a heavier coat.

'What are you doing?' he asked.

He was probably a little older than Jennifer, though it was hard to tell through the gloom.

'I'm looking for my son,' Jennifer said.

'Ain't nothing here for you here, lady,' he replied. The man was chewing on something, or perhaps trying to clear something from between his teeth. She couldn't quite see his eyes through the shadows and it was hard to tell whether he meant it as a threat.

'I just—'

'Ain't nothing here for you.'

It was louder this time. Firmer. A definite threat.

'You should leave the way you got in and forget you ever knew about this place.'

When he stepped towards her, there was a crunch of broken glass under his boot. Jennifer moved backwards, heading towards the door that led back into the rec room.

'You tell anyone you were here?' the man asked – and Jennifer suddenly wondered why he was asking. Was he concerned this refuge might be discovered, or was he wondering whether someone was outside waiting for her? Because if nobody knew where she was...

'I'm leaving,' Jennifer said, as she backed into the rec room. Her foot clipped a mangled chair leg, making her ankle twinge from where she'd gone over on it earlier. She gasped and held onto a broken table, hopping momentarily, as the shadowed man continued towards her. He wasn't speaking now but she could hear the heavy croak of his throat.

Jennifer turned, wondering if her ankle would allow her to run for it, but there was another shuffling movement, another shadow coming into the light. Someone in front of her, someone behind. She was cornered, trapped, with nowhere to go.

The panic began to ripple but then a new voice spoke calmly through the night. 'It's fine, Kev. This is my mum.'

FORTY-FOUR

Jennifer turned to see Daniel standing barely a step away in the rec room. She wasn't sure where he'd come from but he was smiling gently as a crisp shard of moonlight slipped across his face.

'Hi, Mum.'

Jennifer had never seen him as anything but clean-shaven – but a dotted, fluffy beard had formed around his mouth. His eyelids were low, gaze unfocused, looking as tired as she'd felt for the best part of three days.

And then he was upon her, burying his face in her shoulder. She clasped his back as best she could, pulling him in and holding, never ceasing to be amazed by how her tiny baby boy had grown into a man. His warm breath melted her shoulder as Jennifer patted his back gently. She only realised his eyes were wet when he let her go.

'This is Kevin,' Daniel said, indicating the man who'd told her to leave. He was watching them curiously from a few paces away and seemed younger in the new light.

'Hi,' Jennifer managed.

'He's been looking after me,' Daniel added.

'Nah, it's the other way around,' Kevin said. His tone was different now, much lighter than when she'd thought he might be weighing up whether she had someone waiting for her.

'This way,' Daniel said, taking Jennifer's hand and guiding her towards the other end of the rec room. They passed the wretched pile of shattered furniture, ducking under an upturned beam and through a door about which Jennifer had forgotten. She lived one side of Cabot Hall and always took the same steps to leave – but there was another entrance at the other end, with half a dozen or so ground-floor flats.

Daniel led her into another, cluttered, corridor – and then into one of the old student bedrooms.

Jennifer stood in the doorway, reeling from the familiarity. She may have lived a few floors up, but the layout of the room was identical. The small radiator underneath the window, the dresser along one wall, bed on the other. She pictured her own room, even though none of the furniture was left in here. Instead, there was a pile of... *something* on the floor, next to Daniel's rucksack.

'Curtains,' he said, answering the question she hadn't asked.

'Is this where you've been sleeping?' Jennifer asked.

'Yeah...'

The only light came from a crack in the wooden boards that were in place of the windows. Jennifer could taste the damp and she felt her heart shattering at the idea her son had been reduced to this.

She must have sighed without meaning to, because Daniel offered a solemn: 'It's safe.'

Jennifer pictured the warning signs outside and how it might be secure in the moment – but that it would be flat in a month.

Daniel had sat on his pile of curtains and Jennifer wasn't

sure whether to follow. She wanted to touch him, make sure he was real.

'You look tired,' she said.

That got a snort of disbelieving laughter. 'You reckon?' He ruffled his hair and batted away a yawn, almost as if his body wanted to show her how right she was.

Suddenly, Daniel was on his feet.

'I'll get you a chair,' he said.

It was as if he was a child again, suddenly remembering his manners. Before Jennifer could say anything, he had slipped past her into the hall. Moments later and he was back with two plastic chairs. He placed them both next to his makeshift bed and then yawned loudly as he slumped into one.

Jennifer sat in the other, watching him as best she could given the murk. 'Are you OK?' she asked.

He might have shrugged, though it was hard to tell. 'Sort of. I can't sleep. Keep seeing Ella on my bed.'

Jennifer almost reminded him that she'd once seen a young woman dead on a bed. Not the time, though.

'I had to turn off my proper phone,' he said. 'They can track SIM cards, something like that. I borrowed Kev's phone to text you. He'd shown me your video but there's no electricity here, so you can't charge stuff. He goes out during the day and uses a plug in the Asda Café. I couldn't keep messaging you, 'cos it's not my phone. I did wonder if you'd get my clue...'

There was the merest hint of a smile, though it disappeared almost immediately.

'I got it,' she said, even though it had taken a while.

'I didn't know if someone was watching your phone, or intercepting the messages. I don't know how it works. I wanted them to think you were going home, maybe I wanted you to as well.'

He sighed and yawned once more, his entire body sagging.

'I visited Ella's mum,' Jennifer said. She'd thought about this moment, trying to consider what Daniel would want to hear. 'She doesn't think you did anything wrong.'

Daniel was already somewhat slumped, but now his entire body slipped forward until he was on his knees. From nowhere, Jennifer's little boy was sobbing into his hands.

Jennifer tried to comfort him, though he didn't want it. The only person he wanted was the one he'd found on his bed. Jennifer sat at his side, resting a hand on his back and letting him cry.

Daniel and Ella were so young. Maybe they would have broken up at some point, maybe not. But to lose a girlfriend in the way Daniel had was so far outside the natural order. Tears over a girl should be because she'd dumped him; for some normal, everyday reason. Not because she was dead. It was so cruel.

Time passed, it didn't matter how long.

When he was sitting up again, he spoke: 'You should have gone. It's not safe in town.'

'I've done OK for myself.'

Jennifer knew that wasn't quite true. Nick had shoved her in a car boot and then, later, she'd needed an accused drugs trafficker to save her. Just now, she'd felt unsafe when she wasn't sure of Kevin's intentions.

'Have you met Gary?' Daniel asked.

'He was almost the first person I met when I got here. I was trying to figure out what happened and I had your old messages about tutoring. I traced it back to him, then knocked on his door.'

There was a breathy, curious pause. 'Did he ask where I was?'

'I can't remember but I think so. Nick asked, too.'

Daniel didn't react, as if he knew as much. She didn't tell him about the tracker on her car. That might be for another day.

'Gary killed Ella,' Daniel said quietly – and she believed him.

'Do you want to tell me what happened?'

Jennifer had no expectations and would have settled for simply sitting in silence. It was enough, for now, that Daniel was safe.

But then he told her anyway.

FORTY-FIVE

Daniel took his time laying out everything that had happened, or at least the parts he knew.

It had started innocently enough. He and Ella were looking for ways to make money that didn't involve one of them working in a call centre, stacking shelves, working in a bookies', or serving drunks. 'Not that there's anything wrong with that,' he added humourlessly.

Jennifer knew what he meant. There wasn't anything wrong with any of it – but that didn't mean people *wanted* to do those jobs.

Ella was making money from the band, but not much, and she was giving most of it to charity or homeless people anyway. Daniel had shrugged at that, not quite disapproving but perhaps not understanding, either. It wasn't as if they were rich.

He had set up the tutoring website, advertised with posters, plus on local Facebook pages, and even had something on Mumsnet, until it got removed. Gary had approached them after they'd asked to put up a poster at The Mission. He told them his son was introverted and had trouble making friends – but he was also very interested in music.

Charles was their first student, although Daniel winced a fraction at the mention of the word. 'Student' made it sound a lot more formal than it was. Probably made him feel old, too, which allowed Jennifer a gentle smile. She knew that feeling.

As the weeks passed, Ella and Daniel had been tutoring Charles a couple of times a week – and it was as both Gary and Harriet had said: the boy had started to open up. Not only did he love Ella and Daniel but they were enamoured with him. He'd write them little songs in their days apart and had started to understand how rhymes worked.

'He always tried to get the word "fart" into songs,' Daniel said with a smile. It was apparently the funniest word imaginable. Jennifer had to remind her son that there was a time in which he also thought trumping was the funniest thing imaginable.

From there, Ella and Daniel would often be asked to hang around past the tutoring time. An hour here, ninety minutes there. Gary and Harriet would say they were out working at The Mission, though Daniel didn't know if that was true. Gary would pay the full rate, so they acted as glorified – well-paid – babysitters, often putting Charles to bed when it was time.

Almost two weeks before, Daniel and Ella had been at Gary and Harriet's house doing the same thing they'd been doing for months. The parents were out, so they had spent an hour working on songs and music with Charles – or as well as his attention span would allow – then they had let him play on his iPad for a bit, before putting him to bed.

Except, on that night, Charles had fallen asleep. Rather than wake him, or try to carry him, Ella and Daniel had left him dozing on the sofa. Ella had picked up his guitar to take it upstairs but returned a few minutes later, eyes wide, mouth open. Daniel had never seen her so panicked and confused. She told him to 'come look' and then led him up to Charles' bedroom.

They had been inside many times before. The walls were decorated with prints and stickers of Marvel characters and he had a Spider-Man duvet. A giant box of Lego sat in one corner, underneath a desk on which there was an iPad charger. Each of them had sat in the room, reading Charles a story before bed.

But, on that evening, as Daniel entered behind his girl-friend, the rug had been pulled back and the giant box of Lego was on the other side of the room. Ella said she'd been walking across the room to put the guitar on the rack near the window when it felt as if her foot went through the floor. She was worried she'd broken something, so pulled back the rug to make sure. At first she couldn't see anything wrong. The floorboards were all in place – except, when she looked closer, she realised one of the boards was loose, with no nails in the gaping holes. She showed Daniel, then lifted the board to reveal what she had found.

Cash.

Lots of it.

Daniel said her eyes had sparkled as she'd plucked the bundles of used notes from the space and started to count. Within seconds she'd said she was holding five-thousand pounds. It was more than either of them had ever had in an account, definitely more than they had ever seen as cash. As they both looked into the gap under the floorboards, they could see there was so much more money there.

Before Daniel could say anything, Ella was pulling out more of the cash. He wasn't averse, either. They removed bundle after bundle, until Ella found a sealed sandwich bag, buried among the notes. She opened it, holding up a driving licence that belonged to Ben Davies. They knew him, though not well. He helped out at The Mission, as did Ella on occasion. He'd been to a few of her gigs and she was sure he fancied her. He had tried to start a brawl with Daniel in a beer garden one evening, saying Daniel would fight for his girlfriend if he was a real man. Before anything could happen, they'd both been thrown out, even though Daniel hadn't done anything.

Or that's what he said. Jennifer sensed there might have been a little more that he was keeping back. He'd been drinking and someone had been goading him by saying Ella was too good for him. Jennifer didn't think her son was violent but she could imagine that there were words exchanged at the very least.

Either way, not long after that, Ben had disappeared. Yet, more than a year later, they had found his driving licence in a sandwich bag, hidden among a pile of cash that was stashed underneath a child's bedroom floor. There was a phone in the bag, too, although it was turned off. They'd tried turning it on but it was out of battery.

Jennifer already knew the final item that had been in the bag, though she didn't let on that she'd visited Daniel's locker. She let him tell her they'd found a key.

Daniel had been curious about Ben's driving licence as Ella kept pulling things out from under the floorboards. Underneath the cash were rows of number plates, all lined up. She'd removed one but there were so many more there.

And there was so much money.

They had sat together on Charles' floor, asking one another what was going on. What they'd found. It probably should have been obvious but it took Ella googling the number plate. She found a Facebook post from a nearby town, in which someone said their Range Rover had been stolen from their driveway. They'd listed the plate and asked people to look out for it. Daniel and Ella both knew that stolen vehicles was a problem in the area. There were always news stories about it, plus someone Ella's mum knew had woken up to find her year-old Ford taken from her driveway. They had been in town the week before when the police were giving some sort of awareness training in a car park about vehicle security.

By that point, they were both thinking the same: that Gary,

Harriet, or Nick were involved with all the thefts. Maybe all three of them. It felt wildly unlikely and yet there was so much evidence at their feet.

And so much money.

It was hard for them to have any degree of a normal conversation when they were sitting next to something so flabbergasting. So incredible.

Daniel said they should put it back, but he didn't make the first move and neither did Ella. They just sat.

But then there had been a noise from downstairs. They had looked to one another because Charles was supposed to be asleep on the sofa, and then Daniel had rushed to check on him. The boy was in the kitchen, groggily trying to open the fridge and get himself a drink. By the time Daniel had poured him something and cleared up, Ella was back downstairs, saying it was fine to put him to bed.

Daniel knew what she'd done. He hadn't wanted to ask but he knew. A part of him was even glad. He was picturing a proper place of their own, not simply that room in the shared house, where the walls were thin, where the ceilings creaked. He thought they could buy new instruments for her band, maybe even book their own venues, and have some time in a recording studio. They wouldn't go crazy, that wasn't their way, it could really help. He thought all that, while knowing Ella would want to give most of it away.

But he said nothing.

When Gary and Harriet had got home not long afterwards, they were as flustered and apologetic as ever. They said they'd been at The Mission, and maybe they had – except Daniel saw them in a different light than he had before.

Gary paid them extra for the inconvenience of them being late. Daniel had felt guilty about taking additional money in the past but he didn't say no that time, knowing they could definitely afford it.

Gary offered them a lift home, as he had many times before. Daniel would have accepted but Ella said no. She told him it was a nice night, that they'd walk, even though it wasn't and Daniel knew for a fact she didn't want to walk that far.

But she lugged her bag onto her back and Daniel watched her pretend it wasn't so much heavier than when they'd arrived.

Gary didn't seem to notice. He thanked them, saying he'd see them the following week.

And so they left – and they were only at the corner when Ella stopped to sit on the wall. It was cold and she told Daniel she was sorry. Then she unzipped the bag to reveal what Daniel already knew was there. She said she'd taken as much of the money as would fit – and asked him to carry the bag because it was too heavy.

It was *so* heavy.

But they walked and they talked about their dreams and their hopes. She wanted them to get a place together. She wanted to book some studio time for the band, and maybe get Pickle a new guitar. She wanted to give her mum a bit at a time, perhaps even convince her to leave Collier Tower, even though she doubted she would. And, of course, she wanted to give away as much as possible, without making it too obvious. Give a hundred quid to a homeless person here, maybe drop off a thousand in the mailbox for the food bank in town.

Definitely nothing to The Mission.

They swapped the bag from his shoulders to hers a couple of times but Daniel carried it most of the way.

They lived in a fantasy world for an hour. Daniel hadn't known it, but Jennifer did as she listened to him explain. They were young and in love. They had good intentions but there was no way any of that was going to happen, even if for a wondrous, joyous, time they'd convinced themselves it would.

A catastrophe was coming.

By the time they'd reached Daniel's house, they were

convinced they were in the clear. They counted the money on his bed and there was a fraction under ninety-thousand pounds. Ella had also packed the sandwich bag with Ben's driving licence, the key and the phone. They immediately put that on to charge. Ella was going to turn it on but Daniel said not to do it in the house, in case someone was tracking it. He'd check it somewhere else. When he'd done that later the next day, he'd realised there were no contacts, messages, or anything that could identify it – so he'd turned it off again.

Jennifer knew some of the next bit, not that she told her son. Later that night, early the next morning, really, they had lugged that rucksack to his locker – and stuffed everything inside. They'd returned to his house, backs aching, with an empty bag, and at least some of the potential consequences had started to dawn.

Ella had asked what would happen if Gary found out they had taken the money. Neither of them knew, though it would be hard for him to be certain it was them. Daniel said that if they'd stolen the money, Gary and Harriet could hardly report it as stolen. At the time he thought it was from selling stolen cars, even though he wasn't sure why it would be *actual* cash.

Jennifer was ahead of him at that point. She knew whose money it was. There had been half a million in the back of Lance Williams' car when it was taken and, somehow, it seemed, from everything Daniel was saying, that cash was underneath the floor of the boy he'd been tutoring.

Not that she said any of that either. It wasn't her story to tell, not yet anyway – and she could sense from the speed at which her son was speaking that he'd been desperate to get it out.

On the night they had taken the money, Daniel and Ella had sat up, almost until the sun had risen. They wondered what might have happened to Ben, though it seemed ominous he hadn't been seen in a year. They both suggested going to the police with the licence and telling them where they'd found it... Except there was all that money. Plus what would the police do? And how could either of them prove they'd found the licence where they said? They were kids, while Gary was an elder at the church and ran a charity.

As they talked, at one point, Ella had said that they couldn't take what had already been taken, and Daniel said it sounded like a lyric. They ended the evening as they had so many others, with Daniel quietly strumming some simple chords, while Ella sang her new lyrics.

There was so much money.

But they left it for much of the next week. Daniel told nobody and Ella said she'd kept it to herself, too. They had dreams of better days but they had to take their time. Make sure they weren't under suspicion... and the first part of that was to head back to Gary and Harriet's for another tutoring session one week later.

'Last Monday,' Daniel said, hauntingly, ominously.

He was nervous, he explained, his stomach twisting in the way Jennifer's had so often that week. Ella had sounded breezy and confident but he'd seen the nervousness in her, too. They needed to get through one night and then they'd know they were clear.

Gary answered the door as he usually did – welcoming them inside and offering drinks, snacks, whatever. He was always a good host. They were in the hall as he offered to take their coats, because he always did that too. But there was a moment in which his gaze lingered on Ella a fraction too long. Less than a second, probably. There and not – but Daniel wondered. Had he done that before? Was Daniel watching their host under a new light and seeing things that had always been present?

He shouldn't have wondered, he should have run. They both should have done.

Except it lasted for no time at all and then Gary said that Charles was in the lounge. He led them along the hall and opened the door, waiting for them to head inside before following them in and closing it behind.

There was nobody in the room.

Daniel knew but he couldn't speak, couldn't really move. He was on a train in a tunnel, with only one way to go: desperate to run with feet glued to the floor. Ella asked where Charles was, still keeping up her chirpy façade, but Gary didn't reply. He pulled out a remote control from his back pocket and turned on the television.

An image was already there: a frozen top-down still shot of Charles' bedroom. Gary said there was a hidden camera in the light and then pressed play.

They both knew what was going to happen.

They watched as the rug was drawn back and Ella crammed armfuls of cash into the same rucksack she was holding at that very moment.

A week later and it was a lot emptier.

The footage stopped and Gary calmly switched off the TV. He placed the remote on the table and rubbed his hands together, nodding towards Ella's bag and asking if there was any money inside.

She had to say 'no', of course – so he asked where it was. He was so calm but Daniel found that far more worrying than if he'd gone crazy. He'd rather have threats and hurled items. He would have understood that, perhaps even found a way to deal with it.

Not this.

Daniel had looked across to Ella, thinking they should probably say the money was in his locker. They could offer to give it back and pretend it never happened. They would never tell a soul what they'd discovered.

Except there was defiance in Ella's eyes. The same defiance

she had on stage when she was being her truest self. When nothing else mattered.

Maybe it would have been all right if they'd simply given back the money. If they'd apologised and promised to never come over again. But Ella was never going to return it. The moment she'd seen those stacks of banknotes, she had been transfixed – and Daniel had gone with it. They were good for one another but, in that moment, with that decision, they were the worst.

And so, when Gary asked where the money was, Ella stared him down and responded to the question by asking where Ben Davies was.

In that second of backchat, Daniel knew nothing would ever be the same. Gary's features were granite. He was no longer the man who doted on his young son, paid them generous overtime, gave them lifts home. That man was gone, if he'd ever existed.

Gary told them emotionlessly that Ben stole cars for them. They had a garage near the auction house, right on the docks. It was in the perfect place that, once night fell, the cars could be moved directly into shipping containers and then sent off to the Middle East to be sold. Things had been going well and everyone was happy, except the original car owners, of course – but then Ben stole the wrong vehicle.

It wasn't Ben's fault. He didn't know to whom the car belonged: none of them did. But when Ben got it to the lock-up and they had a proper look inside, there was a lot of money in the back. More money than any of them had ever seen before, or knew what to do with. If Ben had never seen it, everything would have been fine but the problem was, once he'd spotted it, he wanted what he called 'his' share. Except what turned out to be half a million pounds was only ever going to be split one way – and that wasn't Ben's.

Daniel had been watching and listening, transfixed. Gary

didn't seem capable of it all, yet he spoke with such clarity and authority that Daniel realised he had drastically underestimated him. He and Ella should never, ever have taken the money, let alone returned a week later as if nothing had happened.

Perhaps it was because she needed to hear it but Ella asked directly whether Gary had killed Ben and the first reply was a bemused shrug. A silent, *of course – what did you expect?*

He told them that he'd given Ben a chance in the first place, over at The Mission. If it wasn't for Gary, Ben would have never been making that extra money anyway. He'd have been border-line homeless and relying on handouts.

Daniel knew they needed some sort of plan. Gary wasn't going to tell them all this and then let them leave – and maybe Ella knew that as well. She simply kept talking. She said that she thought Gary was a good guy because of everything he did with the church and The Mission. For a moment, with the way Gary looked at them, Daniel wondered if a part of him still was. He wasn't explaining because he was going to hurt them but because he wanted them to know a part of who he once was still existed. Everything else he'd said had been so calm and calcu-lated but, for the first time, he seemed hurt. He said that when Covid hit, when they were running out of money, nobody had come to help. He'd spent decades assisting others, literally building a support network in the town. He had won awards, been featured in numerous articles and TV news reports. But then – when *he* needed someone – nobody came. He was going to lose everything but it wasn't only him. It was his son's home. His wife's. And nobody cared.

But then someone he knew who'd moved to Dubai made an offer. It wasn't an outlet to sell antiques but there *was* an oppor-tunity for nearly new cars, if he knew somewhere to get them.

Gary accidentally stumbled into a way to keep his family's life together, knowing it was wrong, but doing it anyway. His family was more important than anything.

The whole time he spoke, Daniel was trying to think of a way out. Gary was blocking the main door that led back to the hall and the front of the house. If Ella and he could get around the sofas quickly, and in unison, there was a second door that led through to the kitchen. From there, a patio door was on the furthest side, past the island. He had no idea if those doors were locked but, if they were open, they might be able to get to the side of the house and then loop back to the front. They would need a lot of things to go their way but if he could somehow get Ella to follow him, they had a chance.

As she kept Gary talking, Daniel was trying to catch Ella's eye. He'd taken the smallest sideways shuffle towards the gap between the sofas, but she hadn't followed.

Ella asked how Gary had known the cars didn't have trackers, which was something Daniel knew nothing about. She said her mum had been looking into getting a newer vehicle and that the woman at the dealership was trying to upsell her to something with a tracking system. Gary said it helped to know someone who worked in insurance, though didn't expand.

In that crumbling university dorm, Jennifer had been quiet for such a long time that her voice croaked as she interjected to tell Daniel that Nick worked in insurance. Daniel stared at his mother for a moment, before nodding slowly. They both understood now. Nick would identify vehicles that hadn't declared a tracker on the insurance. He'd know where the newer ones were located and how much they were worth. Ben would do the thieving, Gary would sort out shipping them to his contact in Dubai.

A tight operation until Ben had taken the wrong car.

Mother and son settled for a moment until Daniel was ready to go again. Then he was back in the lounge at Gary's house: where Ella had been stalling but Daniel had not been able to get her attention.

At that point, it was as if Gary remembered where they

were. He again asked them where the money was and, when neither of them answered, he sighed and said he wished it hadn't got to this point.

Then he reached across to a small desk on which a lamp was sitting. He slipped open a small drawer, momentarily turning away from them, before pulling out a pistol.

It was the first gun Daniel had seen in real life, outside of police at the airport. Gary said he'd never shot it but that it was loaded and they could take their chances if they wanted. He even stepped to the side, showing them the door that led to the front.

All those ideas about rushing the side door and escaping through the back were gone. Daniel knew that Gary had been ahead of them the entire time. He lifted the gun, pointing it at Ella, while watching Daniel. Then he asked, again, for what he said was the final time, where the money was.

Daniel didn't wait for Ella that time. He said that he could get it, knowing that the location was the single piece of valuable information they held. If he told Gary where it was, he'd have little reason not to shoot them. Daniel half expected Ella to argue, except she had gone quiet and perhaps it had sunk in for her, too.

Gary seemed to accept the answer and it felt to Daniel as if he didn't particularly want to use the gun. He told them he wanted their phones and keys – and said to place them on the coffee table. It felt so surreal to see the gun in Gary's hand, while they put down their phones and keys, next to a lifestyle magazine on which the cover promised the top ten tips on how to renovate a bathroom.

Domestic bliss and domestic terror, side by side.

Gary picked up the phones one at a time, turning them off and putting them in the pocket of his jacket, along with the keys. He told Daniel to move across to the radiator, next to the bookshelf – and, with the gun still in Gary's hand, Daniel felt he had little choice.

If Daniel was in any doubt over how much of it had been planned, Gary fished behind a large hardback to remove a handful of heavy-duty zip ties. He looped one each around Daniel's wrists and then connected the pair to the radiator. Daniel could move his legs but little else. For some reason, he'd thought he would be the person to take Gary to the money – but that wasn't going to happen.

Gary said that, once he had the cash, he would return with Ella and let them go. Daniel wasn't sure he believed him, though had little choice. Ella seemed resigned – or, if she had a plan, Daniel had no idea what it was. Gary told her to leave via the door that led into the kitchen but there was a moment where she paused in the doorway.

Back in the crumbling halls, Daniel stopped talking and took a breath. He couldn't meet his mum's eye and needed a minute. More than that. When he'd regained his composure, his words were stunted and broken.

Because, when she'd paused in that doorway, Ella had turned to look over her shoulder, to where Daniel was secured against the radiator. She mouthed 'I love you' – and then Gary ushered her outside and shut the door.

There was quiet for a short while: the clanking of pipes, the chittering of a large, old house. But then there was a sudden, muffled bang; voices that weren't loud enough to make out actual words. Daniel pulled against the radiator, knowing he couldn't get break the ties but wondering if he could wrench the unit from the wall.

He couldn't – but then there was shuffling in a nearby room. Daniel called a tentative 'Hello...?' that was met by only the creaks of the walls.

Daniel didn't know how long he was stuck to that radiator but it felt like a long time. Nobody came and the house seemed empty. He assumed Ella had taken Gary to the locker. She knew the PIN and would be handing back the money.

But then, with no fanfare, Gary had returned, by himself – although Daniel could see that something had changed. Where previously there was a steely determination, there was now a line of sweat across his hairline, a shortness of breath – and, more than that, a sense that he no longer felt in control.

Gary said Daniel was coming with him – but no Ella. She was going to wait at the house. Daniel asked what had happened but got no response. He said he wanted to see his girl-friend but was told that would only happen once the money was back with Gary.

The gun was loose in his hand second time around – but still close enough that Daniel didn't dare try anything as Gary cut through the ties. He handed Daniel a blindfold and told him to put it on, refusing any sort of protest by pushing the muzzle of the pistol into Daniel's side and insisting he get on with it.

Questions about Ella and what had happened in the previous hour or so were ignored. Instead, Daniel was told to walk, which he did. Gary always felt near, and so did the gun. Before long, Daniel was out in the cold, arms outstretched, fumbling for an open car door that he'd been told was in front of him. He had to climb into the back seat and then lie down.

He did that, too.

Only when he was on his back and blinded did Gary again ask where the money was. Daniel had been sure that Ella had taken him to it but all the other man would say was that plans had changed. He added that if Daniel wanted to see his girlfriend again, then he was going to direct them to the money.

And so Daniel told him the cash was near the university. The building used to be a HSBC and there were around three-hundred lockers across two rooms. Gary asked which number locker but Daniel said he'd tell him when they got there. He knew it was all he had left. There was a pause and then a firm-sounding 'Fine'.

Except it didn't sound fine.

Daniel was again zip-tied, this time to the handle of the door at the back of the car. He lay across the back seat, wincing at every bump and pothole in a way with which Jennifer also felt familiar.

Not that she told her son about her experience in the boot of Nick's car. She wondered if it was the same vehicle Daniel had been in.

Except her son was still telling his story.

He spent the entire time on the back seat of the vehicle being bumped around, while desperately worried for Ella. He'd not seen her since the mouthed 'I love you' and it felt as if something had gone awfully wrong. Despite that, he clung onto the idea that he'd show Gary the money – and then be taken back to the house, where Ella would be waiting safely for him. What else could he believe?

When they stopped, Gary said not to move and that he'd be right back. Daniel felt the boot open and the weight of the car lift, as if something had been taken out. He listened as the boot was slammed but then there was quiet.

Daniel waited – but not for long. He rattled his wrists back and forth hard against the handle of the car door. Nothing happened – but nobody stopped him either.

So he yanked hard, as hard as he possibly could, until the plastic ripped and gouged into his skin. But he kept pulling, kept squeezing... and then, miraculously, his wrists slipped through the binds and he was free.

It took Daniel a moment to realise but he sat up and pulled away the blindfold. The zip ties hung limply from the door handle and his wrists were bleeding. There was nobody in sight but, as he looked through the misting car windows, he realised the vehicle was parked outside where he lived. His housemates were out for the night and it was empty. In his momentary confusion, he thought Gary had driven him home... except he'd not yet revealed the exact location of the money, and he didn't know where Ella was.

Daniel and Ella's mobile phones were both sitting on the passenger seat of the car, and perhaps they'd fallen out of Gary's pocket, or maybe he had simply tossed them there. Either way, Daniel grabbed the pair of them and got out of the car. He was going to call the police. Have them save Ella and then they'd confess everything. At least they would be safe.

But then there was movement from the front of the house, a slamming door, and Daniel instinctively ducked away from the street, hiding behind the neighbour's overgrown bush. He watched through the unkempt leaves as Gary burst from the house and opened the driver's door. He was almost inside when he stopped and leapt back, turning a full circle as panic bled through every part of him when he realised Daniel was gone.

Daniel couldn't work out what was happening, nor why Gary had been in his house. He watched as Gary paced a short way along the road and then ran back. He made a quick phone call, though Daniel could hear none of it. Then there were girls walking on the street, their heels ticking across the tarmac, so Gary leapt into his car, not wanting to be seen.

He drove away as soon as the girls had passed.

Daniel finally let himself breathe as he extracted himself from the web of tangled branches. He was going to call the police, hoping someone could get to Gary's house before he did.

There would be safety for Daniel in his own house, considering Gary had just left. Except, when he got to the door, it was on the latch. Inside and Daniel's key was on the table next to where he and his housemates left their shoes. Along the hall, to where Daniel's door was also unlocked.

Jennifer knew what was inside and didn't need her son to say. He couldn't anyway. Back in the shattered halls, he turned to face the corner, clutching his knees to his chest and rocking gently. Jennifer rested a hand on her son's shoulder, though he didn't react. She left him because there had been a time a long way before that she had looked into a bedroom, in which the only thing waiting was hell.

She could guess a lot of the rest but Daniel eventually told her anyway.

Despite the horror of what was in his room, Daniel knew he couldn't wait around. He could call the police and try to explain but there was likely no evidence Gary had done anything. Maybe there'd be forensics, something like that, but he'd be gambling. He could show the police the money but Gary could deny all knowledge, wipe his security tapes, and hide whatever money was left under those floorboards. Perhaps the police would believe Daniel – but it was far more likely they wouldn't. Far more likely they'd trust the easiest solution – which was that he'd killed his girlfriend.

So he ran.

But he couldn't have his mum thinking he was a killer, so he made one call to tell her – and then he hid. He had seen her old halls on a daily basis while walking to his classes. He knew they were due to be knocked down and hadn't necessarily planned to hide there in any long-term way, except, after breaking in, he'd realised a man was already living there. Kevin had been there for months and didn't know where he was going to go once the demolition happened. In the meantime, he'd offered kindness, safety, and a borrowed phone.

That was his story – but Jennifer knew there were things Daniel wasn't telling her. Things he couldn't. His unmoving stare told her enough. The girl he loved, the one who completed him, was dead in horrifying circumstances. And regardless of who had actually done it, Jennifer's son blamed himself.

Things felt different after that. They filled a few of the gaps. Jennifer asked if Daniel knew Nick and he said that he didn't, not really. Nick had been at the house a couple of times when he and Ella had been tutoring Charles. Daniel didn't know who he was and gasped with shock when Jennifer told him he was the son of Harriet and the man who'd killed her friend when she'd been a student. Daniel asked how that could be true, so she explained that Harriet's real first name was Joanne. She was Craig's girlfriend all those years before, but they each had different names then. Jennifer was a Benson, Harriet was a Vickery. Daniel was a Farley. It was, somehow, a massive coincidence that they had all fallen into one another's lives again.

Not that it solved anything.

Daniel nodded, understanding, but then asked the question to which Jennifer had no answer: 'What do I do?'

FORTY-SIX

Jennifer wasn't sure whether she had an answer. Not a smart one anyway. Daniel asked if Jennifer was hungry and, for the first time in days, she thought she was. There was an upturned dresser outside the door and Daniel pulled out one of the drawers, before returning with a Twix.

'You can thank Kev,' he said.

They took a finger each but there wasn't a lot to say. Her instinct still said they should call the police – but it felt dangerous for all the reasons Daniel had mentioned. Not only that, Jennifer didn't trust Sergeant Sheridan, especially after she'd somewhat twisted the truth to make it seem as if Daniel and Ella had fought.

She had vague, desperate thoughts that she could somehow smuggle Daniel abroad. Maybe they could get him a fake passport, with a new name, although she had no idea how to do that. Even if she did, there would be no justice for Ella and no closure for her poor mum. Daniel's name would never be cleared.

They finished eating and Daniel yawned. He seemed lighter and she didn't blame him. 'You should go,' he said. 'Tell

Dad everything but just leave. I'll hand myself in. I don't know what else I can do. I can't hide forever – and this place is going to be knocked down anyway.'

There was a clarity that he hadn't had before. Perhaps he knew that he wouldn't have got to tell her this truth if the police had reached him first.

Jennifer considered taking him away from Ashington in the car. They could hide out at home... Except the police would surely notice – and he'd look so guilty.

Jennifer hadn't moved, so he repeated: 'You should go'.

There had to be a way.

And then Jennifer thought she had it. Maybe.

'Which car were you in?' she asked.

'When?'

'The night everything happened. When you were in the back seat.'

Daniel blinked, frowned, tried to think. She could see the memories reforming. 'It was black,' he said.

'Was it an Audi?'

A pause. 'Maybe. I think so. I only saw it through a bush. I was blindfolded at first.' A pause. 'Why?'

Jennifer didn't reply because she was thinking herself. If it *was* a black Audi, it was the same vehicle Harriet had been driving when they'd met at the café. There was something she'd said then. Something important.

'I don't like it when you get like this,' Daniel said.

'Like what?'

'Like you're about to do something silly.'

FORTY-SEVEN

FRIDAY

The cool harbour air still smelled slightly of sausages, even though the butty van had gone for the day. Jennifer rested on her own car, forcing away a yawn, watching as Harriet's vehicle pulled to a smooth stop next to her in the deserted car park. Jennifer was so tired. She'd had long weeks in her life but this had topped any of those, even the one where she and Natasha had found Hayley.

She was *so* tired.

Harriet fiddled with her bag, did something on her phone, and then clambered out.

Jennifer gave a gentle smile. 'You came,' she said.

'You said it was important.'

Jenifer nodded to acknowledge the point. When she'd seen Harriet in The Mission a couple of days before, there had been a glimpse of the young woman she used to be. Of Jo. Now, as the wind murmured, with everything Jennifer now knew, she couldn't see any of that. They were a pair of strangers.

'Can we walk?' Jennifer asked.

Harriet stared for a moment, probably confused, although she didn't complain. She picked up her bag from the car, locked it, and then followed as Jennifer led her to the path that ringed the docks.

It was so quiet and the water was still. On the far side, the cranes were still clanking and groaning as seagulls circled.

Harriet wasn't dressed for a chilled stroll along the docks and her arms were folded when Jennifer stopped next to a giant anchor on the path. It was a mix of historical artifact and art installation.

Jennifer pointed across the water. She couldn't quite see Etherington's Auctions but knew where it was. 'Nick threatened me on that spot,' Jennifer said, pointing over the waves.

Harriet looked in the direction but then focused back on Jennifer. This wasn't what she'd expected.

'What do you mean?'

'He said he was going to throw me in the water. He wanted to know where Daniel was and wouldn't believe that I didn't know.'

It was so direct, so honest, that Jennifer felt a thrilling stab of something new. People didn't speak to one another in such a way. She'd spent a week hiding so much and talking around everything that was going on. This was real.

Harriet was stammering: 'My Nick?'

A nod: 'He looks so much like his dad.'

More truth that wasn't expected. Harriet was staring, mouth open. 'I, uh... I'll have to talk to him. I don't know why he'd do that.'

When Jennifer didn't give an immediate reply, Harriet kept going: 'I'll have to talk to Gary as well. He's much closer to Nick.' She flicked her gaze across the water. 'Did he really threaten to throw you in?'

'Why would I make it up?'

Harriet's face was impossible to read, though Jennifer understood. She'd spent a week facing down the worst accusations about her son, wavering between defending him as strongly as possible, while accepting victims and their families had a right not to hear it. Jennifer couldn't figure out whether Harriet knew. Daniel's story was unclear about who was involved and how deeply. There was obviously Gary and Nick – but Harriet might know nothing at all. Or perhaps it was selective? She knew about the stolen cars and the money but not what happened to Ella. She wasn't in the room when Daniel was secured to the radiator, nor the car when Gary took Ella's body into the house. Plus she had said that Nick was closer to his stepfather than he was to her.

'What happened in the end?' Harriet asked.

'A guardian angel turned up. Someone named Lance. He seemed to think Nick owed him money.'

There was a definite gulp. Harriet knew that name. 'What happened then?'

'Not much. Lance told Nick he had a day to come up with the money. I'm guessing he's got a few more hours. Then Lance told Nick to stay away from me. I've not seen either of them since.'

It was hard to know for sure but there was definitely a flicker of recognition from Harriet. Jennifer guessed she likely knew something about the stolen cars and the cash – but not about Lance's recent threat.

'Nick isn't Craig,' Harriet whispered after a while. 'He's not his dad.' She thought on that for a moment, then added: 'Why was he trying to find Daniel?'

'I thought you might know?'

There was a blank look that was either genuine bemusement or good acting. Hard to know. 'He and Gary are close,' Harriet said. 'They don't share everything with me.' A pause. 'But... this Lance. Did he, I dunno... make threats?'

Now she was worried.

'That's why I wanted to meet you in person. I know Nick's your son and I don't want anything bad to happen to him. I didn't know whether Nick had told you what happened and didn't think we could talk on the phone.'

Maybe that was a lie? Jennifer *probably* didn't want anything specifically bad to happen to Harriet's son, but maybe she did? He'd bundled her in a car boot and threatened to throw her in the water. His father was a monster and they looked so similar that it was impossible to separate them in her mind.

'Is this the only reason you wanted to meet?' Harriet asked.

'I think so,' Jennifer said – although that was a definite lie. She had to buy time as well. 'I'm probably going home tomorrow. I've not found any sign of Daniel and don't think I've done any real good since coming back.'

True, false, probably true. That last one was debatable.

Harriet had been gazing over the water, towards the cranes and where Nick had threatened to throw Jennifer into the water. Her stare had barely wavered, other than that mention of Lance.

'It was good to see you again,' Jennifer added. 'I hope things work out for you. I'm sorry this is probably the last time we talk. I would've come to your house but, with Nick and everything...'

There was almost a question there, though not quite. Did Harriet know?

She didn't give anything away as she focused back on Jennifer. She was reaching for her phone. 'I'm sorry about Nick,' she said. 'I didn't know. I wish things had been different.'

There was little else to say. They wavered for a moment, wondering how to end things – but, as they started the walk back to the cars, Harriet was tapping furiously on her phone. The tension and worry hung between the pair.

As soon as they reached the car park, Harriet plipped her car open, muttered a final 'bye' and then got inside. She pulled out of the space with one hand on the steering wheel, the other holding her phone to her ear. Jennifer watched her go, figuring they probably *would* see one another again – though perhaps not in as cordial a circumstance.

She got into her own car and then twisted towards the back seat – where Callum was lying flat.

'How did it go?' she asked.

'Got it,' he replied.

'Will she know?'

Callum shuffled himself into a sitting position and straightened his top, before passing across an SD card. 'I never had a problem breaking *into* cars,' he said. 'Only driving them.'

According to him, when he said he'd been in a car crash, that part was true. It was also why he no longer stole vehicles for Gary and Nick. He had been Ben's replacement after Ben had 'disappeared' – except he'd not been very good at it. That had been Jennifer's guess, given what both Lance and Nick had said. He hadn't denied any of it when Jennifer had asked. Without the side income from the car thefts, he'd gone back to his old ways of dealing pills.

'Why'd you do it?' Jennifer asked. She was watching Callum in the rear-view mirror.

'Steal cars?' he asked. He had been surprisingly honest since Jennifer had contacted him the night before with an idea.

'No,' Jennifer replied. She knew he stole vehicles for the money. 'Why did you do *this* when I asked?'

He didn't need to think. 'Ella,' he said. 'I did it for my sister.'

FORTY-EIGHT

SUNDAY

Jennifer waited on the balcony as Ella's mum welcomed Daniel into her flat. Michelle gripped him hard and pulled him close, nuzzling her head into his shoulder.

'I knew it wasn't you,' she managed, with a croak.

Daniel clutched her back but Jennifer could see the exhaustion in her son. After the week he'd had, he had spent the best part of twenty-four hours talking to the police. It would be a lot for anyone but he was so young. Twenty-somethings might think they knew everything but it was a long life and there was a lot to learn. Daniel had already gone through so much more than most.

Michelle finally released him and smiled to Jennifer with wet eyes. 'I said, didn't I?' And she had.

She led them through to the front room, then asked if anyone wanted a drink. It didn't feel as if she was particularly listening. She was on autopilot as host and disappeared into the kitchen as Daniel solemnly looked at the photos of Ella that still adorned the walls. Jennifer left him with his thoughts. He had done so much talking the day before and the main thing he wanted was to go home.

Real home.

They both knew this was more important, though.

When Michelle returned, she'd made three teas – even though Daniel hadn't wanted one. She placed them on the table and sank onto the seat, taking deep breaths and readying herself.

'Did you see her at the end?' she asked.

Daniel was sitting, too, staring aimlessly towards the wall. He had to go through it all one more time and then he could keep it to himself forever, if that's what he wanted.

'Gary took Ella out of the room in his house,' he said. 'I didn't see much after that. I heard some sort of struggle but I don't know what happened. The next time I saw her was on my bed.'

Michelle nodded along. She'd heard some of it directly from the police the day before and earlier that morning – but none of it was first-hand. 'I don't blame you for running,' she said. 'I told the police that. It must have been awful for you. If you'd waited, none of this would have come out.'

It was hard to know whether that was true – but Lance Williams had inadvertently told Jennifer that Callum was a car thief. Harriet had told her that Gary had cameras in their cars and swapped the memory cards every weekend. Then Daniel had described Harriet's car as the one in which Ella had been transported. It had been a gamble and a guess but, while Jennifer kept Harriet talking by the docks, Callum had used some sort of device that got him into keyless cars. Jennifer didn't pretend to understand, though the methods didn't matter too much. The memory card he'd taken contained all the video Jennifer hoped it would – but in particular of him cuffing Daniel onto the back seat. It felt so baffling that he recorded any movement in his vehicles and house... and yet who knew more about car theft? No wonder he was paranoid.

When the police raided Gary's house on Friday evening,

they found number plates plus a little over a quarter of a million squirrelled around the house. They discovered a pair of stolen cars in the storage unit behind his auction house – and, from there, the entire enterprise was crumbling. By the time Daniel gave himself up and told his story, it was over.

It was still unclear how much, if anything, Harriet knew. Jennifer hadn't been told anything officially but she had overheard someone at the police station saying that 'the wife is denying everything'. Between the memory card and Daniel's evidence, only Gary and Nick had been implicated. There were likely to be others, possibly even Callum. For now, his role in obtaining that memory card was unknown to anyone except Jennifer and Daniel. The card had been delivered anonymously to the police and the footage was on YouTube. At some point, Gary and Nick were going to have to explain who was stealing the cars for them. Ben Davies' name would inevitably come up, especially as they had to explain the money as well. Jennifer still had Ben's driving licence but handing it to the police would mean telling them where she'd got it, and how long she'd had it.

They didn't know what else was in that locker, either.

'They've not released Ella's body,' Michelle said. 'When they do, I want it to be a celebration. I want the band to play. You can be as involved as you want.'

She was talking to Daniel and he took a breath. It would feel real to him now. Jennifer knew that from Hayley. While the police were investigating, while questions were being asked, it was a rollercoaster. When everything stopped, reality would hit. Daniel was biting his lip and stood abruptly, saying he needed the toilet and then he rushed out the room. If Jennifer's own experience from two decades before was anything to go by, he would be spending a lot of time by himself in the coming months.

'Are you OK?' Jennifer asked.

Michelle was gazing at the photos of her daughter. 'I mean... no. I don't know what to say.'

Jennifer had spent much of the past day thinking on such things. Despite the week, despite it all, at least she still had her child.

'I ran into Callum a couple of days back,' Jennifer said. 'I think, maybe, he cared more for Ella than you might think.'

Michelle frowned a fraction, likely wondering why Jennifer would say such a thing. Jennifer could hardly say he'd broken into Harriet's car for her, that the evidence now being replayed on news bulletins came from him. Jennifer doubted he was going to stop dealing – but he had at least done one thing for his sister's memory.

'There's one more thing,' Jennifer said, reaching into the big bag for life she'd been carrying – and pulling out another. She passed it across and waited for Michelle's eyes to widen, as she knew they would.

'What is this?' Michelle asked with amazement.

'I need you to not ask questions,' Jennifer said, knowing it was unfair. 'But that's what Ella was killed for. There's about ninety grand inside but I've not counted it fully. Gary Etherington stole the money from a drugs trafficker who couldn't report it stolen. Ella and Daniel took some of it – and Gary killed her for it. Daniel told the police he didn't know what Ella did with the money but it's yours. You can tell the police you found it in her room and they'll confiscate it. Or you can forget who gave it to you and where it came from. You can never spend lots at a time. Bits here. Bits there.'

Michelle peered into the bag once more. Jennifer knew how intimidating it was to see so much cash in one place.

'This is what got her killed?' she asked.

A nod. 'I think she wanted to give away a lot of it anyway. If you keep it, you can never tell anyone but, if you want, I can hand it into the police. I thought it should be your decision.'

Michelle took a breath and Jennifer knew the weight of it all. Regardless of what was in the bag, it wasn't worth losing a daughter for.

A toilet flushed from along the hall, though Daniel didn't immediately emerge.

'I'm going to drive him home later today,' Jennifer said. 'We'll be back for the funeral but I don't know other than that. There might be a trial. If you ever need anything, you should call.'

Jennifer felt a responsibility for the other woman now. Daniel and Ella would always be connected, which meant they were too.

Michelle had slumped and was staring into the bag as footsteps came from the hall beyond. 'I just want her back,' she said.

Daniel stepped into the room, smiling weakly, his eyes red. Jennifer watched him sit, always marvelling at how her little boy wasn't so little any longer. He would need her now and she would be there for him. Because, when it came down to it, if she had to choose between him and anyone else, Jennifer would always – *always* – choose her son.

FORTY-NINE

HARRIET

So that was that then.

All the years of working her way up to the big house, the rich husband, the important community figure... it was gone. She knew, even if those around her might not realise completely.

Perhaps she'd known it when Jennifer had wanted to meet on the docks. Something had definitely been up and she'd had to play along, even as Jennifer whined on about Nick threatening her. Blah, blah, blah. Of course Jennifer knew where Daniel had been the whole time – how else would she have followed Nick's text message to that green?

That had been quite the shocking phone call when Nick rang to say it wasn't Daniel he'd bundled into the car, it was his mum.

Still, Jennifer had seemingly taken on board those hints that Gary and Nick were close. Any idiot would realise it wasn't true. Nicholas had always been a mummy's boy. Always done what he was told.

At least some things had worked in Harriet's favour. Gary had dropped himself in it with his ridiculous insistence on those cameras in the car. She'd tried to tell him it was asking for trouble but that was the thing when you stole for a living: you always assumed someone would try to steal *from* you. If only he'd considered all that while leaving Daniel and Ella alone in the house.

His mistake – *mostly* – and he would be paying for it.

He could tell the police his wife was in on it but it wasn't her who was caught on camera. His poor, desperate wife had no idea where the money came from and nobody could prove otherwise. It wasn't her with the lock-up in her name. Not her who moved Ella's body. She'd never stolen a vehicle, never removed a numberplate, never bribed that bloke at the port, never taken money from a mate in the Middle East. It was all Gary.

But it *was* Ella who'd brought it all down, of course. So predictable. So greedy. Gary had done all the talking, marching her into the kitchen from the study, saying they were going to collect the cash. But what sort of punishment was that? That girl had to be taught a lesson.

It wasn't the first time Harriet's red mist had descended. She'd grabbed that stupid girl, growling 'You think you can steal from us?!' in her face. Gary had let it go at first, perhaps shocked, perhaps enjoying it. By the time he'd tried to stop things, it was too late.

That stupid girl's eyes had boggled and she'd stopped breathing.

Harriet and her husband had stood in the kitchen, looking over that dead girl, having a whispered argument in case Daniel overheard from the next room.

Gary had been naïve and ridiculous, of course. All that stuff with the pistol he would never shoot. He'd have likely let the pair of them go when he got the money – but only a fool would have trusted them to say nothing. There was no way Daniel and Ella could go back to their old lives, whatever he thought.

They'd have to go into the docks, the same way as poor old Ben. Someone else who couldn't keep his grasping, greedy hands to himself.

Gary had asked what they should do with Ben – and again with Ella. Harriet had told him both times to get rid of them at the docks but she changed her mind with the girl. Not the water for her. They had Daniel's key and could leave Ella as a present on his bed. Tie the lamp cord around her neck for old time's sake. Everyone would think he did it because it was always the husband or boyfriend.

Oh, the beautiful symmetry of it all.

It wasn't ideal but one of them had to teach these kids a lesson, and Gary was too much of a wimp. It had been Harriet.

No.

It had been *Joanne*. Sometimes the old her came back.

Just like with that stupid Hayley all those years ago. Those silly girls and their silly obsession with Craig. Poking their nose into Joanne's business in the university café – although that was partly his fault. He was obsessed with her and she knew it. She'd left that knife on his pillow, saying she wanted him to kill something to prove his love. She'd have accepted a mouse. Anything. But then he'd stomped in, all annoyed, waving the knife around, embarrassing himself.

But those silly girls couldn't mind their own business. Then they had been stalking them all around town. She saw them on the steps, where she had barely been able to hide her annoyance. Then they were in the library, watching her and Craig. Even inside the club on a night out. There was no escaping them. That had been the night she had picked a fight with Craig outside because he'd been looking at the three of them – but especially that Hayley with her tiny dress. Joanne had got in a few slaps and kicks at Craig, before slipping and scratching her arm. Craig had gone off in a huff but then, miraculously, those girls had found her in the alley and blamed him! She hadn't even had to make anything up, because they had done it all by themselves.

Hayley was always going to get what was coming to her. That was the first time Joanne had her hands around another person's throat and you know what they say: the first time's the charm. Some people need to learn the hard way not to steal. Whether that was Hayley with boyfriends, or Ella with money, it didn't matter.

It helped that there was always someone else the police looked at. Craig tried to tell them it wasn't him who'd killed Hayley, that he was with his girlfriend – but Joanne had told them the opposite. She was so worried about how her boyfriend was obsessing over other girls. So frightened of him that she couldn't leave. So terrified that she didn't want to say he wasn't *actually* with her that night.

In truth, they *had* been together – just as he told the police – but only after Joanne had paid a little visit to Hayley's house. Not that she told the police that part. She left that horrible bag he always carried for them to find – then they'd done the rest. Well, them plus silly little Jennifer and Natasha. They'd done exactly what she knew they would.

And then, Jennifer had done it again. Another one who was so predictable. The police might've claimed it was anonymous but Harriet knew her old foe had got that memory card implicating Gary. She had been Harriet's shield for a second time.

But there was one thing none of them knew. Jennifer and Daniel probably thought everything was one big coincidence. Except Harriet had kept an eye on Jennifer for so long. People put everything on social media these days – if not them, then their friends. Harriet knew all about Jennifer's marriage and the name change. All about the son named Daniel.

There was one small twist of fate. Daniel *had* answered that tutoring ad – and the moment he'd told them his name, Harriet knew who he was. Not that she let on. That old part of her, the Joanne part, knew she wasn't quite done with Jennifer.

And there was Jennifer's son, standing right in front of Harriet, in her hallway, with no idea who she was. She thought about how she could use him to get to Jennifer, without really knowing why. It was all a game in one way. Those girls still hadn't fully paid for sticking their noses in.

As soon as Daniel introduced them to his girlfriend, to Ella, Harriet knew *she* was the key. She saw how that girl looked at the house, at the gardens, the cars; how she craved security and money for herself.

Takes one to know one. That had been Joanne once. She had that look before she'd found Gary.

Harriet had left that bedroom floorboard loose so many times, hoping Ella or Daniel would stumble across it. She couldn't know for sure *exactly* what they might do – but she had an idea. If they'd gone to the police, Gary would take the fall; if they kept the money and came back, Harriet would wind up Gary to the point that he'd be ready for them. He might even do the deed himself. He hadn't of course.

There was a time when Harriet thought killing the pair of them would be enough to drive Jennifer mad – but then she'd hit upon a better idea.

Poor Ella, in more ways than one. Fell right into the trap.

And Harriet was so, *so* close to destroying Jennifer. So close to putting her son in prison. To having Jennifer labelled as the mother of a murderer.

So close.

In the end, Gary was going down for this, perhaps Nick, too. That's what he gets for being too much like his dad.

But not Harriet. She had her son, Charles, and the police hadn't found *all* the money. She would start again – and then, maybe one day, even if it took another twenty-five years, she would finally get her hands around someone else's neck.

If she was *really* lucky, it might even be Jennifer's...

PUBLISHING TEAM

Turning a manuscript into a book requires the efforts of many people. The publishing team at Bookouture would like to acknowledge everyone who contributed to this publication.

Audio
Alba Proko
Sinead O'Connor
Melissa Tran

Commercial
Lauren Morrissette
Hannah Richmond
Imogen Allport

Cover Design
The Brewster Project

Data and analysis
Mark Alder
Mohamed Bussuri

Editorial
Ellen Gleeson
Nadia Michael